Raw and Real
LOVE

GEORGIA PRICE

Copyright © 2022 Georgia Price
All rights reserved
First Edition

PAGE PUBLISHING
Conneaut Lake, PA

First originally published by Page Publishing 2022

ISBN 978-1-6624-8667-8 (pbk)
ISBN 978-1-6624-8676-0 (digital)

Printed in the United States of America

CHAPTER 1

Jack

Four years ago

I'm in a foul mood. We lost our last game. Our flight was delayed. The weather is shit, and I haven't been home in five days. All I want to do is hold my beautiful baby girls in my arms and rock them to sleep. I want my wife to be in a fairly decent mood, and I want to sleep in my own bed. While things with my wife aren't great, I'm trying really hard to make them better. She's been struggling since our twins were born, and I'm just trying to be patient. We've had a really rocky year and a half, and some days, I wonder how we're still married. I know it's only because of her pregnancy that we stayed together, and honestly, I think our marriage has been doomed for failure from the start. You shouldn't marry someone because you think you can save them.

I started dating Bree at the end of our freshman year of high school. We had gone to different middle schools and met in our ninth-grade English class. I remember thinking she was so pretty. Bree had developed early and had huge boobs that any heterosexual almost-sixteen-year-old boy would enjoy staring at. I remember gawking at her nipples one day when it was cold for nearly the entire hour. I asked her out after that. From that day forward, we were a couple.

All couples have their differences. I am blessed with a great family. My parents are still married and very much in love. My younger sister and I had everything we wanted growing up. Money was never a concern. It was an affectionate home, and my parents supported and encouraged me to follow my dreams. Bree's family, on the other hand, was shit. She never knew her father. Her mother had a drug problem. Bree had been in foster care for a while before her mother got her back. She'd been sexually abused by one of her foster dads and was looking for love and acceptance. I was looking to get laid. Teenage boys think almost exclusively with their dicks. We messed around a lot and had sex fairly early on. My parents weren't Bree fans. But that girl loved me. She would come to all my hockey practices, beg my parents to take her to away games and tournaments, and spend every waking chance she could with our family. It took me years to realize she was just trying to avoid home and leach onto a family.

By the time our senior year rolled around, I had opportunities to play college hockey all over the country. My dad had played for Minnesota, and I guess we always assumed that's where I'd play too. My dad was my hero, and I'd do anything to make him proud. But then Bree started talking about how much she wanted to get out of Minnesota and go to college somewhere else. She wanted us to escape together and start a new chapter. I didn't really want to escape from anything, but I wanted her to be happy. She deserved some good. The Norte Dame coach was an acquaintance of my dad's and had been pursuing me for years. Bree loved the idea of Norte Dame and convinced me to go. She had decent grades and was positive she could get a scholarship. My mom, the sweetheart that she is, had even helped Bree apply for financial aid and scholarships. My mom repeatedly brought it to her attention that she could get a lot more funding for school if we stayed in Minnesota. But Bree wasn't interested. In hindsight, it was a really dumb move because she had to pay out-of-state tuition and didn't actually get accepted into Norte Dame. Either way, we moved there together, me with my full-ride scholarship and her with her big plans.

When we got there, she was immediately disappointed that we couldn't live together. I had to live in the athletic dorms with my teammates, and she ended up finding some roommates in a shitty apartment off campus. She found a waitressing job and took classes at the community college. She made me tell all my friends she was a Norte Dame student. She'd get jealous at parties when girls would hit on the hockey players and was pretty much on my dick throughout all of college. I didn't complain. She was hot. We fucked like bunnies. After all the years of sex and growing up together, I had fallen in love along the way. I did everything I could to help her. I took the money my grandparents had saved for me for college and used it to help her pay her rent and furnish her apartment. My parents encouraged me to "meet nice girls" and "not get too serious too young." It was too late. I was a goner.

When I got drafted with the NHL after college, we were both ecstatic. I had managed to graduate the top of my class with a degree in business management and finance. I had hoped to work with my father if professional hockey wasn't in the cards for me. Bree hadn't finished her prerequisites for the nursing program at the community college yet. She would take some classes but then want to pick up more waitressing hours because the pay was good, or she would get pissed at her boss because she couldn't get one of my game nights off, so she'd quit and then find another waitressing job. She always felt like she deserved more than she was willing to work for and would constantly remind me of how lucky I was. After a while, I looked at her as someone I needed to take care of. I realized that she really couldn't do it on her own, and I *had* been really lucky in life. The difference was that I was willing to work my ass off too.

All my dreams came true when I got drafted to Seattle. But playing in the NHL was much more intense than I expected it to be. There were meetings upon meetings. I had to push my body harder than I ever had before. I needed to sleep more, work out more, lift weights more, eat better, and marry the game. I was dedicated and determined to make a name for myself in the league. Bree became lonely. She always told me I loved hockey more than her, and if I'm being completely honest, I think she was right. We had moved in together, and while I was busy being a rookie, she didn't know anyone in Seattle besides me. I had encouraged her to pick up with her schooling and see if she could get into the nursing program here. I'd introduced her to all the players' wives and girlfriends. It didn't seem to make any difference. She then became fixated on getting married and was practically demanding an engagement ring. I told her I wasn't ready to get married and wanted to take this time to focus on professional hockey.

I should have realized right then that marriage wasn't in the cards for us. You should want to marry your girlfriend of eight years and not give her excuses because you really, really don't want to marry her at all. Well, Bree figured out a way to fix that. She stopped taking her birth control without telling me. All of a sudden, she was "accidentally" pregnant, and I felt trapped. I decided to man up and propose. She wanted to get married immediately before she "was showing." So we had a shotgun wedding in Vegas the very next weekend with no prenup and no family present. My parents were crushed, and even though they didn't admit it, I could see it. Just like that, I was married at twenty-two with a kid on the way. Shit.

Shortly after our wedding, Bree had a miscarriage. I'm still not sure if she was actually ever really pregnant or if it was a trick to get me to marry her. I know that's terrible to say, but I never saw an ultrasound picture, I never went to a doctor's appointment, and the miscarriage happened when I was on a stretch of away games. She didn't tell me until I got home because she "didn't want to stress me out." Either way, I'm ashamed to admit I felt relieved. I looked at it as an opportunity for us to slow down and reevaluate what we wanted at this point in our lives. Bree looked at it like it was just one more disappointment in her long list of disappointments in life. She became depressed. We started to drift apart. Then I got traded to Chicago, and all hell broke loose. She was furious that "they could just uproot our lives." That was part of being in the NHL. You played where you could and rolled with the punches. It was not like she was leaving a job or school or friends. She basically just hung out around the house and went shopping with my money all the time.

I loved Chicago. My team was really welcoming. I was playing the best I ever had in my life. I was closer to my family, and they'd make the drive for all my home games. I had signed a three-year contract, so I felt some stability for the first time in a long time. Bree hated Chicago. She said she was "over the Midwest" and was hoping

I'd get traded sooner than later. Then one day, I came home early from practice to find an empty house. I went to shower in my master bathroom, and there was a used condom sitting on the top of the trash. Bree and I hadn't used condoms in years. The bed was unmade, and her clothes were strewn throughout the room. I knew without a doubt that she had been unfaithful to me. I had only ever been with her. I felt a pit in my stomach that burned a hole right through me. How long had this been going on? How many other guys had she been with? My whole life, it had always been her and only her. I felt sick. I grabbed my keys and my phone and ran. I needed to clear my head, and I needed physical activity to do that. My body was already sore, and I had originally planned to soak in the hot tub when I got home. Now those plans were long gone, and I ran until I felt like my legs were going to fall off. I'm not sure how many miles I went, but when I was done, I felt like I had some clarity.

Instead of focusing on feeling sad, hurt, and betrayed, I felt like I had the keys to my freedom in my hand. I had an excuse to end this awful relationship without being the asshole who deserted her, just like every other man in her life had. I wasn't deserting her. I was holding her liable for her actions. It was no longer my duty to protect her. I couldn't save her. I couldn't keep saving her from her past if she wasn't willing to work for a future with me. I wasn't able to make her happy, and in turn, I wasn't happy either. I called my attorney while still standing on the sidewalk and figured out my best plan of action.

She came home hours later. She was shocked to see me, and I could tell she was nervous. By the time she got home, I was cool, calm, and collected. I asked her how her day was. I told her I knew she'd been unfaithful. I told her I understood because I had been gone all the time. She didn't deny it. She told me she was lonely and didn't feel like I loved her anymore. I guess we both knew it was over. I loved her, I'd always love her, but I can't say I was in love with her. I told her I wanted a divorce. We had only been married for six months. She freaked out. She told me I was selfish and self-centered. She told me I'd never find a woman who would love me the way she loved me. She reminded me that I'd never love anyone more than hockey and I was destined to be alone. The conversation basically ended with her telling me to fuck off and storming out of the house with an overnight bag. She was served divorce papers the next morning.

The week after, when I was getting all my usual health screening for hockey, I found out I had chlamydia. That was when I finally broke down and grieved the loss of the woman I had been with since I was a fifteen-year-old kid. I called her to let her know she needed to be treated, and she started sobbing. We cried together on the phone. She told me she loved me. She apologized repeatedly. She then dropped the bomb and told me she was pregnant and that I was the father. I didn't believe her. I couldn't. I demanded a prenatal paternity test. This time, I went with her to the OB visits. Not only was she pregnant, but she was pregnant with twins. My mother is a twin, and I have three sets of twins in my family. I knew, at that moment, without even having the results back, that my life was about to change forever. I called my parents. They came to Chicago and helped me sort out the mess in my head. We weighed the options between divorce and staying married. We talked about what drove Bree to her infidelity. When the paternity test from the amniocentesis came back saying I was the father, I knew I couldn't abandon my children. I ultimately decided to give my marriage another chance.

Bree's pregnancy was rough. We spent a lot of time in marriage counseling. I was trying to put everything behind us and take some responsibility for the demise of our relationship. I thought it was bringing us closer, and while we weren't back to where we once were, we were on our own road to recovery. Or so I thought. When the twins were born, I learned what real, unconditional, true love really is.

I now had these two precious baby girls who meant everything to me, and I was determined to give them the best life I possibly could. If that meant staying with their mother and working through our differences, then I was willing to give it a try.

So now here I am, about to walk into my home and say hello to my wife and daughters. I didn't bother calling to let Bree know that we were able to fly tonight. I didn't want to wake her. Being a mother to one infant is exhausting, let alone two. Last she knew, we were still stranded in Calgary due to inclement weather. I'm hoping this will be a good surprise and I can help her with a feed or nighttime awakening. Instead, I walk in to find my wife naked, straddling another man on my couch, tits flopping in his face. I see red. The guy sees me first since Bree's back is to me. His eyes go wide, and he pushes Bree off him. He's bare by the way. No wonder I got fucking chlamydia. Bree turns toward me following his eyes.

"Jack! Oh my god! What are you doing here?"

She throws a blanket around her while the asshole is already putting his pants on.

"What the fuck am I doing here? That's a really good question, Bree. What the fuck are you doing?"

"Shit, Jack. Just calm down."

"Get the fuck out of my house. Get the fuck out now!"

"Jack, can we just talk about this?"

Is she fucking kidding me right now? I grab the crystal vase off the table and lunge it across the room. Glass shatters everywhere. Her eyes go wide. She's never seen me like this.

"Whoa, man. Calm down!" the douchebag who was just fucking my wife shouts.

He's trying to slip his shoe on. My fist connects with his jaw, and I hear the crack. I know I just broke it. I also know that if I punch him again, he's going to be out cold. Bree reaches down to check on him. The blanket is still wrapped around her. He's lying on the ground like a fucking pussy, and she looks terrified.

"Get the fuck out now before I completely lose my shit!" I roar.

She throws on the douchebag's shirt. He doesn't try to fight me and doesn't dare throw a punch. He's already heading for the door. Maybe he knows I'm one of the fiercest defenders in the NHL and could knock him out in a single blow. Or maybe he just sees an angry husband. He grabs her hand, and they head toward the door. One of the babies starts crying, undoubtedly from my outburst.

"I have to get the baby, Jack."

Bree starts to head back toward the twins' room.

"No. No, you don't. You're a no-good fucking whore. Don't pretend to sit here and be mother of the year. You're fucking trash. I'll take care of my daughters. Now get the fuck out."

Tears stream down her face.

"Leave, Bree, and don't fucking come back."

"I'm their mother. They need me."

"We don't need you. You're a dirty cunt, and you disgust me."

I hear the asshole tell her it's time to go. He pulls her out the front door. I turn toward my baby girls' room and don't bother looking back. I walk into the soft pink nursery and pick up a crying Rosie. I sit in the rocking chair, trying to calm down. I'm shaking. I look down at my little girl and breathe for the first time since I walked in the door of my home.

Chapter 2

Jack

I finally drift to sleep when my doorbell rings. It's way too early in the morning. I'm tempted to ignore it. But then it rings again, and I'm worried it's going to wake the twins. I get out of bed and throw on a pair of pajama pants. I don't bother with a shirt.

"Hi. I'm Officer Taylor with the Chicago Police Department. This is my partner, Officer Jacobs. Are you Jack Hannen?"

"Yes, I'm Jack Hannen."

"We're sorry to wake you at this early hour, sir, but there's something we need to discuss with you. Is it all right if we come in?"

"Umm...yeah, sure. What's going on?"

"Let's have a seat."

The officers look at one another, and a new pit forms in my stomach. I sit on one of the chairs in the living room. They sit on the couch, across from me, right where I walked in on Bree last night. I'm just now seeing the mostly gone bottle of tequila and two shot glasses on the end table.

"I'm so sorry, but there's been a terrible accident involving your wife, Aubree Hannen. She was the passenger in a car accident involving a drunk driver last night and died on the scene."

I don't speak. I just sit there trying to absorb the words without puking. Finally, I find my voice.

"I didn't know they were drinking."

I look at the tequila bottle again and put my head in my hands, shaking it back and forth. I only hear bits and pieces of the rest of the conversation. She's dead. He's dead. Poor driving conditions with the snow. Hit a tree. The officers are sorry. Identify the body at the coroner's office. Call if I have questions or need anything. There is more, but I can't comprehend anything at this point. I'm numb. Bree's dead. I go through the motions of getting dressed, waking my neighbor, and getting her to come stay with the girls so I can get to the coroner's office. I replay the last things I said to her. "Dirty cunt, whore, disgust me, trash." I begin heaving in my driveway before I get into my car to "identify her body."

Once I've emptied the contents of what I think is an already empty stomach and the bile has stopped escaping from the deep cervices of my gut, I get into my car and drive. I provide identification. I walk into the morgue and confirm Bree's identity. I stare at her gray body, blue lips, and open, lifeless eyes. I see blood matting her blond hair to her head. Her clothes have been removed, and she's covered by a white sheet. I shudder. I suddenly can't breathe. I run from the building to my car. A woman follows me out, asking me to sit down and try to calm down before I leave. She tries to soothe my nerves, but I can't hear what she's saying. I tell her I'm okay and get into my truck. I drive a mile and pull into a deserted park. I sit in the parking lot and sob like I've never cried before. My whole body shakes, and anger floods my veins. How dare she do this to me? My final words to her were so bad. How in the ever-living fuck is this my life?

I don't remember calling my mom, but apparently, I did, because when I get home, she and my dad are getting out of their car. I must have been gone for hours because I know it's a six-hour drive from their place in Minneapolis to my place in Chicago. The neighbor greets us at the door, gives me a sympathetic hug, and tells me she has to head home but to call if I need anything. She hands Rosie to my dad and tells us Ellie is in the pack and play. My six-month-old daughters are now motherless because I kicked their mom out of the house drunk in a snowstorm. I did this to them. What a piece of shit father I turned out to be. I wonder briefly if they'd be better off without me. I start sobbing again. My dad hands my mom the baby and pulls me in for a hug. When I pull away, I see the tears covering his face too and realize that he's been crying with me.

CHAPTER 3

Jack

Present day

"Hannen? Bro, where you at? Did you hear anything I just said?"

Shit. I don't even realize my teammate Graham Novotny is talking to me.

"Ah, sorry, man. What's up?" I say as I pull my shirt over my head in the locker room.

"I asked what you thought about coming out with us after our game Saturday night. Dude, you need to get laid. It's been too long, man, and I think it'll help clear your head. You've been off lately. Good sex always clears my head. Shit, it doesn't even have to be that good. Just get out there."

My best friend, Jimmy Drake, starts laughing as he throws his gear into his locker.

"Jack, you do need to get out."

Jimmy knew me when Bree was still alive. We've been through a lot together. The other guys on the team only know me as a man whore who fucks anything with a pussy and a decent set of tits. I didn't touch another woman for over a year after Bree died, and then once I let myself "get back in the saddle again," I used sex as a release from the constant demons in my head. Well, that is until six months ago, when some chick I had no recollection of approached me saying I was her baby's daddy. Lawyers and DNA testing later, I found out that she was just looking to score some of my NHL paycheck, but it still messed with me. I've never had sex without protection with anyone but Bree. I'm not foolish enough to think that condoms are 100 percent. I just don't care enough to think too much about it. That little incident, however, made me realize it's time to grow up. That, and the fact that my father pulled me aside, told me my actions have consequences, and it's time to get my self-hatred in check before I ruin my life. Yeah, he didn't mince words there. Now I'm trying to be the kind of guy I'd want for my daughters one day, and sex with one faceless puck bunny after the next isn't exactly a good role model.

"You might be right, gentlemen. I'll think about it. It might actually be good for me to get out. I have been stuck in my head lately."

I don't have to exactly become celibate to be a good role model. But maybe I do need to take the time to learn their names and slow the train down a bit.

"There's a line of puck bunnies who have been waiting for their turn with Jack Hannen, bro. You'll have your pick. Just don't go for Tessa. Rumor has it she gave Jones the clap," Novotny says nonchalantly as he strolls over to the showers.

That, right there, may be another reason I'm better off hanging out at home. I haven't exactly looked for a relationship or even considered getting close to someone since Bree, but with the onslaught of sluts at my disposal, it's hard to weed out anyone who may actually be worth getting to know. The agony I try to hide every day is slowly becoming a dull ache instead of a stabbing, constant pain. My parents have been my one constant saving grace. They retired shortly after the incident and relocated to Chicago. Mom watches the girls frequently, and my dad is constantly tinkering around my house. Without them, I'm not sure I would have survived. I want to be better for them. I want them to be able to enjoy their golden years and not worry about me, the twins, and all the shit I've brought their way over the years. It's time to be the man they raised me to be. I just don't know how.

Chapter 4

Caroline

"Why would he send me a dick pic?" I ask my girlfriends.

We're sitting out on the patio of our favorite coffee shop, Coffee! Coffee! Coffee!, enjoying the last of the warm weather as fall approaches and the cold, unrelenting Chicago winter hits us.

"Oooohhh, let me see it!" my friend Sofia says, extending her hand out for my phone.

Sofia is a few years older than me. We met in Dallas when we were NFL cheerleaders together. She's from Chicago, and we reunited when I moved here. She's Latina with dark-black eyes, gorgeous skin, and thick, dark hair that would make any woman jealous.

"Ew, really? Isn't it like you've seen one, you've seen them all?" I ask as I pull up the picture and hand her my phone.

Victoria shakes her head.

"It's so not like that!"

She starts ticking things off with her fingers.

"There's circumcised or not, for starters. Then you have to factor in length and girth. You need to know if it's a straight arrow or if it curves just a little bit to the right or left. There's also—"

"Oh my god. Just stop!"

What is wrong with my friends? Am I just a prude? I seriously don't understand why any man would think this would be a turn-on.

"Holy hell. He's huge."

Sofia hands the phone around the table where my girlfriends all take in the image.

"Wait, so how do you know him?" my friend Mel asks.

"His name is Kelston Green. We went to the University of Michigan together. He played hockey with my brother and just got drafted from New York to Chicago. He's on the Wolves roster this season."

"I'm going to look him up. I want to see what the rest of him looks like," Ari says excitedly.

Ari is Korean, and I met her when I wanted to learn more about K-pop. She was teaching classes, and we instantly hit it off. She's petite, cute, and ridiculously smart. She's in graduate school, getting her PhD in sociology. She wants to teach at a university eventually.

"Oh! He's kind of hot. I thought most hockey players didn't have all their teeth. Even if some of his teeth are fake, he's still hot."

"Kelston Green is not hot. He's an asshole. He was in college, and he apparently is now. I haven't talked to the guy in years. I don't even know how he got my number. Instead of a 'hey, it's been a while,' I get a dick pic, and then he asks me if I want to hook up later."

"I'd hook up with him," Victoria says, laughing as she grabs Ari's phone. "It's been too long, and I think I'm growing cobwebs down there."

Our table erupts in laughter.

My girlfriends all know that I'm not a fan of professional athletes, and I have serious trust issues when it comes to men. My ex-fiancé, Brandon, is an NFL quarterback and an exceptionally good one at that. He took his team to the Super Bowl last year and won league MVP. Women flock to him, which, unfortunately, is why we broke up. After six years together, Brandon got blackout drunk after a win and ended up sleeping with some random chick from the bar. He apologized profusely and begged for me to take him back, but the damage was done. The trust was shattered, and my heart was broken. We tried to work it out, but in the end, I just couldn't. We started dating our senior year of high school, dated throughout college, and made it one year into the NFL before "there was just too much temptation." While we've remained friends, I will never ever date another professional athlete. I also gave up being an NFL cheerleader. I just couldn't surround myself with players any longer, and cheering for Brandon every week was its own sort of hell.

My thoughts are suddenly interrupted when Ari looks at me and says, "Girl, I say you take a ride on his pogo stick. You haven't had any fun in forever. It's been years since you and Brandon broke up, and you've hardly dated since."

"You ladies are ridiculous! I will not be calling him, but I'll gladly share his contact info with you." I look down at my watch. "Shoot. Sorry, but I have to get to the academy. I'm teaching preschool ballet today."

I start gathering my things to get up and walk the few blocks to the dance studio.

"Awww. I don't know how you do the preschoolers. Every time I teach them, there's just a lot of nose picking," Sofia says, making a face. "But I'm coming with you. I've got a tap class that starts in fifteen minutes."

We say our goodbyes and head to the Academy of the Arts where most of us are part-time instructors.

I've been dancing my entire life. My mother danced in a professional ballet company and had me in ballet slippers as soon as I could walk. I share her passion, and even years after her death, it keeps me feeling close to her. Dancing grounds me. It brings me to my happy place and allows me to get lost in the music. My father thinks it's "a wonderful hobby and display of athleticism but certainly not a way to make a healthy living." He's a world-renowned neurosurgeon who focuses all his energy on his research and patients. Once upon a time, he was supportive of my "hobby," but when Mom died, that piece of him died too.

Now Dad values education above all else. For that reason, I majored in elementary education and minored in dance. I didn't enjoy teaching nearly as much as I thought I would and am a semester away from finishing my master's degree in elementary education with still no desire to be in an actual classroom. I love teaching dance, but I find that the classroom is dictated by state mandates and stifles my creativity. I can't teach the way I want to teach in the public school system. I've decided I'm going to continue my education and become a dance movement therapist. My dream would be to open my own studio, but I can't imagine my father ever supporting that idea. Instead, I'm finishing my current master's degree, which I'll probably never use, and I teach several different genres of dance part-time. My students range from preschoolers to geriatric women and special needs students in between. I teach at a nursing home a few times a month and also volunteer my time for at-risk kids at the community center.

As I walk into the doors of the academy, I'm instantly energized and ready to meet my newest group of preschoolers.

Chapter 5

Jack

"Mom? Are you here? Where is everyone?"

I walk into the living room of my home where my mom is sitting on the couch, putting my daughter Rosie's hair into a bun on the top of her head.

"Daddy! Daddy! You're home!" Ellie squeals.

She comes running toward me, wrapping me in a huge hug with Rosie hot on her heels. I crouch down to hug my girls, who always seem to smell like strawberries and bubble gum. I stand up and smile at my mother, pressing a kiss on the top of her head.

"You're home earlier than I expected. Did you forget that the girls start ballet this evening?"

"Yeah, our meeting after practice was cut short, so I'm here. I can take them and give you a break, Mom."

"How about we go together? Your dad is out golfing, enjoying these last few nice days, and I'd like to see their first class."

"Daddy! It's going to be amazing. We're going to float like fairy princesses!" Rosie says as she twirls around in her pink tutu.

Her blond curls are all tucked into the bun, and she looks angelic with her icy-blue eyes staring up at me.

"I can't wait, sweetheart. You're going to do great. Now let's go so we aren't late."

We all jump into my SUV, buckle the girls into their booster seats, and head across town.

"You know, my sister, Judith, has wanted me to bring the girls here forever. Her neighbor teaches here and is actually the one who will be teaching Ellie and Rosie today."

"Auntie J knows everyone, Mom."

I laugh thinking about my aunt Judith. She's a social butterfly, full of energy, and always on the move.

"Yes, she does, doesn't she? She seems to think you're really going to like her neighbor. I guess her name is Caroline. I'm going to try one of her Zumba classes with Judith too. Judith can't say enough good things about her."

"What do you mean Judith thinks I'm going to like her? Why would I care about the girls' dance teacher?"

"Apparently, she's as sweet as she is gorgeous. I think we'd all like for you to find a nice girl for once."

"Mom, let me handle my love life."

"Of course, honey. You've been doing such a great job at it too."

I raise a brow, and she grins at me in that all-knowing motherly way.

"All right then, it looks like we're here."

Thank God this conversation is over. I pull into the parking lot and help the girls out. We all head in, and I brace myself for forty minutes of twirling.

"Hi! Welcome to the Academy of the Arts! Are you girls here for ballet?" a blonde with a smoking body asks my two little girls.

Holy shit. She *is* gorgeous.

"Yes!" Ellie giggles. "We're so excited."

She and Rosie are holding hands jumping up and down. The blonde kneels down so she's at their height.

"Yay! I'm so excited too. We are going to have so much fun. I'm your teacher, and I can't wait for you to show me your moves. My name is Miss Caroline. What are your names?"

"I'm Rosemary Elizabeth Hannen, but everyone calls me Rosie," Rosie proclaims proudly. "Eleanor is my sister, but we call her Ellie."

Ellie beams at Miss Caroline.

"Wow! Those are some gorgeous names. I think you are going to make great ballerinas, Rosie and Ellie. Why don't you take your shoes off and slip your ballet slippers on? There are cubbies over there for your shoes. Your family can help you. Does that sound good?" she asks with a huge smile on her face.

The girls are ecstatic. They don't bother asking for help but run over to the cubbies and start trying to take their shoes off. Miss Caroline stands to address us.

"Hi, thanks for signing the girls up for my class. Do you have any questions before we begin?"

I'm speechless. I just stare at her like a complete idiot. I've been with my fair share of beautiful women and am usually very comfortable with the opposite sex, but this chick puts every other woman I've ever seen to shame. She's the most beautiful creature I've ever seen, and I've somehow lost the ability to form a sentence. My mom starts laughing.

"I'm Kathy, the girls' grandmother, and this is their father, Jack. Your neighbor, Judith, is my sister, and she recommended your classes for the girls."

"Awww how sweet! Judith is the best neighbor ever! I'm so glad you could join us. We'll chat more later. I see a little one in tears, so I'm going to calm her and greet some other families. It was so nice meeting you both."

She turns and starts talking to another little girl who looks terrified about her first dance class.

My mom looks at me with a knowing smirk.

"She's beautiful, isn't she, Jack?"

That seems to snap me out of my trance.

"Sorry about that. I was just lost in thought. Yeah, she seems nice."

By lost in thought, I mean I'm imagining all the things I'd love to do with Miss Caroline. She's more than a perfect ten. Can I give an eleven? She's got long legs that go for miles, tits that will generously pour out of my hands, a perfect ass, a flat stomach you can only get from hours spent at the gym, and such full lips that I'm already envisioning them around my cock. Shit, I'm getting hard at a fucking dance studio with my mom and daughters. Hold it together, man. Focus instead on that long, shiny blond hair, hair that I want to wrap my hands in and yank. Damn it! She looks like a real-life Barbie doll. I let out a long exhale when my mom starts laughing again.

"Let's see if the girls need help."

We take off shoes and get the girls all ready. Miss Caroline leads them into the classroom, and we watch through the glass. There are full-length windows in all six dance studios, and each one of them has a different form of dance going on. I can't take my eyes off my daughter's teacher. I've literally had a boner for the entire forty-minute class. She's not only gorgeous, but the way she works with the kids is amazing. They all seem to be having the time of their lives, Caroline included. She has such a rich laugh, and I don't know if I've ever been more attracted to someone in my entire life. I'm actually disappointed that the class is coming to an end and already hoping my schedule will allow me to come next week. At the end of the class, Caroline comes out and thanks everyone for participating. She hands out flyers for a dance recital at the community center. She asks us to all come out and support her volunteer work, which is teaching inner-city youth an escape through dance. All proceeds will go immediately back to the program.

"We'll be there," I say, my voice gravelly.

They're the first words I've spoken to her. I can't believe what an ass I am around this woman. It's like I'm in seventh grade again and get a boner when Stephanie Ferris smiles at me. Apparently, I just agreed to go watch a bunch of kids dance on one of my few nights off. Great. That being said, I don't know if I'm really that disappointed about it.

*****

It's been a few days since Rosie and Ellie had their first ballet class. They've worn their tutus every day since and have been parading through the house, asking me to turn up the volume of the music every chance they get. They've been dancing to songs from the movie *Frozen*, and I'm man enough to admit I know the entire soundtrack and even caught myself humming it in the shower.

We're now sitting in the front row for the community center dance recital. The girls are excited, and I'll be lying if I say I am not looking forward to getting a glimpse of the very sexy dance instructor. After making a generous donation, I'm seated on the end with Rosie next to me and Ellie sandwiched in between my mom and Auntie J. My aunt wanted to support her neighbor too, so it's me and my favorite ladies today. The lights dim, and a lanky guy comes out thanking everyone for coming, and then he introduces his cochair, Caroline Britton. Holy shit, I didn't think it was possible for her to be any more gorgeous than she was the other day. She thanks us all for coming and introduces the first group of dancers.

She leaves the stage, and the first dance begins. The recital is actually really good, and I'm amazed at the talent of these kids. The lengthy guy comes out again and says something about finishing the night with a number that the instructors all put together. Immediately, I perk up. She saunters onto the stage, and I'm mesmerized. She comes out laughing with a group of ridiculously hot women.

Lengthy guy introduces them. "Victoria Hudson, Ari Lee, Sofia Rodriguez, Caroline Britton, and Melanie Powell are the female instructors who will be performing tonight. I'd like to especially thank Caroline who brought these other ladies on board to be instructors, helped raise our fundraising sales to the highest ever, and spent countless hours on choreography. We couldn't have done it without you!"

Damn, this chick may be out of my league. She's obviously talented as hell, passionate, sexy, and driven. I can't take my eyes off her as the instructor's dance begins. It's hard to tell with the lighting, but I swear she's looking straight at me. The way she moves her body has me imagining all things I'd love to do to her naked. She's captivating, flawless, and perfect in every sense of the word. She's definitely an athlete. She's everything I'd ever want, and for the first time since my wife died, I am really interested in a woman.

Chapter 6

Caroline

Why does Jack Hannen have to be even hotter in person? Since I met him at the academy a few days ago, I have been shamelessly fantasizing about the guy. The magazine covers he graces are enough to leave a woman breathless, but seeing him here, watching my choreography, I'm *panting*. The man looks like a Greek god. My panties got wet just peeking at him through the curtain. When I met him the other day, I was trying so hard to play it cool. He hardly spoke to me at all, but I kept catching his eyes on me. He's so tall with an athletic build, gorgeous ice-blue eyes that mirror my own in color, dishwater blond hair, and matching stubble across his face. His square jaw screams masculinity, and his panty-melting smirk is only outshone by his gorgeous smile. He's wearing jeans and a tight-fitting V-neck T-shirt that shows off that amazing body. Sofia sees me staring and laughs.

"Girl, get in line! Did you see his spread in *Sports Illustrated*? He's also on the cover of *Men's Health* this month. I would love to get some action from that man!" she says as she shows me a picture on her phone.

It's of a very naked Jack with only his large hands covering his manhood. I let out a mouth-watering moan, and she busts out laughing.

"I know, right?"

Mel turns to us.

"All right, ladies. We're up. Let's go kill it."

It's our turn as instructors to do our routine, and as I walk onto the stage, I can feel Jack's eyes on me. We make eye contact, and I swear I'm dancing just for him. Everyone else in the room seems to disappear. My heart is racing, and I can feel my skin becoming slightly flushed. Neither of which is from the dance but from the man sitting a few rows back. He licks his bottom lip, and it feels like he wants to devour me. Please tell me I'm not imagining this. Why I am so drawn to this guy? I contemplate leaping off the stage and into his arms. We finish our routine and head off the stage.

"Girl, Jack Hannen stared at you the entire time. He couldn't take his eyes off you!" Ari exclaims.

"I'm so jealous! How do you know him? I swear you know all the hotties," Victoria chimes in.

"He was watching *all* of us, and his daughters are in my ballet class."

It felt like his eyes really were just on me, but I'm not even going to let my mind go there. We head back out to the stage, bowing and raking in the applause. Again, Jack's eyes lock onto mine. Sofia nudges my side, and my smile grows. Jack smiles back and gives me a little wave. Seriously? Did he just wave at me? My heart has these little flutters going on, and I can barely think straight.

We head off the stage, and my neighbor, Judith, shoots me a text congratulating me. She asks if I have a minute to meet her by one of the rec rooms. I'm not sure if Jack's still with her, but I quickly make my way over. My knees are shaking as I head over to them. Ellie and Rosie each grab my legs, hugging tightly. They're holding flowers, and each hand me a bouquet. Their blue eyes look up at me as they tell me how much they want to learn how to dance just like me. I kneel down and give them each a hug, thanking them for the beautiful flowers and promising to teach them all my moves. Judith pulls me up and gives me another huge hug.

"I'm so proud of you, sweetie! That was wonderful. I know how much effort you put into fundraising and getting instructors. Your girlfriends are amazing! The whole show was engaging, and it's so easy to see how much those kids love you."

"Awww, Judith, you're going to make me cry! Thank you so much."

I can feel his eyes on me. I look up at him, and I suddenly feel as if I can't breathe.

"Thank you for coming too," I say to him, unsure how I even got the words out, but they're more of a husky whisper. I'm not even sure he heard me.

He smiles down at me, and it's as if my world stops.

"You're captivating. I couldn't take my eyes off you."

He reaches down for my hand and kisses it. He's still holding my hand, and I'm just staring into his eyes, unable to respond. We're interrupted by my girlfriends, who come running up behind me.

"Care Bear! You did such a good job coordinating everything! That was so much fun," Victoria says as she makes her way to me. She then sees Jack holding my hand. "Oh, sorry. I didn't realize you were in the middle of something."

Jack smirks and gently squeezes my hand before letting go. He looks at Victoria and gives her one of those panty-melting grins.

"I'm Jack. I was really impressed tonight. Great work."

"Hi, Jack. I'm Victoria."

Just then, Sofia comes running over.

"Care, Chad's here, and he's looking for you again. How many times are you going to gently let this guy down? He's not getting it. Do you want me to take care of him?" Sofia asks.

"No. He's harmless. You guys, he's really nice. He's just not my type. Jack, will you just play along for a minute?" I ask him quickly just as good old Chad walks up to our group.

Jack doesn't have the chance to reply before Chad starts talking.

"Caroline! You were amazing! Here, I got these for you," he says as he lunges a bouquet of flowers into my face.

He is such a sweet guy. I wish I were even a little attracted to him.

"Oh! Thanks, Chad. It was nice of you to come, and thank you for the flowers."

I grab Jack's hand again.

"I'm so sorry! Where are my manners? I don't think I've introduced you to my boyfriend, Jack."

Jack smirks, lets go of my hand, and pulls me into him, putting his arm around me. My hand goes instantly to his chest, and I can't get over how rock-hard it is.

"Chad. Hey, man. It's really nice to meet you," Jack says as he holds his free hand out to shake Chad's.

Chad reaches for his hand, and then his face lights up in recognition.

"Oh shit. You're Jack Hannen, aren't' you? I'm a huge fan!"

"It's always nice to meet a fan. Are you free tomorrow night?" Jack asks.

I have no idea where he's going with this, but I lean into him instinctively. He smells amazing.

"Umm…yeah, no plans," Chad says a little confused.

"Well, if you want, I can get you some tickets to the game. I have a ton, and we're at home tomorrow night," Jack offers, and I literally think Chad is going to jump up and down like a child.

He's trying so hard to compose himself. It's kind of adorable.

"That'd be great!"

"Okay, cool. What's your last name?" Jack asks as he pulls his phone out, still never letting me go.

"Lincoln."

Jack starts typing in his phone.

"You're all set. I texted my contact. She'll have them for you at will call. I got you four tickets, but if you want or need more, just let me know."

"Wow. Thanks so much! I guess I'll see you tomorrow night. And sorry for hitting on your girl, man. If I had known Caroline was with you, I wouldn't have been pursuing her."

Jack pulls me in close.

"No worries. We just recently became a couple, and I can't say I blame you for pursuing her. She's incredible."

I look up at him, and he leans down and gives me a quick, chaste kiss on the lips. Holy hell! Even something so simple, and sweet, and I'm literally a goner. I want more. I literally want to stand on my tiptoes, pull him down to me, and kiss him senseless. I swear I'm blushing when I look back over at Chad.

"Thanks again for everything, Chad," I say.

"No worries. Maybe I'll see you at the game tomorrow, Caroline. Have a great night, you two! And thanks again, Jack! My buddies are going to be stoked."

Jack nods his head and smiles.

"Anytime," Jack says as Chad starts to walk away.

He grins at me and then leans in for another kiss.

"I just wanted to seal the deal and be really convincing," he says an inch from my face.

"Mmmm…yeah."

That's literally all I can say.

"Daddy! You kissed Miss Caroline two times!" Rosie shouts.

That snaps me out of my trance. I try to pull out of his embrace, but he holds me tight.

"And on the lips even!" Ellie exclaims.

Jack looks at his daughters smiling and then at me.

"I forgot we had an audience," he whispers to me. "Yes, I did, girls. That's because Miss Caroline is my special friend."

"Lizzy says her daddy has a special friend, and sometimes, she sleeps over. Can Miss Caroline have a sleepover with us?" Ellie asks eagerly.

"Yeah! That would be so much fun!" Rosie chimes in.

"I would love that, girls! Let's ask her. Miss Caroline, will you come to our house and be my special friend for a sleepover? Pretty please?" Jack asks me.

Sofia and Victoria, who have been silent up to this point, burst out laughing. I look over to see Judith, and Jack's mom, Kathy, also smiling at me. Oh my gosh. I'm so embarrassed. I can't believe we just put that little performance on in front of everyone. I am so wrapped up in him that I kind of forget about everything else. And did he just proposition me for sex in front of his mother and daughters?

"Oh, I'm sorry, girls, but I can't tonight!" I say, nudging Jack in the side.

He smirks.

"Maybe tomorrow night?" Ellie asks me.

"I don't know if tomorrow is going to work either. I'll have to check my schedule."

What the hell? Is no one going to save me here? I think they're all enjoying this a little too much.

"Okay, you can check it and let us know at ballet on Tuesday," Rosie says.

"I'm looking forward to Tuesday."

Jack looks down at his girls and then back up at me.

"Jack!" I practically shout and swat at his chest.

He bursts out laughing. His mom saves me.

"Girls, why don't we let your daddy finish talking to Miss Caroline, and you can come with me and Auntie J? We'll meet your daddy at the car," Kathy says as she grabs Ellie's hand.

"Okay. Bye, Miss Caroline!"

They hug my legs quickly and run off with their grandma.

"Are you freaking kidding me? You can't proposition me for sex in front of a group of people! When, by the way, some of those people are your daughters and mother!" I say.

"I didn't proposition you for sex, Caroline. I just asked if you wanted to come over. Wow, you need to get your mind out of the gutter! And did I catch you smelling me?"

He's got such a huge grin on his face. I just want to either slap him or kiss him. I can't quite decide. I'm leaning toward kiss him. Yeah, I definitely want to do that again.

Sofia clears her throat.

"This is seriously the most adorable thing I've ever witnessed, but I feel like we're interrupting a moment over here, so we're going to step away too."

She grabs Victoria's arm. They're giggling as they walk away.

I completely ignore their departure, slightly in a state of shock, and look up at him again. He still has me tucked under his arm.

"I totally was smelling you. You smell amazing. And what was I supposed to think when you're asking me to spend the night? I'm sure you have women spend the night all the time."

His smile falls away.

"Caroline, I may have a reputation, but I've never brought a woman home to seal the deal. My girls don't need me parading women in and out of their lives. They've never seen me with a woman. Being a good father is more important to me."

"I'm sorry. I shouldn't have assumed—"

He cuts me off. "Don't be sorry. I just want you to know what this is and what this isn't." He leans in closer and whispers in my ear, "I'd be lying if I said I didn't want you in my bed, but I'm being more careful for my girls, now."

I know he can tell the impact he has on me.

"Ummm, Care. Sorry to interrupt, but they want to get some pictures of the instructors," Ari says.

I don't even realize she has walked up on us. I pull away. Jack grabs my arm.

"Can I take you on a date?" he asks.

I can't believe this is real life right now.

"I'm not sure. I have to go now though," I whisper.

He releases me, and then Ari decides to invite him with us tomorrow night.

"We're going out tomorrow night to celebrate all Caroline's hard work for this show. Jack, you should join us. We'll be at Club Indulgence. I'm sure Caroline would love to see you there," Ari practically squeals.

What is she doing?

"I kind of have a work thing tomorrow night, but maybe a few of the guys and I could stop by after. It would definitely be late. During away games, we don't really leave the hotel or the rink, but because we're home, I could probably stop by for a little bit," Jack says to Ari.

I interrupt because they're talking about me, and I'm standing right here.

"Jack, hockey needs to come first. We can hang out another time. But right now, you have people waiting in the car for you, and I have pictures. Thanks for coming to the rescue with Chad. I'll see you around."

I start to walk away. I need to walk away. Five more minutes with this man, and I'm going to lose all self-control. I'm never like this with guys. I'm always so cautious. I don't know how we even started making out in public.

"Bye, Miss Caroline."

I look back, and he's smiling like a kid in a candy store. He winks at me again. I get butterflies in my stomach. I smile back. He's got me, and he knows it.

"Damn, Caroline," Ari says as we're walking away. "The sexual tension between you two is off the charts."

"I know, and I want to give in to the temptation so badly, but you know I can't. I'm not going to allow myself to be one of his many women. Not only is he a professional athlete and gorgeous, but he has a reputation. I don't want to be with another guy who is on the road all the time and is going to leave me when he finds someone better."

I feel defeated just saying the words, but after the pain of watching the man I thought I was going to spend the rest of my life with cheat on me, I'm terrified of putting myself in that position again.

Ari looks at me sympathetically.

"Caroline, Brandon didn't find someone better. He screwed up and apologized profusely to get you back. He knows what he's missing out on. It's been years. You hardly date. This man is clearly into you. You have chemistry. Maybe let your guard down just this once. Something good might come from it."

"I don't know if I can."

Chapter 7

Jack

I learn a few things from my interaction with Caroline. One, she's single, or I wouldn't have been asked to be the stand-in boyfriend. Two, she comes across as a good girl because she showed genuine concern about other women in my bed as if she were concerned about being a number and not something of sustenance. Three, this girl is kryptonite. She pulled away so fast at the end that I'm not sure what to make of it. I would have liked it if she had committed to wanting to see me again, but I'm going to enjoy the game.

I shoot off a rapid-fire group text to my teammates who are also my good friends. I'm really hoping we win because there's no way in hell any of us would even consider going out after a loss.

> Me: After we win tomorrow night, we're going to hit up Club Indulgence. There's a blond I want to get to know better.
>
> Mike Jones: Fuck Yes. That place is a buffet of hot pussy.
>
> Jimmy Drake: Glad you to see you're taking my advice, bro.
>
> Graham Novotny: Jones, you sure you don't have any more penile discharge?

Mike Jones: Fuck you, Novotny.

Kelston Green: Bring on Chicago's finest.

Owen Miller: I'm in. Just make sure you wrap it this time, Jones.

Mike Jones: Fuck you, Miller. I always wrap it. That chick's fucked half of our team. You might want to get checked out too, man.

Jason Martin: Jones, I'll invite Tessa. Now that you've both been treated, I'm sure she's dying to ride your dick again.

Mike Jones: I wouldn't touch that cunt again with a 10-foot pole…or my 10-inch cock.

Nate Hastings: LMAO. You wish, bro.

After another half hour of banter, these assholes finally stop blowing up my phone. I can't believe I'm planning to go to the club after a freaking game. I'm sure Coach won't love this, but I have to see Caroline again.

I get the girls dressed in their pajamas, read bedtime stories, and tuck them in. I head into my own room and jump in the shower. As the hot water soothes my muscles, my mind starts to wander. I start stroking my cock from the base up to the tip as I imagine taking Caroline right here in the shower, watching her tits bounce up and down as I drive into her hard and fast. Her back is pushed against the cold tile, and her legs are wrapped around my waist. I envision her hot, tight pussy clenching down on my throbbing dick as she screams my name. Just then, my jizum shoots out in long, white strings, and my entire body trembles. I let out a loud groan and put my head against the tile as I stand under the water trying to catch my breath.

I can't wait for tomorrow night. I really want this woman, and I can't remember the last time I've said that.

I get dressed. It's not even nine o'clock. I realize that Auntie J will have Caroline's number since she's her neighbor. Perfect. I shoot off a text.

> Me: Auntie J, do you have Caroline's number by chance? I forgot to get it today.
>
> Auntie J: Well hi, Jack. I had a feeling you two would hit it off. Your mother and I approve by the way.
>
> Me: I'm glad to hear that and you were right.
>
> Auntie J: Jack, she's a sweet girl. Don't hurt her. She can't be one of your one-night stands.
>
> Me: She could never be a one-night stand.
>
> Auntie: I'll send her contact info over. Don't disappoint me.

My phone lights up with Caroline's contact info. I feel like a giddy schoolboy. I try to think of the perfect thing to say. I start texting ten times before I settle on something simple yet clever.

> Me: Hi Miss Caroline. It's Jack Hannen. I figured you'd need your boyfriend's number, in case Chad asks for it.

The three little bubbles start moving instantly, and I know she's typing. I can't wait for her reply.

> Caroline: Hi Jack. That's very thoughtful of you.

Me: I'm a very thoughtful guy. I've been thinking about you all night.

Caroline: LOL. Tell me, does that line work on all the girls?

Me: Ok, I get it. You think I'm a playboy. Relax, I haven't had sex in months. I'm cleaning up my image.

Caroline: That's very noble of you.

Me: I'm very noble

Caroline: Jack, we are obviously attracted to each other but I don't know if this is a good idea.

Me: Why's that? Afraid I'll rock your world?

Caroline: Actually, yes.

Me: I will rock your world but you'll love it.

Caroline: Cocky much?

Me: Confident

Caroline: What exactly do you want, Jack?

Me: I'm not sure yet. I just know I really like you and you're the most beautiful woman I've ever seen.

Caroline: You've got a line for everything.

Me: It's not a line. You are the most beautiful woman I've ever seen.

Caroline: Good night, Jack.

Me: Good night. Can't wait to see you tomorrow night.

Caroline: Wait? You're seriously coming? You have a game!

Me: I do have a game. But you'll learn I can be pretty persistent and I really want to see you again.

Caroline: I'm picking up on the persistence thing.

Me: Good. Want to have that sleepover tonight? The girls are already in bed, but I know lots of fun things we could do while they're asleep.

Caroline: Night, Jack!

Me: Good night, beautiful.

Chapter 8

Caroline

I couldn't sleep after texting with Jack last night. God, if he only knew how badly I wanted to take him up on his sleepover offer. My vibrator got a workout, and yet I could not be satisfied. I tossed and turned almost all night. I blame it on the incredibly sexy hockey player. Lust is overpowering common sense. Now we're all gathered at Mel's place getting ready before we go out. The hockey game is on in the background, which is something I would have never turned on, but Sofia insisted. I haven't really followed hockey since my brother, Cody, stopped playing, but from what I read, Jack's incredible. I have to admit, I am curious to see him play. I've always loved the game, and I can't seem to take my eyes off the screen.

I'm embarrassed by how much time I spent on the internet stalking him in the last twenty-four hours. During my very innocent stalking, aside from all his hockey accolades, I learned that his wife died four years ago in a car accident with a drunk driver. I checked his daughters' registration forms at the academy and realized they were only six months old when their mother died. It looks like after her death, he didn't date anyone at all, but then he went on his man-whoring spree. Just as I feared, there are pictures with him and dozens of women all over the internet. It doesn't look like he's currently seeing anyone, but it just reminds me that I'd be a number even though he seems like a stand-up guy who just went through a tragedy when he was very young.

He's adorable with his daughters, and I can see how much he loves them just by watching them interact. He's obviously close to his mother, who also seems sweet. Plus my neighbor, Judith, is constantly raving about her nephew, Jack, and how we would be perfect for one another. He's active in the Boys and Girls Clubs of America and does a ton of volunteer work for the children's hospital. He's obviously generous as he displayed by so willingly giving Chad tickets to the game. He's a damn good kisser, and our chemistry is an inferno. I'm finding it harder by the minute to not want to see where this will go.

"So, Caroline, are you ready for tonight? Maybe a little sexy time with a very sexy hockey player? I mean you are looking hella fine tonight," Ari snorts as she holds up her mojito.

I haven't divulged to my friends just how much time I've spent thinking about Jack Hannen since I met him. If I had to guess, they might already know. I'm not going to admit that I spent forever shaving my legs and moisturizing and may have gotten a mani-pedi today. Plus I totally got waxed last week, not even knowing that I'd meet this guy, but was thanking my lucky stars that I had opted for a Brazilian. I also got a blowout at the salon today. I totally prepped for the possibility of seeing him.

"Ha ha, very funny! He texted me last night saying he was going to come after the game."

I'm still not sure he's going to want to show up at the club after midnight. Part of me thinks we won't see him tonight. He has a game. He's on TV right now. But just the thought of seeing him again has my stomach doing this weird flipping thing and my heart rate rising. I spent so much time getting ready for tonight that you'd think I was going to the Oscars or something. I'm feeling ridiculously confident in my appearance. It's that feeling you get when you find the absolute perfect dress and heels and you know you're going to turn heads.

"Caroline! How did you fail to mention that you were sexting all night?" Mel asks as she finishes reapplying her lipstick.

Mel's gorgeous dark skin and honey-colored eyes make her a force to be reckoned with. She's biracial. Her mom's white and teaches at one of the local high schools. Her father was African American. He was a police officer for the city of Chicago for years and was shot and killed in the line of duty during Mel's senior year of high school.

It's what drove her to apply to law school. She's beautiful, smart, and driven. But tonight, she's letting loose. Her dress is even sluttier than mine, and when Mel actually lets loose, she's the most fun person in the entire world.

"We weren't sexting! It was just some innocent flirting."

I can't even talk about it without blushing. I'm so pathetic.

"I loved watching you two together yesterday. You may as well just have some fun with him, Care Bear. I have a feeling it'll be the best sex of your life. Tell him to bring some friends too," Victoria snorts.

"I'm nervous, you guys. I just don't want to make a mistake and get hurt."

I swallow hard.

"Caroline, trust your instincts. If it feels right, go with it. If not, that's okay too."

Ari gives my arm a little squeeze.

"Care, you deserve only the best. It's going to be okay. Trust us. Okay, now who's ready for some shots?"

Mel holds up a bottle of vodka, and we all head over to the kitchen island. She pours the shots and hands them to each of us.

"To girls' night!"

We all raise our glasses and take the shot. I chase it with some Sprite. I'm not a big drinker, and I want to have my senses about me if and when I see Jack. The game just ended, and the Wolves absolutely crushed Boston. I'm wondering if that means he and his team really will be out celebrating tonight. We turn the TV off and head outside to our Uber. I'm excited, nervous, and slightly giddy. I think tonight has the potential to be awesome.

Sofia links arms with me as we walk out and whispers to me, "Just so you're not surprised later, I put a bunch of condoms in your purse. I wanted you to be prepared for anything. Now let's get out of here."

My jaw drops as we climb into the car.

Chapter 9

Jack

Hell yeah, we won. I played my ass off hoping to earn my reward in Caroline at the end of the night. Spirits are high as we head into Club Indulgence. They have a VIP section set aside for us, and we head straight upstairs. There's a flock of women with us, but I'm only interested in finding one woman tonight, the one who looks like a live Barbie doll and appears to be as sweet as apple pie. All I really know about Caroline is that we have amazing chemistry. She's hot as fuck, loves kids, and dances like she was made for it. Auntie J says she's a sweetheart, and she's obviously involved in the community. So far, I'm really having a hard time finding anything negative here. I scan the bar and don't see her. I start searching the dance floor when the guys call me over for a round of tequila shots. Jones decides to turn his into a body shot with the abundance of surgically enhanced women surrounding us, and after the round, we're all ready to celebrate. Most of us don't drink during the season, and if we do, we stick to beer. I have no plans to drink anything else tonight. I turn and start scanning the dance floor again.

Jones bumps into me with a woman on each arm.

"Who the hell are you looking for, man?"

"A woman I met the other day. She's supposed to be here tonight."

"Bro, look around. You can have your pick."

One of the bunnies on his arm smiles at me.

"I can be yours for the night!"

"Veronica, you're mine tonight!"

Jones puts his arm around her a little tighter, and she trips in her four-inch stilettos.

"It's Vanessa, baby, but I'll answer to whatever you call me."

The woman on his other arm laughs.

God, how in the hell is Jones not tired of these women? Didn't he just finish his antibiotics from the last one? I look at Vanessa. She's attractive. She is skinny and has fake tits and some collagen fill in her lips. She looks more like a porn star than the girl you want to bring home to your mother, but who am I to judge? Jones is looking for an easy lay, nothing long-term. A few months ago, I'd have been doing the same. I shake my head and laugh.

"You three have fun tonight."

I turn back around when I see her. God, is it possible that she's even more beautiful than she was yesterday? She's dancing with the same girlfriends I met, and there's a group of guys gawking at them. It's like every man in the room wants her, and she's just laughing it up, having a great time with whoever has the balls to approach her. Damn, I need to get down there.

"Whoa! Where are you running off to, Jack?"

Jimmy grabs me by my shoulders. He's my best friend and one of the only ones who calls me by my first name.

"You've been staring at the blonde with the perfect body. Is she the one we're here for?"

"Yeah, there's something about this one."

"Well, all right then. I was going to call dibs when I saw her, but I have a feeling you'd kick my ass."

A surge of jealousy suddenly comes over me. No fucking way are my teammates making a move on this one.

"She's mine," I practically growl.

What the fuck is this woman doing to me? Like I'm a caveman or some crazy shit.

"Yeah. That's pretty obvious. But her friends are smokin', so I'm heading down there with you."

He's got this huge-ass smirk on his face, and I can't help but laugh.

As we make our way to the dance floor, phones come out for pictures, and both men and women try to get our attention, asking for autographs and selfies. I try to ignore everything, keeping my eye on the prize. I plaster a smile on my face so I don't look like too much of an asshole ignoring my fans for one of the first times ever. But tonight, all I want is her. Caroline must have sensed my gaze because she looks up, staring straight at me, and her entire face breaks into a huge smile. I slide over to her, my dick already hard. I lean over so I can talk in her ear.

"Hey, Miss Caroline. I was hoping I'd see you tonight."

I pull her against me, and as our bodies start grinding to the music, I think I might actually come in my fucking pants. Her touch is like a bolt of lightning that shoots straight to my crotch. She smells like oranges, fresh and sweet. Her ass is rubbing shamelessly against my dick. I begin kissing her neck without really even thinking about what I'm doing. It just feels so natural to touch her, get closer in any way I can. She arches her neck, showing me she likes what I'm doing, and I let my hands roam over her body. She spins around, so she's facing me, and I put both of my hands on her ass while she rubs her hands over my chest. She's so full of life and energy. Her eyes sparkle up at me, and I see the same lust I feel. I lean in for the kiss. Her hands go to my hair, and something inside me snaps. I kiss her like it's the last thing I'll ever do.

*****

Caroline

Holy shit! Am I seriously grinding shamelessly and making out with him in the middle of the dance floor? And why don't I care? Probably because I've never been more turned on in my life. Surprisingly, Jack can really move. I should have expected his flexibility, but not everyone has rhythm. Why is he so damn sexy? I must be dreaming. Or maybe I'm hallucinating. His hard steel is pushing up against my thigh, and my god, I think I could get off like this. Maybe that's why I can't think straight. Lust has replaced my normal neurons, which are firing off like Fourth of July fireworks. My nipples are so hard. They ache. He's a full foot taller than me, and even in heels, I feel so tiny next to him. He's holding my ass when our lips collide. I kiss him like a woman who needs his kiss to survive. His tongue is firm, dominating, and frenzied. His hands are everywhere as we start to dry hump to the music. I need more, and I need it now. He must have sensed my desire.

He breaks the kiss and pulls me off the dance floor. He leads me up the stairs into the VIP lounge. I walk by a group of men I recognize as his teammates, vaguely seeing Kelston Green, the asshole who sent me the dick pics. Jack quickly brings me to a corner booth and shuts the privacy curtain. He lifts me and sets me on the table. Our lips once again collide, and my breathing becomes ragged. I've never needed someone like I need this man. It's as if all common sense has left my brain.

"I need to touch you," I say as I begin unbuttoning his white button-down shirt.

He groans as I begin outlining the defined muscles on his chest with my tongue. He yanks me close to him and begins sliding his hands up my thighs toward my core. I'm aching for his touch.

He pulls me to the edge of the table and says, "I want to taste you. Is it okay if I taste your pretty pussy, Caroline?"

I can't even form the words, so I simply nod my head and push my hips toward him.

"I need your words. I don't want to misinterpret anything."

"Yes, touch me, Jack. Please."

He becomes frantic like he can't move fast enough. He pulls my thighs over his shoulders, and I lie back on the table, propping myself up onto my elbows. He pushes my panties to the side. His tongue goes straight to my aching clit. He begins licking, sucking, and nibbling, alternating directions, acting like a crazed man. Just when I feel like my world is going to explode, he inserts his finger, and I lose it. I scream his name and buck against his face. I shamelessly rub my sex all over his face as my thighs clench the sides of his head. I'm panting. How the hell has this never felt so good before? He slows his pace and looks up at me, my juices covering his face. He smiles at me.

"I need to be inside of you."

"Yes. Yes, please!"

It's all I can say as I watch him yank a condom out of his wallet. I begin to unbutton his pants and grab his thick shaft. It's so hard and long. I stroke him, and he stares at me with fire in his eyes. He grabs my hand and pushes it aside as he sheathes himself. I open myself for him. I lean back on the table again. He's so tall that he's got one leg standing on the ground and his other knee is on the table, up by my waist. He thrusts into me, hard and deep. I gasp at the sudden intrusion because, oh my god, does it feel good. We quickly find our rhythm when he takes his thumb and presses on my clit. His mouth goes to my breasts, which are still covered by my dress, and he nips at my nipples through the fabric. I lose it again, coming so hard that I see stars.

"I'm going to come, babe."

He begins thrusting harder and faster, driving his way to a glorious finish.

"Yes, God, yes! Jack, please!" I scream again.

He unleashes his load in me, and we both just sit for a minute panting and staring straight into each other's eyes. Sex has never been so good.

*****

Jack

That was amazing. Best sex of my life. Hands down. I can't believe I just lost control like that. I've never fucked a woman in public before, let alone inside a bar with my teammates standing on the other side of a curtain. She does something to me. I lose control. I never should have been so rough with her though. I was fucking her like a man whose life depended on it.

"Are you okay?" I ask, feeling like a dick for not controlling myself better.

I can't get enough of her. Honestly, there's no way I could have been gentle. I was too desperate for her.

"Ummm, yeah. I'm better than okay. That was so, so good."

She looks up at me with her big, blue eyes. Her lips are swollen from our kissing, her skin is flushed, and her nipples are still pointing through her dress. The freshly fucked look may be her best look yet. God, I already want her again.

"I can't believe we just did that."

"I can't either. I can't control myself around you. You're fucking incredible."

I pull out of her and take the condom off. I tie it up and wrap it in a napkin that was sitting on the other end of the table. Not knowing what to do with it, but not wanting my swimmers sitting on a bar table, I put the napkin into my pocket. I can dispose of it later. She starts straightening her dress, and I help her down from the table.

We look at each other for a minute, and she gives me a sheepish grin.

"Well, that was fun."

She suddenly seems a bit embarrassed. Oh, hell no. I'm not going to let this get awkward.

"Why don't we get a drink? Maybe talk a little?"

"Yeah, I'd like that."

She looks up at me, and I suddenly realize just how tiny she is. I'm a big guy, at almost six feet four inches, but even with her heels on, she barely reaches my shoulder. I grab her hand and open the curtain as we make our way to the bar. It feels like every single one of my teammates is staring at us with a smirk on his face. Oh yeah, they all know exactly what went down behind that curtain. I look down at Caroline, about to say something.

"Wow. I really made a great first impression on your teammates. I feel like I'm doing the walk of shame, and it's not even the morning after!"

She lets out a nervous laugh.

"They're staring because you're the most beautiful woman they've ever seen and because they haven't seen me with someone in a really long time. You have nothing to worry about."

I smile down at her, hoping I've calmed her nerves some. We make our way to the bartender, and I ask her what she's drinking.

"I'm not really a big drinker, but I could use a water."

God, could she be any more adorable? I laugh and ask the bartender for two waters. He hands over the ice-cold waters, and I tip him a fifty. I place my hand on the small of her back as we get cozy on the barstools. We turn to face each other, my legs on each side of hers. She pushes a loose hair behind her ear.

"Twenty questions?"

She laughs, a rich throaty laugh.

"I think we're doing this backwards."

"Maybe a little. Favorite sexual position?"

"Oh my gosh, Jack. I thought the idea was to get to know each outside the sex!"

She slaps my chest, and I immediately grab her hand.

"It is. I just wanted to rile you up. For real, now. How old are you?"

I rub my thumb in circles over her hand. I can't stop touching her. She looks down briefly at our hands, smiles, and looks back up at me.

"I'm twenty-six."

"I'm twenty-eight."

"I know. I'm at an unfair advantage because I can look you up online."

"Like what you saw?"

I grin and immediately get nervous. This is what I hate. They all know everything about me because of my career. They know I'm a widower. They know I'm a father. They know my salary. I can't open up on my own time line. My life is an open book.

"I think there's a lot more to you than the playboy they make you out to be. Although, I have to admit, I never thought I'd have sex in a bar. You're definitely persuasive."

I don't know if she realizes how much she just eased my fears with that statement. She validated that there's so much more to me than a freaking bio online and some pictures of me with different women.

"Well, that was a first for both of us."

She arches a brow, seemingly surprised.

"I've also never had a crush on my kids' dance instructor until now."

She laughs.

"Well, I've never been with a hockey player."

It's my turn to laugh.

"Yeah, me neither. I've also never wanted to kiss someone so badly."

She takes a sip of her water, stares into my eyes, and licks her bottom lip, giving me all the permission I need to kiss her. I bring my head down and kiss her gently, exploring instead of devouring and tasting instead of claiming. I break the kiss before I get carried away again, knowing that my team is watching.

"You make me crazy."

I growl into her ear. She instantly arches into me, pressing her breasts into my chest.

"How do you make me want you so badly?" she asks me breathlessly.

"The feeling is mutual."

She grins and then seems to contemplate for a minute.

"Okay. Talking first. Talking is good. What's your favorite food?"

Ah, she's killing me. I just want to get her the hell out of here and take my time getting to know every inch of her body. I take a big breath.

"Italian. What about you?"

"Mexican. First kiss?"

She's good at this game. She's easy to open up to, and I like that she's taking charge of the conversation, ensuring that we actually get to know each other to some extent.

"Jodi Kerr, seventh grade during spin the bottle. Now yours."

She lights up.

"Mine was also in seventh grade, but his name was Matt Welker, and he had just finished eating a bag of salt and vinegar potato chips. It was kind of nasty."

I can't help but laugh.

"First time going to second base."

"Hmmm… I never really played baseball."

She laughs coyly, and she knows she's playing me. God, I like this girl.

"Kidding. Ninth grade, Steve Pratt, under the bleachers after a football game. Yours?"

"Eighth grade. Jenna Stahl, in my buddy's basement. When did you lose your virginity?"

"Junior year of high school. I was seventeen, and he was my boyfriend."

She looks like she's going to say more but doesn't.

"Your turn."

"Sophomore year. I was sixteen, and she was my high school sweetheart."

I don't want to talk about Bree. I need to change the course of this conversation back to us.

"I think I lasted two minutes. But to be honest, I'm slightly embarrassed by how long I lasted with you tonight too. Do you think I'll get the chance to prove that I've got some stamina?"

She twirls a piece of her hair and looks upward like she's really contemplating what I'm offering and then totally catches me off guard with her bluntness.

"Jack Hannen, I literally cannot wait any longer for you to fuck me again."

Holy shit. I just hit the jackpot. This girl is so out of my league.

CHAPTER 10

Caroline

Someone please pinch me. I look over and see the most gorgeous man lying in my bed and smile. I'm wrapped in his arms, and he has one of his legs over mine. I can't believe last night actually happened. Where the hell did that come from? I *never* act like that! I'm a good girl. I don't do hookups or one-night stands. I have nothing against them, and plenty of my good friends have them all the time, but I have trouble separating sex from love. And when I think of love, I think of getting my heart broken again, and I basically just shut down, hence the reason my girlfriends keep encouraging me to live a little. As I replay the events from last night in my mind, I can't decide if I'm embarrassed, aroused, or ashamed at my lack of self-control. Everything about last night was hot, and he is so, so hot. I have never been attracted to anyone like this. I can't even blame being drunk. I barely touched alcohol last night, wanting all my faculties when he got to Club Indulgence.

We were practically on top of each other during the Uber to my town house. We went through nearly all the condoms Sofia had stuffed into my purse. He bent me over my couch and took me right there as soon as we walked into my living room, discarding our clothes all over the entryway. We made our way into the bathroom where he made me come twice in the shower as he pressed me up against the cold tile. We then had sex on my kitchen island when we went to get ice cream out of the freezer. He covered my body in whipped cream and spent nearly an hour licking me clean. We took another shower and then finally made it to my bed where I rode him until I was screaming and bucking as he pushed me up and down over his long steel rod. It was undeniably the best night of my life.

"Keep looking at me like that, and I'm going to have to have my way with you again before I leave."

I'm so lost in my thoughts. I didn't even realize he was awake and staring at me. I can feel his erection against my belly and suddenly feel the need to give him a lasting memory of me this morning. I smile at him, mustering up the strength to speak uninhibited. I'm not normally so forthcoming, but any self-consciousness seems to go away with him. I know if I can get the words out, he's going to lose his mind.

"Good morning, Jack. I wanted to wake you with my mouth on you, but since you're already awake, I guess I'll just have to tell you what I want. I keep thinking about you coming in my mouth and how that would be the most delicious breakfast I've ever had."

His eyes literally bug out of his head.

"I swear I've died and gone to heaven."

He leans into the bed and pulls me on top of him. We start kissing, and I could kiss him forever, but I want to do this for him. I break the kiss and slowly start kissing a trail down his hard chest, his firm abdominal muscles, that *V* that dips down low, until I reach his cock. I lick it, following the vein down his shaft, and he hisses. I know I have him right where I want him. In this very moment, I feel like the most powerful person in the world.

*****

Jack

She's not real. She can't be real. This is all a dream. Wow! Okay, she's good at this. Shit, I can't come this fast. I need to focus on something else. Sewers, tarantulas, counting. I have no desire to ever leave her bed, which is weird considering I never spend the night with a woman. I'm usually long gone when the sun comes up. The more time I spend with her, the more I like her. Why am I not freaking the hell out right now? Oh yeah, because her perfect, full lips are closing in over my crown, with her big doe eyes looking up at me, staring straight into my soul. I can't think right now, not when her hand is cupping my balls, and her other hand goes toward the base of my shaft. She's sucking me hard, harder than I thought she would. It feels fucking amazing. She quickly finds her rhythm with her hands and her mouth caressing my dick until I'm nearly gone. I'm still trying to hold it together. I put my hand in her hair, guiding her. My hips start moving, and I'm trying to be respectful and not fuck her mouth. She suddenly grabs my ass and pushes me further into her. I feel myself hit the back of her throat. She swallows, and I fucking lose it.

"Care—babe, I'm going to come."

That seems to get her going even more, and she sucks me harder and faster until my load is shooting straight down her throat. I can't take my eyes off her. She's incredible. That was incredible. Last night was incredible. I'm so screwed.

She looks up at me with a satisfied smile.

"How'd I do?"

Is she serious right now? How does she not know what she does to me? I actually don't want her to know what she does to me.

"So good, babe. *A* plus work right there. Your turn. Lay down, and let me eat that sweet pussy."

I've noticed she likes the dirty talk. I thought it would scare her off a little because she's got that sweet and innocent demeanor, but she's really a lioness. The dirtier I talked last night, the more responsive she became. She doesn't lie down but instead sits up and pulls me in for a kiss. I can taste myself on her. I gently push back until she's holding her weight with her elbows, and then I fucking devour her. Breakfast has never tasted so good.

Chapter 11

Caroline

Jack left a few hours ago to get home to his daughters but not before giving me three more amazing orgasms. No man has ever been able to turn my body to putty the way he does. It's like I'm his puppet, and he can make me come on command. My girlfriends are all sitting down to lunch, and I'm just waiting to be berated with questions.

"So, Caroline, you kind of disappeared after you and Jack were dry humping and making out on the dance floor. Care to fill us in?" Mel asks, arching one of her perfect brows at me.

Mel doesn't sugarcoat anything and definitely doesn't beat around the bush. It's my favorite thing about her, but I'm totally going to play this out.

"I have no idea what you're talking about."

I take a sip of my lemonade and smirk. Sofia literally looks like she's dying for details.

"Caroline, spill! Is he huge? Did he leave you utterly satisfied? Did you use the condoms I gave you?"

I can't contain my laughter.

"That man is literally a god. I've never had sex that good, and yes, he's huge. It was the best night and morning of my life."

I sigh dreamily. I expect them to start drilling me, but instead, they give each other worried side glances.

"Honey, I'm glad you had fun, but he's a professional athlete. He probably has lots of experience giving girls the best night of their lives. We wanted you to let loose, but we don't want you to get hurt."

Sofia looks to Mel.

"Care, you haven't dated much since Brandon. You were the one who told us no professional athletes ever again. Remember? You have trouble separating sex and love, and we don't want you falling head over heels in love before you've established what exactly is going on between you two. Last night was sex. It sounds like it was life-altering, best-sex-of-your-life sex, but don't get your hopes up that it's going to turn into something more. His playboy reputation is there for a reason."

Well, great. Talk about raining on my parade.

"Ladies, I know. Don't worry. I'm not going to fall in love with him. I just had a really good time last night. It was incredible actually, but I don't even know if I'll see him naked again."

I'm going to change the subject before I start overanalyzing everything.

"Besides, my brother, Cody's coming into town tonight. I plan to spend my time with him and hang out in the city."

"Your brother is so hot. Don't be mad at me for hitting on him the second I see him."

Ari laughs shamelessly.

"I'm so glad he broke up with his girlfriend."

"Yeah, it was pretty obvious that she wasn't right for him. I have no idea how they lasted two years together."

Just then, my phone pings. It's a text from Jack. My heart starts racing, and my belly does a little flip. I swipe to open it.

Jack: I can't stop thinking about you.

Hmmm, you and me both, handsome. I think I'm going to go with honesty here. Everyone always says that's best, right? I just don't want to seem desperate or crazy or obsessed or all of the above.

Me: Likewise. You're kind of great.

Jack: Can you have dinner with me tonight?

Me: I'm so sorry but I already have plans.

> Jack: I can be very persuasive as you well know. I think you should change your plans.
>
> Me: I don't doubt that, but these plans can't be changed. Rain check?
>
> Jack: I have a home game on Tuesday and then I'll be out of town for a few days for a string of away games. Promise me dinner when I get back.
>
> Me: I promise

I really want to go to dinner with him tonight, but there is no way I'm ditching Cody when he's flying in from New York. I shoot off a quick text to Cody.

> Me: Hey. Still on for some delicious Chicago style pizza for dinner?
>
> Cody: You better believe it. Looking forward to seeing you, lil sis.
>
> Me: I'm not that much younger and you're just freakishly tall.
>
> Cody: Nearly everyone is taller than you short stack. Boarding the plane. Talk soon.

"Ummm, hey there, gorgeous. You still with us?"
Mel starts laughing.
"He texted you, didn't he?"
I'm sure I'm blushing. Gosh, I'm so bad at hiding anything.
"Yes. He wanted to do dinner tonight, but I told him I had plans. I kind of wish Cody was coming tomorrow night instead so I could go out with him."

"Proceed with caution, Care. It's good to make him wait and not rearrange all your plans for him. I'll see you tonight at the academy," Sofia says as she starts gathering her things to leave.

"Ladies, it's been real, but I've got a hair appointment in ten minutes."

She gives us quick hugs and leaves.

I look at my other friends, unsure how they'll respond but feeling compelled to tell them.

"Jack's daughters are actually enrolled in my ballet class this afternoon, but I think his mom, Kathy, is bringing them."

I really hope they don't tell me not to be excited about the possibility of seeing him. I'm not completely naive to the fact that he can hurt me. I just want to believe he's not Brandon, and he's not going to crush me.

"Your first crazy night of sex in who even knows how long, and it ends up being with a guy you're suddenly seeing all the time, know his mother, and are teaching his daughters. I don't think this qualifies as a one-night stand, Care. Knowing you, he'll end up falling madly in love with you, and you'll make one hundred cute little babies," Victoria says as she gives my hand a quick squeeze. "I've got to get to my mom's place. She wants help picking out decorations for my sister's bridal shower."

"You're ridiculous. Have fun with your mama, beautiful. I have to get going too."

I hug Mel and Ari goodbye as they stay to chat. Then I head to the library. I'm almost done with a paper I'm working on, and it's time to use my brain again although I'm not sure how I'm going to concentrate because all I can think about is Jack.

*****

Jack

I'm walking into the locker room and expecting shit from the guys. I haven't responded to any of the hundred texts that have popped up on my phone since last night. I really don't care. I'm in such a good mood. Nothing can bring me down. This girl does something to me, and I like it. She makes me feel alive again like she's waking parts of me that have been dead for years. I'm on cloud nine.

"Ohhhh! Here he is! Have fun last night, man?" Novotny asks, getting everyone else on board.

Jones chimes in, "Where'd you take off to with that hottie? I think Veronica was hoping for a little fun. You disappointed her, man. She really wanted to ride your stick. Luckily, I took care of her for you."

Jimmy follows, "Jones, you douche. Her name's Vanessa. How the hell do I know that when you're the one who fucked her last night? Jack, I'm not going to lie. I was tempted to open that curtain just to make sure you were both okay in there. Those screams were so loud. We heard them over the music."

I laugh out loud at that one.

"What can I say, gentlemen? She's incredible."

"That's all you're going to give us, man? Throw an old dog a bone here," Novotny says with the biggest grin on his face I think I've ever seen.

"I'm not giving details with this one. I like her too much. We went back to her place after the club. We had a really, really good time, and I woke up to her lips around my dick. Best fucking night ever. I'm not giving you anything else."

I can't contain my smile. I'm like a little kid in a candy store, so freaking excited. It's hard to tamper down my enthusiasm.

"I'm happy for you, man," Jimmy says as he pats my shoulder. "You deserve to have some fun, and she's fucking gorgeous."

Just then, Kelston Green walks in. I don't know Kelston as well as the other guys. He was recently traded to our team, and I'm still getting a feel for him. I invited him out last night because he's one of a few single guys left on the team.

"Fuck, Hannen. You stole my girl. I've been trying to hook up with Caroline Britton since I moved to Chicago. I didn't realize she was willing to make the switch from NFL to NHL, so I'd been feeling her out. I gotta know, is she as much of a freak in the bedroom as I've heard?"

"What the hell are you talking about, Green?" I ask, suddenly feeling uneasiness seeping throughout my veins.

"Caroline. The chick you fucked in the bar last night. You know, Brandon Mueller's ex?" he says, looking at me incredulously.

"Brandon Mueller, the NFL quarterback for the Texas Coyotes is Caroline's ex?"

Please tell me I'm misunderstanding something.

"No fucking way! You didn't know, bro. Caroline is a former NFL cheerleader. Rumor has it after she and Brandon broke up, she fucked half the team. I guess she got tired of the NFL and decided to make her way to puck bunny status. You just got to be the lucky one to tap that ass first. So how was she?"

I think I'm going to be sick. How in the hell did I fall for that sweet girl act? The hardworking graduate student who loves children and volunteers with inner-city youth is actually just like every other chick I've been with since my wife. She's not interested in me, just interested in the fame and money. Maybe she'll show up pretending I'm her baby daddy too. How the hell could I have been so stupid? Everyone's looking at me, waiting for a response when our phones all ping. The guys all look down and start scrolling through their phones. I can tell by the sound that it's something involving one of us that made headlines. I don't have to be a genius to guess what it's about.

"Shit. Don't bother looking, Jack," Jimmy says.

"You know I have to."

I swipe across my screen. There are multiple pictures of me and Caroline from the club. They show us all over each other, even one of me closing the curtain. The headline reads "From NFL to NHL?" There's a picture of Caroline kissing Brandon Mueller. He's in his jersey, and Caroline is in her cheer uniform. There's another with her and a group of Texas Coyotes players at a bar. I guess Green knew what he was talking about.

"Let's get on the ice. We're going to be late."

I can't think straight. I'm so pissed. I sure know how to pick 'em.

Chapter 12

Caroline

After being locked in the library all afternoon, I'm excited to get to the studio and work with my students. The physical activity always wakes me up, and dancing brings me to life. I've just finished with my five- through seven-year-old tap class when I see Jack's daughters come running through the door, dressed for my preschool ballet class. Gosh, they are adorable. I have a few minutes before class starts, so I go to greet them. They're both talking a mile a minute, and I love how excited they are to be here. Kathy comes up and gives me a huge hug.

"Caroline! I'm so happy to see you again. The girls couldn't stop talking about you the whole way here. Jack was supposed to come too, but he got held up at practice. He should be here later."

I know he just left my house this morning, but I can hardly contain my excitement. I can't wait to see him again.

"It's great to see all of you, Kathy. I'm so glad the girls were able to get into this class. Rosie? Ellie? Are you ready to come dance with me?" I ask as the two little girls eagerly look up at me, jumping up and down repeatedly. "Let's go!"

I bring the girls into the studio and leave Kathy to watch through the glass. The rest of my class begins to file in. We begin with stretches and then start with some simple basic moves, prancing around to songs they all know. The kids are all having fun, and before I know it, the class is over. One of the moms stops me on my way out to ask if I think her daughter is ready to move up to the next level. As we discuss her progress, I see that Jack is already here. His teeth are clenched, his jaw set hard, and his body tense and rigid. He looks nothing like the man who fucked me senseless this morning. I begin to wonder what could have happened at practice and want to make sure he's okay. I finish my conversation and make my way over to him. He's helping Rosie change her shoes while Ellie is running circles around them.

"Hey there! I'm glad you could make it. Ellie and Rosie were amazing today. They're naturals. I'm so proud of both of them."

I hold my hand out and go to touch his arm when he pulls back and looks at me with ice-cold eyes.

"I'm not sure how you fit it all in, Caroline. It was fun, but I'm all set."

He stands, grabs one daughter's hand in each of his, and walks out the door. I stand, completely shell-shocked when Kathy comes out of the bathroom and sees me standing there staring at Jack.

"Caroline. He normally doesn't let the headlines get to him, but apparently, one of his teammates also had some things to say about you too. I'm sorry, honey. I'm sure it's a big misunderstanding. This is just a sensitive subject for Jack."

She hurries out the door after Jack and her granddaughters. What is she talking about? Just then, Sofia comes up behind me and hands me her phone. My jaw drops. My heart starts racing. How can they get away with such blasphemy? The article makes me look like some sort of whore with no morals. How can they insinuate that I'm just looking to be attached to a professional athlete's paycheck? I'm so mad. I'm shaking. How in the hell can Jack actually believe any of this? Why wouldn't he just ask me about Brandon? Sofia puts her arm around me, and I tuck my head into her shoulder. I'm shaking. I'm so upset.

"Why don't you let me cover your last class, Care? Go talk to him."

Sofia really is the best friend ever. I can't find the words to thank her, so I simply nod and run out the door after Jack.

"Hey, Jack! Can I talk to you for a minute?"

I'm breathless as I reach him.

"No, sorry. We have to run."

I can see how mad he is. But he won't even give me the chance to talk to him.

"I just want a minute."

I sound desperate.

"I'll bring the girls to the park around the block. You can walk over there and meet us when you're finished, Jack."

Kathy comes to my rescue, and I make a mental note to do something nice for her. Jack sighs.

"What do you want?" he asks me.

"Do you really believe the stuff that was written about me?"

"Look, Caroline. I'm no longer interested. I'm trying not to be a dick."

"Too late."

"You're not the first woman who's fucked me because I'm a hockey player. I'm sure you won't be the last. I'm not complaining about it. We had a good time. Now you can go on to your next conquest. Jones is always up for a good time. I can give you his number."

"How dare you? You don't even know me!"

What an asshole. I cannot believe the nerve of this guy.

"I know enough."

"No, you don't. I could care less that you play hockey. It's actually a strike against you. Believe it or not, I liked the guy I met at the dance recital. It just helped that your Aunt Judith has been shamelessly trying to get me to go on a date with you for nearly a year. I've never had a one-night stand, and I made a terrible decision with you."

"Spare me."

He walks closer to me. He brings his mouth down to my ear. My heartbeat picks up, and even though I'm angry with him, he smells so incredibly good that it reminds me of last night. I can feel his breath against my ear.

"Were you thinking what a bad idea it was this morning? I was there. You had zero regrets. Don't expect me to believe you were after anything more than what you got. You're just pissed you got outed."

He stands to his full height, towering over me. I look up at him. How could I have misjudged him so much? I can't believe I slept with this guy. The tears come back, streaming down my face.

"You're horrible."

It's all I can say. I turn back and walk into the dance studio. I gather my things and head home.

*****

I haven't seen my brother in ages, and I've been looking forward to his trip for months. Now all I want to do is lock myself in my town house with a carton of cookie dough ice cream and cry while I watch chick flicks on TV. Instead, I'm doing my very best to put on a smile and not be a total downer during our dinner. He had work meetings all afternoon, so this is the first time I've seen him since he landed in Chicago. I'm meeting him at Giovanni's, our favorite place for a traditional Chicago pizza. As I walk in, I'm assaulted by the smell of garlic and olives. I scan the red-and-white-checkered-covered tables and see my brother sitting alone, staring at his phone, with two glasses of red wine on the table. God, I've missed him.

"Cody!" I say and run over to him.

A huge smile takes over his face. He stands to envelop me in one of his big, strong hugs.

"Runt! I've missed you. Got you a pinot. That okay?"

He pulls out the chair across from him, and I sit down, smiling up at my brother. I was wrong. I don't need chick flicks and ice cream. I need my protective, dependable big brother.

"More than okay. Thanks. You look good, Cody. New York must be treating you well."

"You look like you've been crying. Does that have anything to do with the article of you and Jack Hannen?" he asks me while handing out his phone.

Of course, he's seen it. I don't speak. I'm too embarrassed and so ashamed of myself for being so stupid. I should have never let my guard down. I simply nod.

"You want to tell me what happened? Because I know you're not the woman they're describing in this article."

"Cody, I don't even know where to begin."

"How about the beginning?"

He gives me a half smile. The waiter comes over to our table, and we place our order. Neither one of us bothers to look at the menu. We both know what we want. It's the same thing every time. Large cheese pizza with peperoni, green peppers, mushrooms, and yellow peppers. We always start with a house salad with Italian dressing. As the waiter walks away, Cody starts again.

"All right, Caroline, I'm here to listen."

"You know my neighbor, Judith?"

He looks at me confused.

"Yeah, of course, I know her. She makes me cookies every time I visit you."

"Jack Hannen is her nephew. She talked Jack into enrolling his four-year-old twin daughters into one of my dance classes. I think she actually talked Jack's mom into it, but either way, I've been seeing him at the academy. Then he showed up to my recital at the community center. We talked and flirted for a bit. My girlfriends invited him to meet us at a dance club last night, but I didn't think he'd show. Not only did he show, but we danced together all night. That's where the pictures are from."

"Okay, so you knew him before the night at the club. That makes me feel a little better," he says, taking a sip of his wine.

"Yeah. I didn't know much about him other than he plays for the Wolves, and then when I was looking him up online, I saw that his wife died in a car accident. I was obviously attracted to him, like every other woman in America."

He laughs.

"I wonder why I'm not on the cover of any magazines? Seriously though, it looks like he's attracted to you too. I would rather not have seen these pictures," he says holding his phone up.

I can't help but blush.

"When we started dancing, things got a little carried away. It was so out of character for me. I obviously wasn't thinking. I just—"

"No details, please! Got carried away is all I needed to hear."

He makes a face, and I can't help but laugh. It feels good to talk to him.

"Okay, no more details. He spent the night at my house. We texted throughout the day. He asked me to dinner tonight, and I told him I already had plans, but we were going to get together once he gets home from his stretch of away games."

"Caroline, I'm not really understanding why you were crying. He didn't seem to believe this bullshit any more than I do if he asked you to dinner."

"That was earlier in the day. I saw him this evening after his daughters had their class, and he was an ass. He could hardly even look at me. His mom came over and apologized. She told me he usually doesn't believe the stuff he reads online, but one of his teammates had also said some things about me, and it pissed him off. I tried to talk to him, but he made me feel like a cheap whore."

"What an asshole. Damn. Who on his team would say something? Did you talk to any of the other guys at the club?"

"No one. They saw us together at the club, but that was it."

"Then why the hell would one of them be talking shit?"

"I honestly have no idea."

That's the thing that has really been bothering me. Some stranger wrote a bunch of lies about me, but then someone he actually knows lied about me too? And someone on his team?

"Oh, wait! Didn't Kelston Green just get traded to the Wolves? Remember, he played hockey with me at Michigan? He wanted you so bad. He was constantly asking me when you and Mueller were going to break up so he could swoop in. Maybe he said something to Jack."

"Yeah, I remember Kelston. I was always really nice to him though. I think he's an asshole, but he doesn't have any reason to talk trash about me."

The salad arrives, and we start digging in.

"Believe it or not, he sent me dick pics a few days ago. He wanted to hook up. I've never had anyone send me pictures of their manhood. I was so shocked. I didn't respond."

"What the actual fuck, Caroline? Why didn't you tell me he was harassing you? I'm going to kick his ass."

I put my hand on his.

"I didn't tell you because I knew you'd react like this. Don't worry about it. It was one time, and I haven't heard from him again."

Cody relaxes slightly.

"Caroline. It was definitely him. Asshole was probably just jealous and wanted to have something to say in the locker room. Just talk to Jack."

"I have no desire to talk to Jack ever again. He didn't even give me a chance to defend myself."

"Look, everything just came out with the article. The guy probably has tons of women throwing themselves at him, and he grouped you with them. Let shit settle down, give it some time, and reach out. If nothing else but to demand an apology."

"Yeah, I guess you're right. Maybe it was just bad timing."

"I'm always right."

He grins at me.

"Okay, thanks, Cody. I'm so glad you're here. You always make me feel better."

I grab his hand and give it a tight squeeze. The pizza arrives. We start talking about everything and nothing. I'm actually having a lot of fun, and we're both laughing as we reminisce about all the pranks we used to pull on each other. Before I know it, we've finished a bottle of wine and are heading out with a box of leftover pizza.

*****

Jack

After I talked to Caroline in the parking lot, I felt like absolute garbage. Deep down, I know she's not a whore. Aunt Judith would have steered me far away if she were anything but genuine. I walk to the park and meet my girls.

"How did it go?" my mom asks as I push Ellie on the swing.

"Not too good. I was a jerk."

I let out a big sigh.

"Well, that's a shame because everyone who knows her adores her. Judith's been telling me how perfect you two would be together for months. I didn't believe her at first, but after meeting Caroline, and seeing you two together, I couldn't agree more. Maybe you should apologize."

"I don't think she wants to hear from me."

My mom looks at me with that all-knowing maternal look.

"Jack, what did you do?"

"I don't want to replay it. I was a jerk. We'll leave it at that."

"I guess I don't need to voice my disappointment then."

"No, you don't."

We play at the park for an hour or so before everyone gets hungry. The girls want pizza. We head to Giovanni's, which is hands down the best pizza in Chicago. So now I've been sitting in Giovanni's back booth with my mom and daughters staring at Caroline and her date for the last hour. Of course, she's here. Her back is to me, but I watched her run up and hug him. I saw her put her hand on his. She was laughing like she didn't have a care in the world, looking absolutely stunning. It should piss me off that I still think she's the most beautiful woman I've ever seen. It's like the shit online didn't bother her a bit. Here, I've been sick about it, and she obviously doesn't care at all. I can't believe I thought she was different.

"Why don't you go talk to her, honey?" my mom asks.

Apparently, I'm not doing a good job at hiding my sulking and staring because Mom is onto me.

"There's nothing to say. Plus she's on a date."

Just as I say the words, she gets up from the table. The guy helps her with her coat and says something to her. She nods and heads out the front door. The guy acts like he's heading to the bathrooms and then quickly turns toward me. He's staring straight at me and knows I've been watching him. He approaches our table.

"Hey. You're Jack Hannen, right?" he asks me.

"Yep."

I have no reason to be polite to this tool, so I'm not going to sit here and make conversation easy.

"Would you mind if we talk for a minute privately?"

He looks over at my mom and daughters.

"Yeah, I would mind. I'm kind of in the middle of dinner with my family."

"Look, Jack. I was trying to be cool with you, but you've been shooting daggers at me for the last hour and staring at me like you want to kill me. To be honest, I should be the one who's pissed at you for treating my baby sister like garbage."

His sister? What the hell is he talking about? I raise my brows at him. He must have sensed my confusion.

"I'm Cody Britton, Caroline's brother."

Oh. Did not see that one coming. Her brother. Not a date. Not at all. I wonder if he knows that I had my dick inside his baby sister less than twenty-four hours ago. Shit.

"Cool. Nice to meet you. We're trying to eat, so if you don't mind—"

He cuts me off. "Yeah, I do mind." He throws my words back at me. "I guess we're doing this here. You're in the news all the time, Jack. You know not everything that's written about you is true. Just like not everything that was written about Caroline is true. You should give her the chance to explain herself without accusing her of being something she's not."

"I really don't want to talk about this right now, but if you must know, I had a source confirm what was written. Maybe you just don't want to believe what was written about your sister."

I give him a tight smile, and he actually starts laughing at me. I'm trying to watch my language in front of my daughters and not be a total asshole.

"A source, huh? Let me guess. Kelston Green? Yeah, I'm glad he's your teammate now and not mine. He and I played hockey at the University of Michigan together for four years. Three of those years he spent obsessing over my sister. He's had a thing for her forever, and she's never shown an ounce of interest in the guy. She was with Mueller and crushed Green's ridiculously large ego."

I admittedly don't know Kelston Green that well, but his timing was impeccable. He obviously has some sort of history with Caroline. But her brother also just confirmed that she was with Mueller.

"There are pictures with her and Mueller all over the internet, and you just confirmed that she was with him."

"Do you honestly know nothing about my sister? I knew you were a playboy, but damn, I kind of figured you talked to your women at least a little bit first."

He looks disgusted at me.

"Caroline and Brandon Mueller dated for six years. They were engaged when he cheated on her and left her absolutely devastated. She was never with any other NFL player. She quit cheering after they broke up. You're something else, Hannen."

He turns to leave when Caroline comes running up to him.

"Cody! What are you doing?"

She looks at him and then me and then over to my mom and the girls.

"You said you had to use the bathroom and would meet me outside in a minute," she says through gritted teeth.

Oh, she's pissed. I actually feel kind of bad for her brother.

"I didn't need to use the restroom. Just wanted to set the record straight with Jack here."

Caroline glares at him and then looks at me again.

"Jack, I'm so sorry. I had no idea you were here."

She looks at Cody.

"You knew he was here the whole time, and you didn't say anything to me?"

"I didn't want you stressing out any more over the guy," he says nonchalantly.

"Cody, I'm a big girl and can fight my own battles. I appreciate you trying to set the record straight, but seriously? Not cool."

Caroline looks like she's about to cry. My mom starts to get up and make her way out of the booth.

"Rosie? Ellie? Why don't we let your daddy talk to Miss Caroline for a minute?" she says.

"Kathy! No. I'm so sorry. We should never have interrupted your meal. We're leaving right now. Aren't we, Cody?" Caroline says as she puts her hand on Cody's arm.

"Yes, ma'am. I'm really sorry for interrupting your meal and for discussing all of this in front of you and your granddaughters. That was extremely rude of me. I shouldn't have had this conversation here," Cody says, keeping his eyes on my mom and not bothering to look at me.

He allows Caroline to push him toward the doors of the restaurant. Once they're out of view, I let out a big sigh. My mom opens her mouth to speak, but I can't handle it right now. I cut her off.

"I know, Mom."

I honestly don't know what else to say. Maybe I did screw it up. I've been trying so hard to stop being a playboy and start being a role model for my daughters. I think tonight's dinner conversation just set me back a few months of hard work. I don't know what to think. I definitely don't know what to do about the whole Caroline situation. Even if I do try and have a normal conversation with her now, I doubt she'll talk to me.

Chapter 13

Jack

It's been a little over a week since I saw Caroline and her brother at Giovanni's. I feel like an asshole, but I have tried to contact her and apologize. I left her a voice mail and texted an apology. She hasn't responded. Then she completely ignored me when I brought the girls to dance last night and tried talking to her in person. She still treated my daughters with nothing but kindness, but she wouldn't even make eye contact with me. Both my mother and Auntie J are furious with me.

A group of the guys are all heading to O'Neils for some burgers after our team meeting. My mom took the girls to a movie, and then they were heading to Auntie J's for dinner. I find myself with a few free hours, and while I could head over to Auntie J's, I have no desire to hear the wrath of two angry women. We head into the restaurant, and the hostess brings us to a large corner booth. We pile in and place our orders. Mike Jones surveys the area and wastes no time looking for pussy.

"You guys see that table of hotties directly next to us? They keep looking over here. Maybe I should go introduce myself."

Jones is one of the best wingmen in the league, a great friend, and funny as shit, but he's not the guy you want anywhere near your sister.

"Shit. Jack, isn't that Caroline?"

Jimmy's looking at the group of women, and sure enough, Caroline is sitting right in the middle of the table glaring at me.

"Caroline Britton's here? Jack, since you already had your chance, I'm calling dibs, man."

Kelston Green is literally drooling as he looks at her. She's surrounded by beautiful women, but it's as if none of the others even exist. I can only see her, and if Kelston thinks he's making a move, he doesn't realize how badly I'm going to pummel his ass.

"The hell you are," I nearly growl.

"Whoa, bro, she looks pissed at you. If looks could kill, you'd be six feet under."

Jones starts laughing. "What did you do?"

"Last time I saw you two together, you were fucking at Club Indulgence. I'm guessing you called her out about that article, huh?" Novotny chimes in.

"Incoming."

Jimmy feels the need to announce the dark-skinned beauty who just left Caroline's table and is heading straight toward us. She's staring right at me, and I feel like she's coming to chop my dick off. I instinctively drop my left hand to cover my manhood.

"What the hell are you doing here, Jack? Haven't you messed with my girl enough?"

She takes her beer and lunges it at me.

"Holy shit! This is awesome!"

Jones is laughing hysterically. I'm dripping in beer, and he's laughing his ass off. At least the rest of the guys look shocked for a minute before they all start laughing too.

Caroline comes running over.

"Mel, are you serious right now? Why does everyone think I can't fight my own battles? Jack, I'm so sorry! Are you okay?"

I can't believe she's actually worried about me right now. I deserved the beer to the face.

"Care, it's not that we don't think you can fight your own battles. You're just too sweet. Your sweetness is your best quality, babe, and I love you for it. But he called you a whore and he—"

"No need to apologize. I'm fine, and I deserved it. I am sorry about the misunderstanding, Caroline."

I look over at the dark-skinned beauty whom I now know goes by Mel.

"You're right, Mel, I am a piece of shit when it comes to Caroline."

Mel looks slightly triumphant, but Caroline looks mortified.

Jimmy starts to get out of the booth, making room for me to slide out.

"Maybe you two should go talk."

"Nope. Not necessary. Jack said everything he needed to say to me already. I know exactly how he feels about me. Mel, I'll meet you back at our table. I'm going to run to the bathroom really quick."

She turns abruptly and practically runs to the bathroom. I totally fucked this up. Jones stands up and introduces himself to Mel.

"Hey there, honey. What do you say about us combining tables? I'm sure Jack would love to apologize to Caroline, and I know I would love your company."

"Are you serious right now, *honey*?"

Mel looks like she wishes she still had beer in her cup. But then one of the other women chimes in.

"I think that's a great idea. Caroline deserves some closure. You boys can do the heavy lifting."

Green readily stands up and helps Jones move their table.

"Are you sure Caroline is going to be okay with this? He called her a whore," Mel says.

"You called her a whore? What the fuck is wrong with you, Hannen?" Novotny asks me.

Before I can reply, the women start talking.

"This may be a good thing, Mel, and we can always leave. Caroline might need this push, or she's never going to talk to his ass again. She has to see his family all the time, and I know she's been stressing over it."

This comes from a Latina-looking woman. It's like they don't realize I'm here, or they don't care.

"Girl, you are beautiful. How did you know I love Italian women?" Jones says as he shamelessly checks her out.

"One, you're an idiot. Two, I'm not Italian. I'm Latina. Three, don't call me girl. I'm a grown woman."

She raises a sculpted brow in Jones' direction, and I notice Jimmy immediately zones in. She's 100 percent his type. He likes them smart, sexy, and sassy. It's as if she were made for him.

"Damn, feisty. I like it. And guess what? I like Latina women too. I don't discriminate."

Jones gives her one of his panty-melting grins that I've seen countless women fall for. This one shakes her head and turns to look at the bathroom door as if she's telepathically willing Caroline to come out.

"Down, boy. I think she might be out of your league," Jimmy says to Jones. "Excuse me, miss? On behalf of the rest of us, I'd like to sincerely apologize for our friend's disrespectful comments. He's had a few concussions and sometimes speaks without thinking."

The Latina woman smiles at Jimmy, but it's Novotny who brings the conversation back to me.

"Jack, you didn't honestly call her a whore, did you?"

Does he seriously have to ask again? I'm about to reply when Caroline comes walking over to the now joined tables. I'm positive she just heard the question. All eyes shift from me to her and her to me. The table grows silent.

"What's going on?" Caroline finally asks.

I can see the worry written all over her face. She's plastered on a fake smile, but she's not fooling anyone. I should say something to lighten the mood, but I'm still sitting staring at her with beer dripping off me.

"Sorry, Care. We thought we'd give Jack a chance to apologize, but we can ask for our drink bill. It will only be for a few minutes," one of the women says to Caroline.

Caroline nods and sits down, unease written all over her face.

*****

Caroline

I sit down at the table completely bewildered that my girlfriends managed to infiltrate this NHL table in the few minutes I spent in the bathroom trying to compose myself. Did they honestly think I'd want to sit with him? I'm going to bail. I look in my purse for some cash to contribute to my drink so I don't have to wait for the server when Jack tells everyone he's going to grab another shirt out of his car and will be back. He stares at me the entire time, and I hate that a single look from him still gives me goose bumps. I'm about to announce my departure when the guy sitting next to me leans in.

"I'm sorry we didn't get the chance to meet earlier, Caroline. I'm Jimmy Drake. Jack's my best friend."

"Hi, Jimmy. It's nice to meet you. Are you the Uncle Jimmy Rosie and Ellie always talk about at dance? I think Rosie may have a crush."

He chuckles. Just because he's Jack's friend doesn't mean I need to be rude to him too. He's actually a really good-looking guy, and I'm kind of annoyed that I can't appreciate how handsome he is because all I can think about is Jack. Jimmy leans in so that only I can hear him.

"Caroline, I only have a minute or so before he comes back, so I'm going to be direct here. That guy knows he screwed up. He's one of the best men I know. He's loyal to a fault, generous, and, unfortunately, a little fucked up. He's a single dad who has been through a lot. Trust me, if you give him another chance, you won't regret it. He just needs someone to be patient with him."

He looks at me earnestly, and I want to believe him. Seeing Jack tonight is messing with me. I was holding out strong. I've listened to his voice mail every day but have managed to not call him back. I've read and reread his text almost one hundred times and have typed and deleted a reply more times than I can count.

"I appreciate your insight, Jimmy, but Jack and I will not be reuniting under any circumstances."

I know I deserve more respect than Jack gave me, and I am not going to give Jimmy any indication that I'm becoming weaker by the minute.

"I'm going to head out."

I get up to leave and bump right into Jack's hard chest. He's got a new shirt on, and it looks like he may have splashed some water over his face and hair in the bathroom. He's gorgeous. I immediately feel the connection, the pull to him. We stare into each other's eyes. His eyes are magnetic. I feel like every significant interaction we've ever had has started with us staring at one another. He reaches down and pushes a piece of hair behind my ear. My traitorous body tingles with anticipation, apparently forgetting that this guy is an asshole. I swallow the lump in my throat. I'm sure he can see what he does to me no matter how hard I try to hide it.

"Please don't touch my hair again," I whisper.

"I'm sorry. I didn't mean to make you uncomfortable," he says, eyes full of remorse, and I'm so pissed at myself for still being attracted to him.

"I'm leaving. Take care."

I turn toward the table.

"I'm heading out. Have fun everyone."

"Care, we're sorry, babe. We can all leave," the pretty Asian-looking woman says.

"No worries. I have class in the morning anyways. Good night!"

My friends all exchange a look, but I know if I don't get out of here soon, I'm going to regret it.

"Hey, Caroline, I can leave. Why don't you stay with your friends?" he asks me like he actually thinks I would want to stay now.

"I was leaving anyways. Bye, Jack."

Just stay strong, Caroline. You can do this.

"I'll walk you to your car."

Why? Doesn't he realize I have no desire to talk to him?

"That's not necessary."

I begin walking toward the door but am hyperaware of the man who decides to walk uninvited next to me. Everyone turns to look at Jack. A few people stop him and ask for autographs. A woman even asks him to sign her chest. I'm feeling lucky that he's getting held up by his fans. I walk out the back exit toward the parking lot. The air is especially cool, reminding me of the impending winter that is right around the corner. I'll shoot the girls a text once I'm home, asking someone to grab my coat that I left inside. There's no way I'm going back in there, and this way, they won't try to talk me into staying. I'm just getting into my car when Jack comes running out the door over to me. So much for my clean break.

"What are you doing, Jack? Your friends are all inside."

"I don't want to be with my friends. I want to be with you."

He scoots into the passenger seat, rubbing his hands together to keep warm.

"Can we please talk?"

*****

Jack

I'm taking a huge risk here by following her and jumping into her car, but I don't care. There's this compelling pull I have toward her, and God, even though I shouldn't, I want her. She puts her head on the steering wheel. I give her a minute, willing her to speak first, knowing she's about to kick me out. But when she looks up, I see vulnerability.

"Jack, why are you doing this? You obviously don't think very much of me. Why are you trying so hard to get me to talk to you?"

"I screwed up. I panicked. I really liked you, and prior to that article, I was on cloud nine. I believed that shit because it was easier than admitting that I might actually like you. I haven't had a relationship since my wife died, and I sabotage anything good that comes into my life. Caroline, I really am sorry."

Damn, I did not plan to drop that much of a truth bomb on her. I have fucking diarrhea of the mouth. Her face softens.

"I'm sorry that you've had a difficult time since your wife's death, but what you said was cruel. You really hurt me."

"And I regret that. Most of the women I've been with recently are after my paycheck or being with a professional athlete. I shouldn't have grouped you with them."

"No, you shouldn't have, but I understand where you're coming from."

"If you give me the chance, I promise I will do my best to make up for it."

"You want me to give you another chance?"

I can see how skeptical she is and want to try and smooth things over.

"We don't have to sleep together. Maybe we could be friends."

Fuck, I don't want to be her friend. I want to be inside of her again already.

"You want to be my friend?"

Smart girl, she knows I don't really want to be her friend, but she has no idea what I really want to do to her.

"Sure. Now let's go back to your place. I heard you say you have to be up early tomorrow for class, and I know we're both hungry. I'll cook for you."

"Okay."

She looks as if she doesn't have any fight left in her. Then she backs out of the parking spot, and we head to her place. I can't believe she's letting me come over. I cannot fuck this up. We don't say much on the drive. She pulls into her garage, and we walk in. I look around as if I've never seen it before. It's warm and welcoming. Everything is tidy, and it smells like vanilla.

"Last time you were here, we were a little preoccupied, so I didn't show you around. Welcome to my home."

She actually blushes.

"Thanks for having me. I like it."

I can't say that I liked it better the first time when I stripped her naked the second we walked through the door. I remember bending her over the couch and taking her right there. The sex was rough and unforgiving, and she gave back everything I threw at her. I'm hard just thinking about it. She must be thinking the same thing because I notice she's flushed as she looks from me to the couch. Yeah, she remembers. I clear my throat.

"All right. I'm going to peek in your fridge and see what I can make for us. Why don't you get a glass of wine and relax?"

I see she has a chicken breast, tons of veggies, and a box of noodles in the pantry. I quickly get to work, cooking the chicken and making a white cheese sauce that I can put over some steamed vegetables, the chicken, and the pasta. I feel at home in the kitchen. She sits down at the island and quietly watches me as I chop the vegetables.

"You don't have to do this, Jack."

"I want to do this for you, Caroline. Let me. Do you teach dance every night?" I ask, wanting to take her mind off of what I'm doing.

"I teach dance part-time. I'm getting my master's degree, so I have class and study in the mornings. I teach classes from noon to six PM during the week and spend my weekends volunteering with the community center."

"That's great. I was surprised by how much I enjoyed your show at the community center. Some of those kids were amazing."

I'm trying to be supportive and keep the conversation on her so she stops thinking I'm a self-centered prick.

"They really are! It's been a lot of fun. I feel like it makes a positive impact in a lot of their lives. I saw on your profile that you do quite a bit of volunteer work yourself."

"Yeah, I'm pretty active in helping raise money for the children's hospital downtown. My best friend growing up had leukemia, and I spent a lot of time visiting him in the hospital as a kid. I just remember how tough things were on all of us during that time. I figure anything I can do to make it better for some other kid and his loved ones is worth it."

"Jack, I had no idea you had such a personal connection. Did your friend pass away?" she asks with concern all over her face.

"Nope. He's been in remission for years. We thought we were going to lose him for a while there. He's a great guy. He lives in Minnesota still. He and his wife just had a baby boy last month. I've been wanting to get out there to see them."

"I'm glad he's doing well. You definitely should get out there and see him. I'm sure they'd love it. I'm guessing you won't be able to do that until after your season's done though, right?"

"Yeah, we're pretty busy during the season. All right, food's done."

I put the plate of pasta in front of her. She smiles.

"I'm impressed. I don't think I've ever had a guy cook for me."

She looks up at me with her gorgeous blue eyes. They're blue like mine, but mine have a stormy gray in them, and hers remind me of ice-blue. They're so light. They match the sky on a cloudless day. She's fucking beautiful.

"You're kidding me? Well, as your newest friend, I promise this won't be the last time I cook for you."

I smile back at her, and I feel that connection we had the first time we met. The sexual tension is starting to mount, and I'm trying not to think of her naked. The harder I try, the more I fail.

"Thanks, friend. This is delicious."

She giggles. I'm totally going for it. I lean in closer to her.

"Are you thinking dirty thought right now too?"

Her eyes go wide. Her pupils dilate, and her cheeks redden. She takes a quick sip of wine.

"Um, we both know that's a terrible idea."

Her body doesn't seem to be agreeing with her words. I lean closer and whisper in her ear.

"Is it though? Our misunderstanding has been cleared up. Maybe we should get back to where we were before it."

I moved a little too fast on that one. She instantly backs away, putting space between us.

"Hey there, Mr. Charmer. Let's be real. It's going to take more than an apology and making me dinner."

I can see her determination in her set jaw. It's freaking adorable. I'll play along.

"You think I'm charming?"

"Oh my gosh. Is that all you heard?"

"Nope. Just the only part I'm going to comment on. So now are you thinking dirty thoughts?"

I love pushing her buttons. It's so easy to do.

"Oh my god, Jack!"

She starts laughing now.

"What? You can't blame me for trying!"

She's fun. Auntie J might have been right. This one is different than the other women I've been with over the years. We flirt for the duration of our meal. I'm really having a lot of fun with her.

"It's getting late, Jack. I think it's best if you go home. I can give you a ride."

Damn, and I thought I was doing so well. She's basically kicking me out.

"I'll grab an Uber. You don't have to drive me."

Just then, Jimmy texts, asking me where I'm at. I shoot him a quick response, asking him to pick me up at Caroline's.

"Actually, Jimmy's going to swing by and pick me up. He lives a few houses down from me."

"Great."

She looks around awkwardly and starts to clean up the dinner mess.

"You know, while we're waiting for him, we could hang out in your bedroom for a bit."

"Jack! You're persistent. I'll give you that. Now get your butt in here and help me do the dishes."

She has no idea how persistent I can be.

Chapter 14

Caroline

I love puzzles, riddles, and games. I'm good at them, and I'm usually good with people. But Jack Hannen is an enigma to me. He has taken residence in my brain, and I don't like it. I am spending way too much time thinking about him, and I can't stop no matter how hard I try. It's like when your mom tells you not to eat the cookie until after dinner, but then all you can think about is how badly you want to taste the cookie.

No single person has ever made me feel close to the way he did. I'm pretty inexperienced sexually. Obviously, I was intimate with my fiancé, but it took me a full year before I dated again after Brandon. In the three years that we've been broken up, I dated one guy for a little over six months and another for eight months. I had sex with both of those guys, and while I enjoyed it, it was nothing like Jack Hannen sex. Jack Hannen sex is raw, dirty, and addicting. It leaves you utterly satisfied but then makes you crave more. It's the kind of sex you read about but think is fictional like, girl, it can't be that good. But with Jack Hannen, it's that good and more. I can't stop thinking about the things that man can do with his hands and, holy hell, his tongue. The things he whispered in my ear are a recurrent fantasy I keep replaying in my head. He talks dirty, and I can't believe how much I liked it. I may be ruined for all other men.

God, I need to stop. The guy is ridiculous. When my neighbor Judith—or as he calls her, Auntie J—suggested I date her nephew, I wasn't interested. I wasn't interested because he is a professional athlete. I wasn't interested because he's on the cover of magazines, has guest appearances on late night comedy shows, and is literally the Zeus of men. Why would a guy like that choose me? Fame and money destroyed my first serious relationship, and this guy has plenty of both. The main reason I kept telling Judith I didn't think it was a good idea though is because Jack Hannen is known to be a playboy. He's slept with probably more women than he can name, and I really, honestly, can't believe I'm one on that long list. I'd like to say I'm disgusted with myself for not holding out, but damn, then I'd have to give up the best sex of my life, and I can't go back now. I have no idea what came over me that night at Club Indulgence. I've never wanted someone the way I wanted him that night. I've never had that strong of a sexual connection with someone. I don't think I could have stopped it if I tried.

But then after the best sex of my very inexperienced life, the playboy, himself, has the audacity to insinuate that I'm a slut. What the actual hell? I read the articles. I don't know who I pissed off for them to write those things about me, but wow. I understand why Jack freaked out. I didn't know about the chick pretending he was her baby's daddy until I started internet stalking him. I can see why he wouldn't trust women. I can also see how those articles would make me seem untrustworthy. Then add on his teammate, whom I am guessing was Kelston Green, backing the articles and talking trash about me. Yeah, it looks bad. But I'm not some random woman. I'm a friend of his family. I take care of his Aunt Judith's diabetic cat when she's out of town. I teach his daughters ballet, and I've met his mother. He should have at least talked to me. While I accepted his apology, I'm still not willing to jump into the guy's bed again.

He has texted me every day since the night he apologized and made me dinner. Most of the texts are ridiculously sweet, all are flirtatious, and if it weren't for the way he reacted to those articles, I'd probably have one enormous crush. The problem is I slept with the guy the first chance I got, and he basically called me easy because of it. Every text he sends is loaded with sexual innuendos. Trust me, I would love to have sex with him again, but I don't trust myself to make good decisions around him. Texting is one thing, but to actually be in the same room with him? No, I'm not that strong, and I'll cave for sure. I know the pleasure he can give my body, and despite what my mind says, my body is begging for more.

*****

Jack

I've texted Caroline every day since we had dinner at her house. We haven't spoken, but I think she's forgiven me for being a prick. It's been almost a week, and I've been out of town for hockey, but I can't stop thinking about her. I'm not sure what it is that makes her different. I know the sex was incredible. Unforgettable, really. Best-sex-of-my-life sex. Sex I'm still fantasizing about weeks later. But that's not why I keep thinking about her. She's special. Before Bree's death, I was always a one girl kind of guy. Through my grief and self-hatred, I found sex to be a release. I didn't want to know the women I was fucking. It didn't matter. They served a purpose. But now I actually want to get to know Caroline, the blond-haired, blue-eyed angel that makes my heart skip a beat. She makes me want more and makes me want to be better.

I don't know exactly what I want from her. I like her, but I don't do relationships. I think my one and only chance at love, as fucked up of a love as it was, died with Bree that night. Sometimes, I feel that this is karma's way of payback for her death. I'm not allowed to love or be loved again. I don't deserve that honor. What happened with Bree will haunt me for the rest of my life. Caroline is just a reminder of that.

We just finished a four-day stretch of away games, are home for another three, and then are on the road for another four. We got back last night. I'm already back in the locker room this morning. My nanny has been out of town visiting her family, and my parents have had the girls. My mom seemed exhausted after I got home from my game last night. I know she's getting tired of my schedule even though she loves my girls. I'm going to have to see if I can get a second nanny to help out some. It reminds me of what I'm missing by not having a wife and a motherly figure for them. It's this constant internal war, and I'm just waiting for the grenade to go off at any time. I'm heading into the locker room for practice and a team meeting, and I hear Novotny call my name.

"Hannen! Did you see your boy, Brandon Mueller, was on *Sports Today* talking about Caroline?"

Damn him. I just want to put this shit behind me.

"Nope."

I did a pretty simple internet search and found out that Brandon and Caroline were engaged and broke it off for undisclosed reasons. The shit her brother, Cody, told me seems legitimate. I'm not sure if watching his interview is going to make things better or worse between us.

"Well, that's a damn shame because I think it'd be good for you to watch. According to him, she's not a whore, man."

"I know that. I was being a dick to her without knowing all the facts."

Why the hell am I talking about this?

"Is she still pissed at you?"

"I hope not. I'm trying to get in her good graces again, but she's making me work for it."

Jimmy walks up to me with the interview pulled up on his phone. He looks at Novotny and gives him a nod, like they both know some shit I don't.

"Just watch it."

He hands me his phone, and I press play against my better judgment. The screen shows Brandon Mueller sitting across from the host, Alyssa Whytt. They've got coffee mugs in front of them, and for the first few minutes, they talk football. I'm about to turn it off because I could really give a flying fuck about this guy's season when the conversation shifts.

> ALYSSA. Brandon, your ex, Caroline Britton, was recently seen with NHL player, Jack Hannen, of the Chicago Wolves. She got eaten alive by the paparazzi, and there were

some pretty terrible things said about her. What are your thoughts on the matter?

BRANDON. I called Caroline after this all surfaced. She was obviously upset. I don't think she and Hannen are together any longer, which is definitely his loss. She's one in a million. She and I were together for six years, and I screwed it up. I'll always love her and have tried to win her back more times than I can count. In the end, she made the right call by dumping my ass.

He chuckles and rubs the back of his neck like he's still uncomfortable talking about it.

ALYSSA. Well, she's lucky you still have her back. Do the rest of her former NFL lovers share your sentiments?

BRANDON. There weren't any others. She's a really good girl. As far as the pictures of her and Hannen, I don't know what went down there. She didn't want to talk to me about it.

ALYSSA. Maybe I'll have to have Jack Hannen on the show soon to find out.

BRANDON. Just let him know I'll kick his ass if he hurts her.

They both laugh, and the segment wraps up with some more football talk. I stare at the phone feeling oddly at peace that he confirmed what I desperately wanted to be the truth. Maybe she really is the good girl I initially thought she was. Hearing confirmation that she really wasn't whoring it up with every NFL player with a fat contract definitely works in her favor.

"Jimmy!" I shout. "Take your phone back, man."

He comes waltzing over, naked as can be. The guy is always naked.

"Dude, cover up. We have towels."

He just laughs as he wraps a towel around himself.

"Jack, don't be jealous, man. So are you going to pursue this chick?"

"I don't know, but it's good to hear she wasn't spreading her legs for the entire NFL."

Even as I say the words, I feel like a dick.

"All right, since you have no definite plans to go after her, do you mind if I make a move then? She's fucking gorgeous, and since Mueller has her back, I know she's not just after our bank accounts. Listening to her screams in the club makes me think she's pretty fucking wild with her sexuality, and by the way, you were on cloud nine after your night with her. I wouldn't mind hitting that."

I see red. I'm going to kill him. My fists clench, my jaw tightens, and my breath is ragged.

"Are you fucking kidding me?"

"Yeah, I am. Just wanted to prove to you that you have it bad for this chick. Call her, man. Now come on. We've got to get on the ice."

He starts putting his gear on, and we don't say anything else as we head onto the rink. We go through our drills, and I try to get my head on straight for tomorrow's game.

After practice, I spend as much time as I possibly can with my daughters. I pick them up from preschool and take them to lunch and then the children's museum. There's nothing that grounds me more and reminds me of what's important in life than them. We've been playing with bubbles. The girls stand on a platform. There's a Hula-Hoop thing surrounding it. The hoop is sitting in a huge pool of bubble mix and is tied to a string. When you pull the string, the hoop goes up, a bubble forms over the platform, and the girls are inside the bubble. It's pretty freaking cool, and they love it. We have a great day, and I'm starting to feel better about everything. We get into the car and start to drive home.

"Daddy, what did you do that was so mean to Miss Caroline?" Rosie asks me with a curious expression on her face.

Kids pick up on everything.

"Yeah, everyone is mad at you."

This comes from Ellie. This is definitely not the conversation I want to be having with my daughters.

"No, girls, it's okay. Miss Caroline and I just had a disagreement. We're not mad at each other. We're still friends."

"I heard Grandma and Grandpa talking about it, and Grandma told Grandpa that you were mean to Miss Caroline," Ellie says, looking at me with big doe eyes.

I should have known my mom would have discussed this with my father. A pit forms in my stomach.

"I said something I shouldn't have said to her, but I apologized. You know how important it is to say you're sorry when you do something wrong. I promise, we are all better now. She's a very good teacher. Did you know you have show-and-tell at school tomorrow?"

"Yay!" Rosie screeches.

Luckily, that's all it takes to distract my four-year-olds from the topic at hand. We spend the rest of the drive talking about what they should bring to school. Just as we pull into our driveway, I see my dad's truck is already parked in front of the house. The girls go running out to greet Grandpa. My dad talks to the girls for a few minutes while I get the stuff together to make spaghetti. After they've talked Grandpa's ear off, they ask me if they can watch an episode on TV while I make dinner. I turn the TV on and see my dad studying me.

"How've you been, Dad?"

I figure I may as well take the lead on this one.

"Fine. I ran into Caroline today. She had a flat tire in the parking lot of the pharmacy and was pretty close to tears. I fixed it for her and asked her a few questions about what's going on with you two."

"All right, Dad. Lay it on me."

"You know what gets me about that girl? She took your side. She told me you were right to judge her. She made poor decisions the night you two went dancing, and if one of her teammates told her stuff about a guy she just met, she'd believe him too. Then she said the article would have sealed the deal for her, and she'd never have talked to you again."

"That was my initial plan, but that plan changed. Did she tell you I apologized?"

I'm honestly dumfounded. I didn't expect this conversation to go this way. The fact that she's seeing things from my perspective is also intriguing. In all the years Bree and I were together, she never once tried to understand how I was feeling.

"She did. I think it's going to take more than that though. Don't mess it up with this one, okay?"

"That's what everyone's been telling me."

"Jack, I can't tell you how to live your life. You're a grown-ass man. I can hope that I raised you to be the kind of man who makes solid decisions and lives his life with integrity. Other than that, I can be here for you when you fall flat on your ass. But I've got to tell you, there's something special about her."

"I know. Being with her made me feel alive for the first time in years, Dad. When I woke up at her house that morning, I was happier than I've been in ages. And not just because of the sex. It was because I felt some kind of bond to her as soon as I met her. It just felt right. There's something about her that draws me in. I can't really explain it, but after all this shit went down, my guard is up. I don't want to bring drama into my life. After all the shit I went through with Bree, and then Lyndsey claiming I was her baby's daddy, I'm weary."

"You really think that she's going to bring you drama?"

"I don't know. Don't they all?"

I sigh and run my hand through my hair.

My dad laughs.

"When you find the right one, Jack, you'll know it. Drama or not."

*****

Hours after my dad left, I'm still lying awake in bed. I should be asleep, but I can't get a blonde out of my head. I've already jacked off to thoughts of her, and it's still not enough. It's too late to call or text, but I've decided I will after my game tomorrow. I need to talk to her. I feel like I've just drifted off to sleep when my alarm goes off.

I throw on a pair of pajama pants and check to make sure the nanny is here. Sure enough, she let herself in and is making breakfast before the girls get up for school. We talk for a bit about her trip visiting her family. I wake the girls up and help get them ready for school. I let the nanny take them and then decide to go back to bed for a few hours before I have to be at the rink.

When I finally wake up, I feel better than I have all week. I take my time getting ready to get to the locker room. I set my gear down when Jimmy greets me.

"First time I've seen you smile in a while. Should I assume you cleared the air with blondie?"

"Something like that."

"Good. You deserve some happiness, man."

I laugh at him.

"I don't know about that."

"I do, man. It's long overdue."

"All right, enough of this shit. Let's focus on the game and not my love life for now."

"Done."

We finish putting on our gear, go and listen to Coach, and then start warming up for the game. I skate around the rink, loving the cold air that fills my lungs. It's early still, but I look around the stadium when suddenly I see her. Just like something out of my dreams, Caroline is sitting there in the stands. She's with her brother, and he's ordering beers for them. She's wearing jeans that hug her tight ass, a sweater that fits her curves like it was made for her, a red hat, a scarf, and mittens. She looks beautiful. Damn it. I can't walk away from this one. She glances up just then, and our eyes lock on one another. It's like that first night at her dance recital. I don't see anything but her. She takes my breath away. I smile and wave a gloved hand at her. She bites her lower lip and gives me a small, shy smile. She waves back. We're still staring at one another when Jimmy comes over and hits my helmet. It shakes me out of my trance. He's laughing.

"Stop staring at your woman. You're drooling, man."

Shit. I probably am. I don't even care. I can't wait to talk to her tonight.

Chapter 15

Caroline

I wish I could stop staring at him. I have no idea what the score is. All I see is him. I'm even staring at him when he's not playing, taking a second to catch his breath, and grabbing some water from the bench. I wish I could turn off this attraction. I wish I could just forget about him and our time together. I keep trying to convince myself that I'm better off without him, but after he made me dinner, I softened a little. His texts keep getting sweeter. I get a "good morning, beautiful" text every morning. Then throughout the day, there's little funny things the girls did, questions about my day, and random pieces of trivia. I look forward to his messages like a giddy little schoolgirl.

Cody was glad Jack apologized, but I haven't told him that he keeps texting me. His project is wrapping up, and after two weeks of being here in Chicago with me, he'll be heading back to New York tomorrow. I'll miss him, but I know he's eager to get back. He looks over at me.

"Care, thanks for coming with me tonight. I know this whole Jack thing screwed with your head. Part of me feels like we should have just bailed on these tickets."

"Don't worry about it. I know how much you love the game. You've played your whole life, and we catch a Wolves game every time you're in town. Plus we've had these tickets for months."

"Yeah, but that was before this shit went down. Brandon even called him out on national television, showing his support for you."

Just then, my phone pings. I look down to see a group text from Kathy and Judith. They're texting me to come to their family box.

"Judith and Kathy are texting us to meet them in their box."

"Kathy?"

"Kathy is Judith's sister and Jack's mom. The one you met at the restaurant."

"Oh. I still feel like an ass for that. Maybe we should go for a little bit, just to smooth things over."

"Do you think that Brandon's interview is the only reason his family invited us to watch the game with us in their box? They're always so nice to me, but I feel kind of weird about it."

"You've been Judith's neighbor for a while now, and she knows the real you. Plus Jack's parents have seen you teaching their granddaughters ballet for a few weeks now. If they really thought you were a bad influence, they would have taken the girls out of your class."

"I love his family, Cody. His daughters are absolute sweethearts. Judith and Rick are great neighbors, and I've actually started to really like his parents too. His dad even changed my flat tire while you were held up in your meeting yesterday."

"Let's go up to their box for a few minutes then. You're obviously going to be seeing these people a lot. Avoiding them makes you look guilty. Hold your head high and be the bigger person."

"Do you think Jack will assume I have ulterior motives if he sees me sitting with them?"

"Fuck his presumptuous ass. Like you said, Rick and Judith are your neighbors. His dad obviously likes you, and his mom has texted you three times during this game saying her granddaughters want to see you."

"You're reading my texts now?"

Of course, he is. My protective older brother can't help himself.

"I'm sitting right next to you. I just so happened to see the screen. I'm not trying to be a dick. Come on, let's go."

My brother stands up and offers me his hand. I reluctantly grab it, and he yanks me up quickly as if not wanting to give me a chance to stay rooted to my seat. We head over to the box. The smell of chocolate grabs my attention as soon as we enter. Ellie and Rosie are eating chocolate cupcakes, and I'm desperately wanting one. We're instantaneously greeted with hugs from everyone. Jack Sr. is a really nice man, and we've actually talked quite a bit. I can't help but like him. He looks like an older version of Jack with salt-and-peppered hair, crow's feet, and the same beautiful smile. He sees me eyeing the cupcakes and laughs.

"Caroline, you must be inflicted with the same ailment my wife has. Chocolate addiction is a serious health issue of hers."

Kathy smiles and turns to me.

"Honey, every woman loves chocolate! Now let's get you a cupcake."

"How can I say no to that?" I say with a big smile on my face.

Ellie and Rosie come running up to me.

"Miss Caroline! Miss Caroline! Can you sit with us?"

They are looking up at me with chocolate all over their mouths and eager, pleading eyes. They're grabbing my hands to steer me toward their seats. I look at Kathy and laugh.

"And how can I say no to that?"

She gives me a warm smile.

"You really can't. Go sit down. I'll bring a washcloth over for their faces."

I look over at Cody. He's talking business with Rick and seems to be enjoying himself. I get cozy in my seat and smile as Ellie snuggles in on my right and Rosie on my left. I eat my cupcake and notice Ellie is getting tired. She lays her head on my lap, and I start playing with her hair like my mom used to do to me when I was tired. She slowly drifts off to sleep. Rosie gives me a sleepy smile. I put my arm around her and rest my head on hers. She's out within a few minutes. I sit there with the girls, feeling totally at peace for the first time in what feels like forever until I see some guy trying to take pictures of me inside the box. Unease settles in. I'm sure these will be posted all over the internet in no time with some headline about me trying to win Jack's heart.

After the first article circulated, more and more pictures of me and Brandon in high school and college surfaced, me with guys from Brandon's teams, and pictures with guys from my brother's hockey days at Michigan. Basically, every article said the same thing. I'm a whore who screws athletes. While it couldn't be further from the truth, people believe what they want to believe. None of this would have ever even come up if Jack were a normal guy, but instead, he graces the covers of magazines on a regular basis. I'm so caught up in my own head that I hardly realize the game is over with a Wolves victory. I slowly ease myself out of my spot, careful not to wake the girls. I don't want to linger with Jack's family at risk of running into him after the game. I graciously thank them for their hospitality, grab Cody, and do my best to escape unscathed.

*****

Jack

I saw Caroline in my family's box. I'm not really sure what to make of it. She's managed to win my protective family over effortlessly even in the face of controversy. Even before Brandon's interview, both my mom and dad stuck up for her and urged me to talk to her. Tonight, there is something about seeing my two little girls sleeping soundly in her arms that tugs at my heart. I want that for them. I want them to have a woman who loves them as if they're her own. I just haven't thought it was in the cards for me to find that someone.

I try to make my way out of the locker room as quickly as I can after a win. I stop to talk to a few reporters, then answer questions about the game, and thank the fans. I head into the locker rooms.

"Nice game, Hannen. I'm glad the shit with blondie didn't mess with you too much. She looked smoking hot tonight."

Leave it to fucking Jones to bring up Caroline the second I walk into the locker room. I don't bother answering him and instead turn my attention to Kelston Green.

"So, Green, I've got to know. Are you full of shit or is Branden Mueller?"

"Good game to you too, bro. I just told you what I heard. She was always at all the parties with athletes in college. I don't know how many guys she fucked. She and Mueller dated for like a decade or some shit."

"Are you kidding me?"

"Look, Hannen. If you were an asshole toward her based on what you heard from me, that's on you. Her picture is plastered all over the internet with athletes. I was looking out for you."

"Do me a favor, and let me look out for myself."

Green's right. He's not responsible for me treating her like shit, but I wouldn't have paid as much attention to those articles if he hadn't said something first. Even after apologizing to her, I still feel like an asshole.

Jimmy puts a stop to the conversation.

"Gentlemen, relax. We just killed the Panthers. Let's act like a team and celebrate."

"I've got to take care of some shit. You guys have fun without me."

I head over to the showers, get dressed, and get the fuck out of there in record time. Of course, I missed Caroline. As I head out to my car, I shoot off a quick text, trying not to overthink it.

> Me: Hi. I saw you at the game. Thanks for coming.
>
> Caroline: Hi. My brother's a big fan and asked me to go with him while he's in town.
>
> Me: Well tell your brother thanks. I was happy to see you. You looked beautiful tonight.
>
> Caroline: Thanks. We had fun. You played well.
>
> Me: I was hoping I'd see you after the game.
>
> Caroline: Yeah, sorry. Cody has an early flight.
>
> Me: Are you sure you're not avoiding me?
>
> Caroline: Why would I avoid you?

Me: I don't know. We haven't talked since I was at your place and I was really hoping to see you. Can I come over tonight so we can talk now?

Caroline: It's late. I don't think that's a good idea.

Me: Can I take you to dinner this week?

Caroline: I'm not sure that's a good idea either. I forgive you for the whole misunderstanding, but I don't think we should be going on dates, Jack.

Me: Why not?

Caroline: Because

Me: How about we don't call it a date but two people meeting for a meal. We both have to eat. Plus, we're friends now. Friends eat together.

Caroline: True, but most of my friends don't text me asking me if I'm wearing panties.

Me: It was an honest question.

Caroline: Dinner will not lead to sex, Jack.

Me: I'm not asking for sex. Although, if you offer, I definitely won't say no.

Caroline: I'm not offering.

Jack. Fair enough. Dinner tomorrow night?

Raw and Real Love

Caroline: Would you be asking me if Brandon didn't have my back during his interview? I'm assuming you saw it.

Jack: I did see it, and yes, I would have asked you anyways. Seeing you in my box made me want to talk to you.

Caroline: I hope I didn't overstep. Your mom invited me.

Jack: Are you kidding? I loved that you were there. Now, I know you said you liked Mexican food. How about 6pm tomorrow at The Big Sombrero? I just want to talk to you.

Caroline: I have a class but I can meet you there at 7.

Jack: Thanks for giving me that second chance. Can't wait to see you.

No response. I'm not going to lie. I'm really freaking excited to see her. I have tomorrow night off and then have another game the next night. That being said, I should have thought this through. I can't take her to dinner. My mom watches the girls too much as it is, and my nanny asked for the night off months ago. Plus with how much I'm out of town during the season, I really should spend my night with my daughters. This is another reason I don't do relationships. Being a single dad is hard enough, but add my travel schedule in, and most women aren't going to want to deal with this shit. I send her a text.

Jack: Hey Caroline. I'm really sorry but I was so anxious to see you that I didn't realize that I need spend tomorrow night with the girls. I've been gone a lot for games and tomorrow is my only night off before I leave again. Want to come over my house for a taco dinner instead?

Fuck. What am I thinking? I can't invite her over. I've never invited a woman over for dinner. Although, the girls already know her, so maybe it's okay. I'll be having a friend over, not a random woman. I really don't know what I'm doing. I'm in uncharted waters here.

Caroline: The girls definitely need their daddy time. I don't want to impose.

Jack: You're not. They already love you. They'll be ecstatic.

Caroline: Are you sure?

Jack: Yeah, I'll text you my address.

This may be the worst idea I've ever had, but I need to own up to my mistakes and see where this takes me.

Chapter 16

Caroline

I said goodbye to Cody this morning. He wrapped his project up and is heading back to his consulting firm in New York. I'm hoping business brings him back here again soon. My brother is my rock. Growing up, we only had each other. He became my best friend and protector. We are what you call "Irish twins," meaning that even though we aren't actually twins, we were born in the same calendar year. Cody is eleven months older than me, and I idolized him growing up. I was so relieved when Brandon got an offer to play at the University of Michigan. Cody was there already for hockey, and it was like a dream come true when Brandon accepted their offer. It felt like fate to be there with my two favorite guys. Now having Cody here during the Jack fiasco was nice too. I like having a guy's perspective on things. He refused to let me get too upset about it. I'm headed to Coffee! Coffee! Coffee! to meet Mel and Sofia. I'm curious to see if they're going to have the same advice for me.

"All right, ladies, I need your help."

Sofia, Mel, and I have just sat down in front of our piping hot cappuccinos.

Mel's golden eyes go wide.

"Please tell me you found a sexy, sweet guy who will make you forget all about Jack Hannen."

"Ummm...no, but it *is* about Jack Hannen."

I cringe, knowing they aren't going to be happy with me for agreeing to a date only after Brandon's interview.

"Wait. What? I thought we hated him after calling you easy after the most amazing sex of your life? We're still not fully accepting his apology, right?"

Sofia looks utterly confused, and I don't blame her. I am too.

"He keeps texting me and invited me to dinner at his house tonight. I'm not sure I should go."

I should probably say I'm afraid to go, afraid of how much of a pull he has on me, afraid that I'm even considering knowing that my lady parts are screaming for his attention, afraid that I don't trust myself around Jack, and afraid that I'll make a mistake and end up heart broken. I don't know why I still want to give him a chance.

"Girl, you get this look on your face every time you mention his name. I had a feeling you would have some kind of announcement after going to his game last night. Then there are the pictures of you cuddling with his daughters. Brandon's interview just sealed the deal. Of course, he reaches out now."

Mel's smart.

"What pictures?" I ask, already having a sick feeling in the pit of my stomach.

Sofia shows me the pictures of me cuddling with Ellie and Rosie last night at the game while talking to Jack's mom. Is this why he's asking me to come when the girls are there? Does he want to have the girls there as a buffer? I'm confused.

"I hadn't seen those. Can't people just mind their own business?"

"Look, Care. He doesn't want to be friends. He's trying to get back in your good graces. You don't go from hottest sex of your life to zero sexual chemistry just by snapping your fingers. What if he makes a move after you've talked? Caroline, you don't do casual sex. You do picket white fences," Sofia says.

"I'm not going to have sex with him."

I can say it with confidence despite the traitorous ache between my legs trying to disagree with me.

"I've never seen you even consider putting out for a guy the first night you met him. And especially not in a nightclub! What is it about this guy? I mean, besides the obvious. We all know he's hot as Hades."

Mel has a devious smile on her face.

"I honestly don't know. In this situation, if it were any other guy, I'd never talk to him again."

"But it's Jack, and we all know you're going over there tonight," Sofia says as she takes a sip of her chai tea. "Let us know how many orgasms you have after your talk."

Damn it. I don't know if I'm happy or disappointed that I'm doing this tonight.

*****

Something is wrong. Ever since I left Coffee! Coffee! Coffee! I've felt off, but as the day progressed, I just kept feeling worse. My stomach is killing me. My head is throbbing. I have terrible chills, and I can't seem to get warm no matter what I do. Two of the parents asked me if I was okay at dance tonight. One of them even suggested I cancel class and go home. Ari walked into the studio, took one look at me, and made me leave. She ended up teaching my class for me, and now I'm lying on my bathroom floor because I'm pretty sure I'm going to puke, and I don't have the energy to get up. My phone is lying next to me. It rings. It's Cody. I debate picking it up, but then I want to make sure he's okay.

"Sis, what the fuck? Are you as sick as a dog? I spent the whole damn flight in the bathroom, got home, and literally have been shitting my brains out since."

"I haven't started with the diarrhea yet, but I know it's coming. I feel like death," I say.

"Damn it. I was hoping you were spared. Shit. I gotta go!"

The line disconnects, and I lay my head back on the cold tile floor. Suddenly, I have the immediate sensation to go to the bathroom. I pull down my pants as quickly as I can and empty the contents of my entire colon. I then have to grab the trash can and puke because I can't get off the toilet. This is miserable. After crawling back onto the floor, it suddenly dawns on me that I'm supposed to be at Jack's. I decide to shoot him a text because I can't imagine talking to him on the phone like this.

Me: I'm so sorry to cancel last minute, but I am so incredibly sick.

Jack: Are you ok?

Me: I have a stomach bug thing.

Jack: Do you need some sports drinks and saltine crackers?

Me: I can't imagine putting anything in my mouth right now.

Jack: There's so many ways I'd like to reply to that. Do you want me to come to you?

Me: You cannot see me like this.

Jack: Feel better, beautiful.

I lie back down and fall asleep. There's a loud knocking on my door that startles me awake. Who would be banging on my door right now? I'm tempted to not answer it, but then a bunch of smaller, faster knocks start. It takes me a minute to stand. The room is spinning, and I have to catch my bearings. It takes me a while, but I manage to make it to the door. I open it to see Rosie and Ellie banging relentlessly on it while Jack holds a bag of groceries.

"Hey. Sorry to drop in unannounced, but you had me worried," he says.

"I'm okay."

It's all I can muster out. I hold on to the door for support.

"Caroline, no offense, but you're not okay. You're paler than the white leotard thing you're wearing. We're coming in."

"I don't think that's a good idea. I don't want you to catch this."

"Lucky for you, I don't get sick."

He walks into my town house with the girls following behind him.

"Girls, do you have the movie you picked out to watch?"

"Yes, Daddy!"

Ellie hands him a princess movie.

"All right. Sit down on the couch and get comfy. I'm going to help Miss Caroline feel better while you watch your movie."

He puts the movie in and gets the girls situated.

"You need to sit down, babe," he says to me.

I nod in agreement and make my way back toward the bathroom. I'm too weak to fight him. Walking is not a good idea. I've caught the spins and start throwing up again. When there's nothing left in my stomach, I stare at the toilet trying to catch my breath. A hand comes up on my back. I had forgotten Jack was here.

"I'm so sorry, babe. Do you think you could drink any of this? Maybe just a sip?"

I start to shake my head to protest, but he holds it up to my lips, and I take a small sip. He puts his other hand on my forehead.

"Caroline, you're burning up. I'm going to draw you a cool bath. I'm guessing you won't be able to keep any Tylenol down, but the bath should help with the fever."

He sits on the edge of the tub and turns the water on. He lets the water run over his hand, waiting for the right temperature. As the tub starts to fill, I simply sit and watch the water climb. It hurts to think.

"I'll be right back. I'm just going to check on the girls."

I hear some shuffling in the other room.

"Hey. Sorry about that. They're passed out on your couch. I knew they'd be tired coming over here so late, but I didn't expect them to fall asleep that quickly. Let me help you get in the tub."

I shake my head.

"Caroline, please let me help you."

"I don't want you to see me like this."

"We all get sick, babe."

"I know, but I don't want to get naked in front of you either."

His smile reaches his eyes, and he lets out a chuckle.

"I've already seen you naked, and I really liked what I saw. But this isn't sexual, Caroline. Let me help you."

I know he's right. There's no way I can get in the tub myself. I try to stand, and he grabs my hand to help me up. I put my other hand on the counter near the sink to steady myself.

"I'm going to help slide this arm out first."

He pulls on the elastic of my leotard and brings my arm out. He steadies me, switches arms, and does the same to the other side. Then he gets on his knees and pulls it down the rest of the way. As I lift my foot, he gently takes it out of the fabric. He then gives the same care to my undergarments. When I'm completely naked, he lifts me up and sets me in the tub with such care that you'd think I was fine china. The water feels better than I expected it to. My head is still spinning, and I lean back and close my eyes.

"Take another sip for me, Caroline."

He holds the sports drink up to me, and I take another sip of the bright-orange liquid.

"Want me to help you wash your hair? I'm pretty good at it. I do the twins' all the time, and I think you have some puke in it."

"Of course, I do. The sexiest man in America wants to wash puke from my hair. This is awful."

I draw my knees up and bury my face in them. I'm so humiliated.

"Caroline, don't be embarrassed. I once shit my pants on a Ferris wheel when I was sick. You should have seen people's faces when I got off that ride."

He shakes his head, and I can't help but smile.

"You're not at all who I thought you were, Jack."

"Shhh… I've got a rep to protect, babe."

He winks at me. He then grabs the shampoo and starts massaging it into my scalp. It feels so good. I lean back and close my eyes. He uses the shower attachment to rinse my hair.

"Conditioner next?"

"Yes, sir."

"Got it."

He grabs the sports drink.

"Take one more sip for me first."

He conditions and rinses my hair. Then he washes my body, making me take sips every so often. By the end of the bath, I'm feeling a little bit better. He lifts me out of the water and wraps me in a towel. Then he brings me to my bedroom and sets me on the bed. Every action is done with so much tenderness. I'm not sure why he's doing this for me. I know he's used to taking care of people. He's been a single dad for years, but we aren't even dating.

"Jack, thank you for this."

I don't honestly know what else to say.

"Don't worry about it. My mom was a nurse before she retired, and I think she instilled some of those nurturing skills in me. We're fixers. It's what we do. Plus, you honestly looked like you needed the help."

"Yeah, I would have just slept on the bathroom floor all night."

"This is way better. Where do you keep your underwear?"

"What?"

I'm so confused. Is he one of those fetish guys? Like he wants my underwear for something?

"Caroline, you're naked. I wanted to give you a pair of underwear to slip on. I don't know. Do you want to just sleep naked?"

"Oh! Okay. Top drawer on the left. I thought you wanted them for yourself."

He looks at me like I've grown a second head and grabs a pair off the top.

"Not my thing, beautiful. Are these okay?"

I nod at the pale pink panties he pulled out.

"Pajamas?"

"Second drawer on the right."

He grabs a pair off the top and brings them over to me.

"Thanks."

I slowly dress myself with his help. He sits on the bed next to me and then makes me take another sip.

"You look a little bit better. Do you want to try a cracker or anything?"

"Not yet."

"Okay, do you want to lay down and try to sleep?"

I nod my head. He pulls the blankets down, and I slip into bed. He covers me up, makes me take another sip, and then sets the drink on the nightstand. He scoots over to the other side of the bed.

"I'll stay with you a little longer and slip out after you're asleep."

"Don't you need to get the girls home?"

"Nah. Once they're out, they're out. They'll sleep here, in the car, or at home. It really doesn't matter."

"You have a game tomorrow?"

"Yeah, I'm sorry. I won't be able to stay with you all day."

"Jack, I wouldn't expect you to."

"Maybe I wouldn't mind. Now close your eyes."

He starts rubbing circles on my back, and I slowly drift off to sleep. When I wake up, he's gone. There's a note on my nightstand. All it says is "feel better, sleeping beauty." The blankets the girls were using on my couch are folded. My refrigerator is full of sports drinks, and there are three different kinds of crackers sitting on my kitchen counter. There's no way that just happened.

*****

Jack

When Caroline bailed on dinner at my house last night, I thought she just got cold feet. I really went over to her house to call her out. I grabbed some crackers and sports drinks on the way over just in case she really was sick and had planned to just drop them off if that was the case. One look at her though, and I was afraid to leave her. She looked as white as a ghost. She was so weak, she couldn't even answer the door without leaning against it, and I could tell she was dizzy by the way she kept trying to rest her head against the doorframe. I was legitimately worried. I tried to help as much as I could, and at least when I left, I wasn't worried that she was hypoglycemic anymore. I would have stayed all night if I didn't have the girls, but I had to get them to school this morning. The nanny is at the house now, and she'll be there for the next three days. She basically lives with us, but I like being alone with the kids when I'm home. I'm heading to the rink. Our away game is close tonight. Detroit is about a four-and-half-hour drive and only a little over an hour flight. I had called my favorite deli and have them delivering chicken noodle soup and a baguette to Caroline's house for lunch. I'm hoping she can tolerate it.

Jimmy sits down next to me for our travels. We both usually have our headphones on, but he looks like he's in a talkative mood.

"Hey. How'd dinner with blondie go last night?"

"It didn't. She got sick, so I brought her some sports drinks."

"Guess you didn't get laid. Stomach thing?"

"Yeah. She looked like she was dying, Jimmy."

"You better hope you don't get that."

"I never get sick."

"You're going to jinx yourself. You know, she still owes you dinner. Maybe you can collect on dropping off the sports drinks."

"It's a little fucked up because I really like this one."

"I noticed."

"Nothing can come of it. It's like I'm teasing myself."

"Why can nothing come of it?"

"Jimmy, you saw how miserable I made Bree, and we both know how that ended. I don't think the whole marriage thing is in the cards for me again."

"You didn't make her miserable. She did that to herself. And I never said marry blondie. Just have some fun."

"I don't want her thinking I'm game for some committed relationship thing that's actually going somewhere. I think she wants the picket white fence."

"So tell her that. Who knows? Maybe she'll want to be fuck buddies instead."

"She really doesn't come across as that kind of woman."

"Shit. After those articles came out, that's all you thought she wanted."

"Yeah, I fucked up there."

"Invite her over for dinner. Offer sex, nothing more. If she takes it, cool. If she doesn't, you saved yourself a headache."

"Seems fair enough."

"Keep me posted."

Chapter 17

Caroline

I'm feeling 100 percent better. The diarrhea lasted an additional twenty-four hours after Jack left, but I finally feel normal again. Jack's been gone for three days. I haven't stopped thinking about him. I think I'm more confused by him now than I was before. The way he took care of me was the nicest thing any man has ever done for me. But we're not dating, we're barely friends, and I don't know why he did all of that for me. Is he really just that nice of a guy? I wouldn't have believed it before, but now I'm starting to second-guess if I really know him at all. There are so many layers to him, and I feel like I'm just starting to scratch the surface. He invited me over tonight for the dinner we were supposed to have the night I got sick, and I have butterflies in my stomach. I'm excited, nervous, and maybe a little embarrassed on the drive to his place.

As I pull into his neighborhood, I see one mansion after the next with beautifully landscaped yards, fountains, and mature trees. When I get to his house, I have to pause and just breathe. These homes are not so different from the one I was raised in, and yet I still feel anxious as I walk up the steps to knock on the door. I'm sure it has nothing to do with the opulence of the house and everything to do with the man inside. The door flies open, and I'm greeted by Ellie and Rosie, both of whom are already hugging my waist and welcoming me into their home. As I'm swept in, Jack comes over to greet me. He takes the box of cookies out of my hand and gives me a kiss on the cheek. I swear every fiber in my body stands at alert.

"I guess you'll be getting the grand tour before dinner," he says, laughing at his daughters' excitement as they drag me along. "I'm going to finish up in the kitchen. When you girls are done showing Caroline around, will you please bring her into the kitchen for dinner? It'll be ready in ten minutes."

"Sounds good. I'll make sure we're back in time."

We stand there staring at one another for a second, and I feel as if all the oxygen is sucked out of the room every time I am close to him.

"Thanks again for coming, Caroline."

He must see me blushing because I can feel the warmth rising in my chest and up my cheeks. I forgot how incredibly sexy he is this close up.

I'm eventually nudged along, and after lots of *oohs* and *aahs*, we make our way back to the kitchen. His house is gorgeous. It's large but warm and homey. Ellie's room is lavender, and Rosie's in a pale pink. Both have canopy beds with white bed spreads and little fairy lights dangling. There are white desks full of art and craft supplies and white dressers. Along the wall, each girl has a bookshelf full of well-read books. I'm guessing he had a professional decorator or maybe his mother got free reign, but whoever conceptualized this house did a fantastic job.

There are the most delicious smells wafting up the stairs, and I start to tell the girls how hungry I am. They happily bring me back to the kitchen. Jack has an incredible spread laid out, and I'm seriously impressed by his cooking skills.

"Wow! I didn't expect you to cook me dinner again. I just assumed we'd get take out. This is a really nice surprise. Can I help?"

"No need. Everything's done. I love cooking. I learned out of necessity, and it's become a hobby of mine. Why don't you help yourself to a glass of wine?"

I pour a glass of wine and study Jack as he moves effortlessly through the kitchen. He's wearing jeans that fit his ass perfectly. He has a long-sleeved, black Under Armour shirt that advertises his incredibly defined muscles, and I'm seriously trying not to salivate.

"Can I get you or the girls something to drink too?"

"I have a bottle of water already, but I know the girls would each love a small cup of chocolate milk."

"I'm on it."

I pour two glasses half full of chocolate milk and bring them over to the table.

"Thank you, Miss Caroline!" the girls say in unison as they rush over to their seats.

"No problem. Now I want to hear all about your day at preschool. What did you do today?" I ask, glad that the girls are here.

I've always been really comfortable around children even if I'm not fully comfortable with the beautiful man in the room. It seems silly that I'd be uncomfortable around someone I've been so intimate with only days ago. Dinner goes by quickly with the girls monopolizing all the conversation, and I fall a little bit more in love with them. They're so sweet, but I can't help but think of all the things that they're going to wish they had their mom around for. I remember that longing especially during the times when I would have to ask one of our many nannies questions when most young girls could just go to their mother. Changes in my body, prom dress shopping, talks about boys, getting ready for my dance recitals, putting makeup on, the list may never end. At least the girls will have each other like Cody and I did. I swallow a lump in the back of my throat and try to focus on the present. After dinner, Jack tells the girls it's time for bed.

"I'll clean up while you get them situated."

I stand and start clearing the table.

"No, Caroline. You're my guest. Just leave everything. I can do it later."

He stands, stretches, and grabs one of the many plates off the table. Our hands brush against one another, and I feel a bolt of electricity travel down my spine. I shiver and look up. Jack licks his lips, and I know for sure he felt the same connection I did.

"Go upstairs. I've got this."

I give him a playful nudge with my hip. His lips quirk into a grin, and he leans over and kisses my cheek again. Damn him for being so irresistible.

"Thank you." He turns and shouts, "Last one upstairs is a rotten egg!"

He takes off toward the staircase with the girls, giggling and racing after him.

"Daddy! I'm going to win tonight!" Ellie screeches.

"It's my turn to pick out the stories!" Rosie exclaims as she tries to catch up.

I watch as the three of them scamper off, laughter filling the hallways. It tugs at my heart, making me want a family of my own. I can tell what a good dad he is as I listen to them interact. I continue to eavesdrop as I put the food away, wash the pots and pans, and clear the rest of the table. Jack did a good job of cleaning as he cooked, so the mess really isn't too terrible.

I'm loading the last of the dishes when I feel his hands on my waist and the heat from his chest on my back. He nuzzles into the crook of my neck, and I swear my lady parts are screaming for attention.

"I'm so glad you're feeling better."

"Me too. Thank you so much for coming to my rescue."

I open my neck to him and welcome the warmth of his body.

"It was my pleasure," he says as he kisses my neck. "I wish I could have stayed all night."

He's slowly making his way up to my ear and nibbles on my lobe.

"Hmmm...yep."

He snickers, and his hands make their way up from my hips to my aching breasts. His kisses move to my jaw. I turn into a puddle of mush from his touch. I push my ass toward him and can feel his steel length against me. I don't know which one of us wants this more, but it excites me to know that I can do this to him.

"I have a really hard time keeping my hands off you," he whispers into my ear.

My nipples are standing into hard peaks as his thumbs brush over them, caressing each bud through my bra.

"I kind of like your hands on me."

He spins me around, and his lips come crashing down to mine. I don't know how far I should let this go. It feels so good, and I'm losing my ability to stay strong by the millisecond. I break the kiss.

"We need to talk first," I say it breathlessly, almost a whisper.

He effortlessly picks me up and sets me on the kitchen counter. Our foreheads come together, and he looks at me, his eyes searching.

"Let's talk."

"Jack, I don't know where to go from here. I want you, but I want your respect. I've only been with three men before you, and it took them months to get me into bed. It took you hours, and now I feel like you're always going to think I'm easy."

"Caroline, I was a complete asshole. I freaked out because of the recent baby daddy accusations and finding out she wanted to tie herself to an athlete. I know that article about you wasn't true. Brandon Mueller even declared it to the world. I also know that Auntie J would have never have tried to get me to ask you out a thousand times if she thought there was anything to be concerned about. I was a dick, and I'm sorry. I have a lot of respect for you."

"Thank you. But please don't disrespect me again. If you want me, you treat me right. Brandon crushed me. He broke my heart into a million little pieces. I may not be broken in the same ways you are, but we all have our demons."

With that, I seem to have opened a window to his own broken heart, but he quickly shuts it again. He lets out a shaky breath but continues to hold me close. He picks me up and moves us to the couch. He sets me down on his lap.

"I have no intentions of hurting you."

His hands come up to my face, and he cups my cheeks in his hands. Our foreheads stay together, and our eyes never wander from the other's. It's as if he's looking deep into my soul.

"Promise?"

He lets out a ragged exhale.

"I promise. But, Caroline, I'm not at a place where I can give you a relationship. I want you. I've never wanted someone the way I want you. Not even my wife."

I don't know what I expected him to say, but it isn't this. What the hell does he want then?

"How about right now, we just play a game? I want to get to know you a little better. How about for every question you answer, I'll take off a piece of clothing, and vice versa?"

I start kissing his neck again, waiting for an answer.

He hesitates for a minute. I can sense him contemplating my proposal.

"Uhhh, okay. What do you want to know?"

He starts nibbling on my ear. It feels so, so good. Everything about the possibility of an "us" is fragile. I can't imagine what he went through losing the mother of his children, and I know he's not ready for a relationship, but I want to understand why. In this moment, all I can do is kiss him. The kiss begins slow, tentative, like he's letting me explore and see if I want what he has to offer. It quickly becomes more passionate, heated, and frantic. Our hands start roaming, and I try to regain some of my self-control. I break the kiss. We're both breathless. I wrap my arms around his lower back and dip them under his shirt.

I need to start this off with an easy question. He already told me he doesn't trust women, and I know there are some huge walls erected after his wife died. If there is any chance at all of moving forward, I need to get him to open up. I already know where he grew up, thanks to my internet stalking, admittingly, not my finest moment.

"Game first. Where did you grow up?"

"Born and raised in Minnesota. Shirt off."

I smile and take my time slowly teasing him while I unbutton my blouse. I lean into his chest so that my breasts are pushed up against him as I straddle him on the couch.

"God, you're sexy. What about you? Where did you grow up?"

"I was actually born in Chicago but grew up in Boston. We moved there when my dad graduated residency. I was only a toddler. I came back here for school. Now your shirt."

He backs up slightly, pulls the black shirt over his head, and tosses it to the ground. He continues stroking the outer edge of my thighs with his thumbs. I immediately put my hands on his chest. I begin tracing his pecs with my fingers.

"Where did you go to college?"

I know this answer too, but he's responding so well to me. I think I'll give him one more softball.

"Norte Dame. I got drafted right after graduation. Your bra."

I reach behind and unclasp my bra. I let it fall off my shoulders and drop to the floor. He sucks in a breath.

"May I?"

I nod.

His big calloused hands begin fondling my breasts. I push my chest toward him and close my eyes. I can barely concentrate.

"Next question, Jack."

My voice is husky, a little more than a whisper.

"Hmm?"

His eyes are dark and filled with lust.

"It's your turn to ask a question."

"Oh right."

He continues to fondle me but doesn't speak. I moan as he leans down and takes one of my nipples into his mouth. He bites gently and then quickly kisses the pain away. He begins to shower his attention on the other breast. I can feel my panties getting wetter with each swipe of his tongue. I pull back, placing my palms on his chest to push him away momentarily.

"Question, Jack."

"Right. Um, okay. What's your biggest fear?"

This guy is full of surprises. I'm not sure if my answer will freak him out. He's looking at me. I swallow. If I want to start this off on the right foot, I need to be honest. I'm sure he can see the nervousness in my eyes.

"I'm afraid I'm never going to find someone who loves me as much as I love him."

I bite my lower lip. Why did Brandon have to screw me up so badly?

"Caroline, you must be joking. You've got heartbreaker written all over you. I'm pretty sure you could pick any man you wanted, and he'd be in love with you within minutes."

His hands have moved up to my face, and he's cupping my jaw. It's so sweet and intimate that I want to cry.

"They may fall for me, but I'm not enough to keep them."

"What are you talking about?"

"Brandon and I dated for six years, Jack. Senior year of high school, four years of college, and his first year in the NFL. He asked me to be his wife and then cheated on me during his first season. That's all it took. One season. Once he made the league, I was just one of many. There was nothing special about me. I wasn't enough to keep him from finding another woman."

I look away from his eyes, too embarrassed to say more.

*****

Jack

Damn, I've lost respect for Brandon Mueller. How the fuck could he cheat on her? Like any guy in his right mind would give her up? Hell, I hardly know her, but I know enough to know she's incredible.

"Brandon was an immature dumbass who didn't realize what he had. For a lot of guys, rookie year is full of mistakes. I'd say he made the biggest one of all."

I wait for her gaze to meet mine, and I bring her in for a gentle kiss to show her just how special she is.

"Don't you ever for a second think you aren't enough. Any bastard would be lucky to have you. Mueller even admitted that the other day."

She looks at me with sad eyes. I want to make her smile. I want to convince her that she's enough, but shit, I just told her I don't want a relationship with her. Nothing like sending mixed signals. I wasn't overly excited about this game at the start, but now I get why she wanted to do it. I've got to get us back on track.

"Now, Caroline, what am I taking off?"

She grins.

"Pants."

I take off my jeans. My erection is tenting my boxer briefs, and I feel like an ass for being hard as a rock when she's upset about her ex-boyfriend. I give her a sheepish smile.

"I guess it's pretty obvious how much I want you."

She reaches down and begins to rub her hand up and down my length through my underwear. It feels so good that I'm worried I'm going to cream my pants.

"Okay, babe, what's your question for me?"

If I don't hurry this along, I'm going to embarrass myself.

"Same question. What's your biggest fear, Jack?"

"That's an easy one for me. The two little girls sleeping upstairs mean more than anything else in the world to me. I don't know what I'd do if something ever happened to them. The thought of it gives me palpitations."

She brings her lips to my chest and kisses right where my heart sits. She looks up at me with those gorgeous baby blues. I think the walls I've erected are going to be hammered down quickly with this one if I'm not careful.

"You're amazing with them. They're lucky to have you as their father."

"Thank you. Now take your pants off."

I can't help but laugh.

"But now that I mention those two little girls upstairs, I'm thinking we should do this somewhere more private in case someone wakes up. I'm taking you to my bedroom where we can shut the door. Making you come on my couch will have to wait for another time."

She smiles at me and then grabs my hand.

"Take me to your room, and then I'll take my pants off."

I pick her up and carry her to my bed. I lay her down, and she reaches to unbutton her jeans. I take over, and she lifts her hips while I slowly pull them down. I stare there admiring her wearing only her light-blue panties.

"Looks like we're down to our undies, handsome."

She props herself on her elbows. God, I love her confidence. I'm losing self-control.

"You've got one minute to ask me a question before I say fuck the rules and take you right here."

She laughs.

"All right, Jack. Where do you see yourself in five years?"

Ah, of course. She wants to know if I plan on having all the shit women want, marriage with the big happy family with a yard and a dog. She doesn't know that's a sore spot for me. I center myself over her. My dick is pressing against her panties, and if we were naked right now, I'd slide right in. I start sucking on her earlobe and kissing down her jaw. I know I can distract her without fully answering her question.

"I'm twenty-eight, so in five years, I'll be thirty-three. I hope to still be playing hockey."

I make my way down her neck, over her collarbone.

"The girls will be nine and hopefully still as sweet as they are now."

I begin paying special attention to her breasts.

"I hope that they're happy, and maybe I'll have a puppy by then."

She moans as I clamp down on her nipple. I reach down and start removing her panties. She lifts her hips, making my job easier. Once her panties are off, I lick her folds. She moans again. I suck her clit into my mouth. She's unbelievably wet. I add a finger, then two, continuing to lap her sweet pussy. She's rocking against my face. I want to stick my dick in her so badly, it hurts. Her legs start quivering, and I know she's close. I move my fingers faster, rhythmically pumping in and out of her. I can feel her muscles tightening around my hand and her sweet juices pouring out all over my face. Her hands fist the sheets. She cries out my name. Those cries are like music to my ears. My ego may have just grown a little bigger. I gently bring her back down. She's panting, and I'm quite pleased with myself. My hard cock is dripping inside of my boxers. She smiles at me and begins rubbing little circles over my back with her fingernails.

"Jack, you're way too good at that. But you cheated."

"What do you mean?"

"You didn't finish answering my last question."

She looks into my eyes, wanting more. I can't give her more than that.

"Yeah, I did. Now I get to ask you one last one, and then I plan to have you screaming my name again."

"All right, hit me."

The look of disappointment flashes out of her eyes as quickly as it came. She locks her ankles around my hips and pushes herself under my aching cock.

"You want me to spank you?"

I grind against her.

"Is that your question?"

She looks up at me sweetly, fluttering her lashes, her hands moving up and down my back.

"Nah, but when you said 'hit me,' that's where my mind went. I'll figure out the answer to that one on my own."

I'm really having a hard time focusing here.

"Okay, last question, chocolate or vanilla?"

Her hands go toward my boxer briefs and begin to push them down. I quickly stand up to pull them down and reach for a condom out of the nightstand.

"Always chocolate, Jack. Now please get inside me."

I can hardly breathe. I better not come like a high school kid. What is it about her? I sheathe my cock, position myself on the bed, and look down at her.

"You are so incredibly beautiful."

I begin to kiss her, and she suddenly pulls back as if she's no longer wanting to do this.

"Hey, are you all right?"

"Jack, if we're going to do this, I need open communication. What I'm trying to say is if this is going to become something we do regularly, I'm not comfortable being with a guy who is having sex with other people. When you leave for a stretch of away games, I don't want to be in your bed one night and find out you have someone else in your bed the next night. I can't do that."

I guess it may be time for me to speak some truths too. This may be the most real I've been with anyone in years.

"Caroline, I haven't had sex in six months. Until you. I went through a phase when I couldn't even look at a woman without feeling guilty after Bree's death. Then I made some poor decisions. I found myself suddenly single with women at my disposal. I'm not going to lie. I've been with a lot of women, and I'm a little screwed up. The baby daddy drama put a stop to that lifestyle. I've been pickier lately. I want to be the kind of guy who's a role model for my daughters, an example of the kind of guy I'd want for them one day. I promise you that while we're doing this, it's only going to be me and you."

"Deal."

She puts her hands on my cheeks. The moment is getting too intimate, which is weird considering what we're about to do, but physical connection and emotional connection are two very different things. I can't let myself get too emotionally involved. I need to remind myself what this is. I start to kiss her again, but she gently pushes me away.

"One more thing, Jack. Let me just make sure I'm clear on the terms here. We are agreeing to sleeping together and exclusivity, but you don't want a relationship, so what is this?"

"Does it need a label?"

"I guess I just want to understand what we are and what we aren't."

She sighs and looks up at me. I can see the vulnerability in her eyes, but I'm never going to be the guy who gives her the fairy-tale ending.

"How about we work on becoming better friends? Getting to know each other better, and while we work on our friendship, we have a lot of sex."

I smile down on her, and she laughs.

"So like a friend with benefits arrangement?"

"Yeah, I think we could be great friends."

I begin kissing a trail of kisses down her chest and stomach, working my way to her core. This time instead of pushing me away, she puts her hands around my back and pulls me closer to her. Our eyes lock. My cock brushes the opening of her center, and I look into her eyes.

"I need to make sure you're ready for me before I—"

She cuts me off. "I'm ready."

She puts her hands on my ass, and as I start to slowly enter her, she pulls me all the way inside her. We both gasp. She's so wet and tight. I need a minute before I start to move, or this is going to be over before it even starts. She begins rolling her hips underneath me, prompting me to thrust in and out of her. Each time, I draw myself out as far as I can go without exiting her body and then thrust back in deep. We find our rhythm, and to my relief, her muscles begin to clench down on me.

"Oh my god, I'm going to come."

I watch in awe as she comes apart in front of my eyes, hair splayed over the pillow, face flushed, eyes half closed, lips parted. She's like an angel sent down to me from heaven. The sight of her climaxing brings me over the edge. I come so hard I feel it down to the tip of my toes. We lie there breathless for a minute or an hour, I'm not entirely sure, but I realize that keeping this purely physical is going to be damn near impossible.

Chapter 18

Caroline

I don't know if last night could have gone any better. Not just the sex either. The sex was amazing. We were up until the wee hours of the morning, and I feel slightly guilty knowing he has a game tonight. He assured me he'd have time to nap before the game and gave me more orgasms than I thought was humanly possible in a night. But aside from the sex, I'm learning about the many layers of Jack. It seems like each layer is better than the last, and I'm excited to see where this could go. He's obviously afraid of commitment, but the fact that he is open about his fears makes me think that he's aware of his own confines. If I'm the one he could finally trust enough to let his guard down, then I'd consider myself the beyond lucky. He's a catch, and he seems oblivious to it. He looked at me with such reverence this morning that I know, with certainty, he feels something special between us too. I left before the girls woke up to eliminate any confusion, but I already wish I were back in his bed.

After napping and studying all day, I'm meeting the girls at Ari's place for a ladies' night. I have exams this week so this will be the last of me socializing for a while. Ari, Victoria, and Mel are here. Sofia is out with her boyfriend. We're sipping our wine, laughing, and chatting about a guy who has it bad for Mel when Victoria asks me how my dinner with Jack went.

"Did you thank him for taking care of you when you were sick?" Mel asks.

"I did. We actually talked a lot."

I can't help but smile.

"And?" Ari asks.

"I'm trying to figure him out. He's like this puzzle of sweet and sexy mixed with dark and guarded."

"Get to the part where he gave you a thousand orgasms last night!" Victoria says with a smile on her face like she's in the know.

"Yeah, that did happen. Multiple times. The sex just keeps getting better with him. He told me he can't do a relationship but wants to be friends with benefits."

I look around, waiting for a reply, and see three shocked women staring at me.

"Care, you're like the epitome of a Disney princess. You're not a friend with benefits kind of girl. I'm worried you're going to get crushed, sweetie," Ari says softly.

"You're the sweet, good girl of the group, honey, and we love you for it. But you're breaking all your normal rules for this guy. Why?" Mel asks.

"How do you know he's going to be exclusive with you? We know how important that is to you after Brandon," Ari gently adds.

"We talked about being exclusive, and he agreed. Look, ladies, I understand your concerns, but I know him better than you think. I know his family. I know what an amazing father he is to those two little girls. I know he's been through tragedy and lost his wife way too young. Not only did he come to my rescue when I was sick, but he cooked Mexican food for me because he knows it's my favorite. He's thoughtful and kind. He's a generous lover. He makes me feel bold, and I act out of character with him because he excites me."

I could go on and on about this man, but I need to reign it in before they start lecturing me about not falling for him.

"Oh, Care. You've got it bad for him," Mel says as she pours me another glass of wine.

"Are you sure you're capable of this sleeping together with no label thing you've got going on?" Victoria asks sincerely.

"All I know is he's a single dad who lost his wife and has been repeatedly screwed over by women who want him only because of his NHL status. Right now, I'm willing to do things his way. I'm not going to pressure him into something neither of us is ready for.

I want to be his friend, and I think he just needs to believe in love again."

I take a sip of my wine, confident in my decision. This man makes me want things I haven't wanted in a very long time, and I'm willing to be patient.

*****

Jack

After two wins at home, we're on the road again. I already miss Caroline. I talked her into coming over again last night before I had to leave, and damn, she's incredible. We're sitting on the tarmac waiting to get off the plane, so I shoot her a text.

> Me: Hey beautiful. Made it safely. Will you be watching my game tonight?
>
> Caroline: Hi handsome. I'm glad you made it safely. I've been thinking about you. Of course, I'll be watching.
>
> Me: Good. I'll call you after, but don't wait up. I know you need your rest for studying and I don't want to interfere with that.
>
> Caroline: I'll be up, Jack. XOXO
>
> Me: Talk to you soon.

"Hey, Jack. What's up with you? You're staring at your phone like it's Fourth of July fireworks."

I swear nothing gets by Jimmy.

"Caroline came over last night. I took your advice, man."

"She's down to get dirty with no strings attached, huh?"

"Yeah, surprisingly."

"So I'm guessing you fucked her senseless, and that's why you can't stop smiling?"

Jimmy already knows the answer, but he loves giving me shit.

"Something like that."

"It's good to see you happy, man. She seems to have that effect on you."

"Yeah, she does."

"So this isn't going to be one of those hit-it-and-quit-it type of situations?"

"No, man, we agreed to mess around for a while. No expectations of anything more than that."

"You sure about that?"

"You know me, man. We talked about this. I can't do more."

"Jack, it's been four years. Eventually, you're going to be ready for more."

"Don't rain on my parade right now, all right?"

"Gotcha. Let's go kick some ass."

We both stand to get off the plane. The weather in Buffalo isn't so different from Chicago. The gray clouds and cold rain seem to have followed us. I shoot my mom a quick text telling her I made it and to kiss Ellie and Rosie good night for me.

*****

We got our asses kicked. My whole body hurts, and my eye is already turning purple. I took a pretty nice right hook in the second period. The locker room is unusually quiet. Everyone's pissed, and I think we all just want to get back to the hotel and put tonight behind us. I lean over to check my phone and make sure my mom didn't have any issues with the girls. Instead, I have a text from Caroline. It's a selfie she took. She's wearing some sexy librarian glasses with her blond hair in a messy bun on the top of her head. She got an oversized shirt on that's coming off of one shoulder, exposing a hot-pink bra strap, a pile of books in front of her, and her laptop open. I wish

I could throw all those books on the ground and fuck her right there at her desk. Then I read what she wrote.

> I'm sorry about the loss, babe. I wish I were there to kiss that gorgeous cock of yours and make you forget all about it.

I hear laughing behind me.

"Novotny, what the hell, man? Why are you reading my texts over my shoulder? Give me some fucking privacy."

"Can she kiss my gorgeous cock? I know I'd feel *a lot* better right now."

I start laughing because I feel like the luckiest bastard on the planet right now. She does that to me.

"Sorry, man. She's taken."

"I'm glad you two worked things out after the paparazzi shit."

"Me too."

"Maybe we should all get together with her friends again. There are some fine-ass women in that group," Jimmy chimes in with a knowing smile on his face.

The bus ride is quick, and I basically sprint to my hotel room. As soon as I walk in the door, I call her. She answers on the first ring.

"Hi, handsome."

"Hi, beautiful. I'm not waking you, am I?"

"No. I couldn't sleep. There's this really sexy guy I was hoping would call me before I went to bed."

"Damn, what I wouldn't give to be him."

She chuckles.

"How's the eye?"

"Ugly. Can I FaceTime you?"

"Of course."

The screen switches over, and she's wearing exactly what she was in her text, but now she's lying in bed.

"Hi."

"You really are beautiful."

"Aww…thanks. That eye looks like it hurts."

"It's not so bad. Novotny saw your text."
Her face reddens.
"Jack! That was supposed to be for your eyes only."
She's got this adorable smile on her face.
"Not my fault. He was snooping behind me in the locker room. But I promise no one can see you now."
"You don't have to share a room?"
"No. One of the perks of being a more senior player."
"That is nice."
"Have you ever had phone sex?"
"Umm, a few times?"
"You continue to surprise me. Let me guess, NFL days?"
"Yeah. Not like it stopped him from straying, but we tried it."
"Hey, when are you going to realize that his straying had nothing to do with you and everything to do with him?"
"Anyways, how many games until you're home again?"
Her sudden change of subject doesn't go unnoticed, but I let it slide. I don't want to talk about her douchebag ex either.
"Miss me?"
"I do, but lucky me, I get to see Ellie and Rosie tomorrow."
"I'm jealous."
"Yeah, they're pretty great. I think it's because their dad is such a cool dude."
"Cool dude, huh? Nice choice of words."
She laughs.
"So how about we try that phone sex you mentioned earlier?"
It's my turn to laugh.
"Ah, so that's why you miss me."
"Well, Jack Hannen orgasms are like no orgasm I've ever had before."
"And how's that?"
"Maybe stronger? More intense? Somehow all around better?"
"Damn, girl, you trying to stroke my ego?"
"I'd rather be stroking something else actually."
"All right, dirty girl. I'll play along. Can you take your shirt off for me? I'm dying to see that hot-pink bra that's been teasing me."

She sets her phone down on the edge of the bed and props it up with a pillow. Then with this coy look, she slowly lifts her shirt, and damn, I'm already sporting a semi.

"That is one sexy bra. Do the panties match?"

"Hmmm... I guess you'll have to wait and see. Because before I take anything else off, I'd love for you to take your shirt off too."

I set my phone down and rip my shirt off.

"How's that?"

"Your body is seriously a work of art. I want to lick those muscles, and I'm not even joking. So hot."

I think one of my favorite things about her is how she expresses herself. She's not afraid to speak her mind, and she makes me laugh.

"What can I say, babe? I work out."

She's laughing now.

"Is that so? I would have never guessed."

"So can I see those panties now?"

"You show me yours. I'll show you mine."

"Deal."

She reaches down and pulls her tight-fitting yoga pants off. The bra *does* match the panties. They're both lined with black lace, and her push-up bra is making me want to fuck her tits. She notices where I'm staring and slowly traces a finger over her breasts.

"You like?"

"Yeah, babe. I like a lot." My voice is husky. "Just like that. Reach behind yourself and unclasp your bra for me."

She obeys and her tits spill out.

"Perfect. I want you to pinch those nipples for me now. Good. Roll them between your thumb and index finger."

She's got her hands exactly where I want them and lets out a whimper.

"That's great, Care. Now a little rougher."

She pulls on her nipples harder, and I slide my hand into my boxer briefs to let my dick out.

"Look what you do to me, honey."

She gasps.

"It feels so good, Jack."

I begin to stroke myself up and down as I watch her.

"I want to see your right hand touch your pussy and keep your left hand on your breast. Good, Caroline. Now I want to see how you touch yourself. Will you show me what you like?"

She brings her hand down to her clit and swirls her first two fingers over her clit in a circular motion. She moans and moves her hands over the sensitive spot again. I keep stroking myself. I want to watch her come apart for me.

"That's it, babe. You're so fucking hot. I'm getting close already. Put your finger inside yourself."

She slides a finger inside her core and gasps. She begins rhythmically moving in and out, matching the speed of my strokes on my dick. Her eyes never leave mine.

"Jack, oh my, oh my, I'm coming."

Her legs are quivering, and her eyes flutter closed. Her lips part, and I'm in awe. I quicken my strokes and shoot my load all over my stomach. I take a minute to catch my breath. She's staring at me with a look of sheer satisfaction.

"Why is it always so much better with you?"

"I don't know, babe. But that was awesome."

I grab my T-shirt and wipe my come off my stomach. I pick the phone up off the pillows where it was propped so that mainly my face is on display.

"Agreed."

She rolls on her side and brings the phone to her face.

"That totally helped clear my head."

"You have a lot on your mind?"

I assume she's going to talk about school stuff.

"My mom's birthday is next month. I just made dinner reservations for it. Even though she's gone, we still celebrate every year."

"What do you mean she's gone?"

I feel like an ass. Is her mom dead and I didn't know?

"She got a really bad headache one night after school. She was always so full of life and energy, but that night, she was lying on the couch with a cool rag over her eyes. Cody told her he'd make dinner. When Dad came home a few hours later, he took her to the ER right away. She was diagnosed with an inoperable brain tumor that night. She fought hard, but even with treatment, we lost her a month later. My dad is a world-renowned neurosurgeon, and even though there was nothing he could have done, he blamed himself. She was the love of his life. In a way, we lost both of our parents when she died."

"I can't imagine how hard that must have been for your whole family."

I never would have imagined Caroline had lost her mother. She's so upbeat and sweet all the time that she has this innocence to her. It's hard to imagine her facing such adversity at such a young age.

"So you still celebrate her birthday?"

"Dad hasn't celebrated it with us in a few years now, but Cody and I still do every year. Every year on her birthday, we would go for a fancy dinner as a family. She was never one of those moms who wanted a night to herself although no one would have blamed her. She wanted us all to dress up and experience high-end dining. She absolutely loved trying different foods and flavors. Her idea of fun was going to street fairs and hole-in-the-wall restaurants or dive bars for unique foods. But on her birthday, we always went fancy. It might have been more Dad's doing than her request, but the tradition stuck. Now Cody and I go out to a fancy dinner every year on her birthday."

"That's a nice way to honor her memory, Caroline."

"Yeah, she was amazing. I still miss her every day."

I swallow. The only woman I've ever lost was Bree, and I can't say I miss her. How fucked up is that seeing as how I vowed to love until death do us part. I guess our situation was so bad up that I felt guilt more than grief when she died. I do feel bad that my girls never got to know their mother, but I think the love was long gone from our marriage, if it was every really there at all. She must mistake my silence because she looks at me so exposed.

"I'm sorry. I don't even know why I just told you all of that."

"I'm glad you did. You're an incredible woman. You know that, right?"

She laughs.

"Maybe I'll start believing it one day. Are you ready for bed, handsome?" she asks with a yawn.

"It looks like you are. I'm pretty beat too. That game was rough. Good night, Caroline."

"Good night, Jack. Sleep tight."

She ends the call, and I lie in bed thinking. She's beautiful, smart, funny, and strong. She makes me want things I haven't wanted in years. That scares the shit out of me. I don't know if I'm ready for more, but I don't want to let this one go.

Chapter 19

Caroline

"Okay, class! Let's all sit down and read our book for today, *Giraffes Can't Dance*."

My preschool ballet class is for three- and four-year-old children, and we always begin with a story. Jack's still out of town for away games, but I know Kathy is supposed to be bringing Ellie and Rosie. They haven't arrived yet, and I've already given them a few extra minutes, so I sit down crisscross applesauce and begin the story surrounded by tutus. My students all look up at me with curious eyes, totally engrossed in the story, as I make the characters have funny voices. Ellie comes running in first.

"Hi, Miss Caroline!"

"Hi, Ellie. I'm glad you could come."

"Grandma is sick, but we begged her to let us see you!"

"Oh no. I'll have to check on her after class. Okay, now shhh! We need to finish our story."

"Hi, Miss Caroline!"

I have to laugh. We're never going to get any dancing done at this rate.

"Hi, Rosie. Sit down so we can finish our book, okay?"

I read the last few pages and then lead the class through their routine. Most of them are starting to remember some of the steps, and they're all adorable. After class, I head out to the observation area to see Kathy. On Tuesday nights, this is my last class of the day, so I don't have to set up for the next group. I see Kathy across the room, and she looks awful. Her skin is ghostly pale. She looks like she's shivering despite the fact that she's wearing her winter coat, and it's warm in the studio. I feel her pain especially when I was just sick myself.

"Hi, Kathy. I hear you're sick. Are you okay?"

"I think I just have a cold or something," she says as she starts coughing.

It sounds as if her lungs are going to pop out of her chest. She shakes her head and gives me a weak smile.

"I'm so sorry. I've been fighting this for days. It just keeps getting worse."

"I think you need to go home, drink lots of fluids, and rest."

"I can't. Jack's still out of town for his game. Jack Sr. is gone this week for his annual golf outing with his college buddies. Rick and Judith are at their time-share in Florida, and Jack's nanny called me because she's in the hospital having gallbladder surgery. The nanny agency Jack uses has a backup, but I know he gets nervous having a nanny he hasn't met before in the house with the girls while he's on the road."

"Do you want me to watch the girls for you so you can rest?"

"Caroline, I can't ask you to do that."

"You're not asking. I'm offering. In fact, why don't we put their booster seats in my car right now? I'll take them home and plan on spending the night. I can get them to preschool in the morning."

"Sweetie. That is way too much. I'll be fine."

"Grandma, please! Can we have a sleepover with Miss Caroline? Please, please, please!"

Rosie is jumping up and down with excitement.

"See, they want me to come!"

I insist.

"Caroline, I—"

"Kathy, you're going home."

"Thank you, honey."

She starts coughing again and reaches into her bag for a tissue.

"I'm so glad you and Jack worked things out. He told me he had you over for dinner to apologize. I was happy to see you didn't let him off the hook too easily."

"We all need to be held accountable for our actions, right?"

"You're good for him."

She pauses as if she's going to say more and then things better of it.

"I'll let him know I asked you to do this. All right, let's go get those booster seats moved."

"Yay! Miss Caroline, can we stay up late and watch movies?" Ellie asks me as her eyes shimmer with excitement.

"We'll see. We're going to stop by my house first so I can pack a few things for my overnight bag. You'll get to visit my house again. My friend, Sofia, is staying with me for a little bit until she gets her own place. She makes the best food ever. Maybe if we're lucky, she'll make us something delicious."

I already know that she's been tinkering in my kitchen all day. She cooks when she's stressed. She texted earlier telling me to come home starving, so this will be perfect. I'm not really sure what's going on with Sofia. She just moved out of her boyfriend's apartment, and when she asked if she could stay with me, I didn't hesitate to let her. She's refusing to talk about the breakup, and I'm worried about her. She said they just needed some space from one another, and she wasn't ready to talk about it.

We give Kathy hugs, and I urge her to jump right into bed. Then the girls are loaded up, and we talk about our favorite things to do in the fall. Before I know it, we are pulling into my driveway. The girls start bouncing in their seats.

"You live by Auntie J!" Rosie says.

"I do. She's my neighbor, but she and your uncle Rick aren't home."

"I know. They're in Florida, and they promised to bring us a present home!"

"Oh, that will be so nice."

I help the girls out of the car, and as we enter my town house, we are immediately greeted by the most amazing smells. Sofia sees the two little girls and raises a brow at me.

"Well, hi there, and who are you?"

"I'm Ellie Hannen, and this is my sister," Ellie says as she points to Rosie.

Sofia raises a brow at me.

"Oh! Hi, girls. I've seen you at dance class. I'm sorry I didn't remember you right away. It's nice to see you. Would you like to try some homemade ice cream? I've been working on some new flavors."

"Ice cream? Yay!" Rosie shouts.

"Here, try some," Sofia says as she laughs.

She fills two small bowls with lemon ice cream and puts a spoon in each.

"Caroline, can you come check on something in the living room with me?"

I follow her into the living room.

"What are you doing, Care? He's out of town, and you two just established that you aren't in a relationship. Why do you have his girls?"

"His mom is sick. She was watching them and looked awful. I offered to take them for the night so she could rest."

"For the night? They're sleeping here?"

"No, I just came to pack a bag. I think they'll sleep better in their own beds."

"And where are you going to sleep?"

"Jack's house is huge. I'll just crash in one of the spare bedrooms."

"Does he know about this plan?"

"I was going to call him on my way to his house and tell him what's going on."

"Care, are you sure this isn't going to freak him out? Like too much, too fast? Are you sure he's not going to think you're trying to play mommy to get him to commit to some sort of relationship?"

"That's not at all what I'm doing. His mom's sick. I didn't have plans, and I love his girls. I thought I'd just offer to help."

"I think you should call him right now and make sure this is okay with him before you make any further plans."

She's right. I've never been with his children alone. Maybe this will freak him out. I pull out my phone to call him. He answers on the first ring.

"Hey, Jack."

"Aww, what? No hey handsome? I kind of liked that nickname."

He makes me smile. Just hearing his voice reminds me of all the dirty things we did last night.

"Well, handsome, I'm calling because your mom is sick, and I offered to watch the girls for her. She looked awful when she brought them to dance and was coughing up a storm. I wanted to make sure you were okay with me watching them."

"Ummm…sure, I guess. You don't mind? I feel bad. I didn't know she was sick. Is she okay?"

"I don't think she wanted you to worry. It seems like it's just a nasty head cold and cough right now. She looked miserable. I really don't mind watching them at all. I can bring them to preschool in the morning and check in with your mom then."

"Is that going to interfere with your schooling though?"

"Nope. I start class after their drop off. My teaching load is light tomorrow afternoon, so I'll be able to pick them up if your mom is still under the weather."

"Okay. Thanks, Caroline. I'll be back as soon as possible. I have to go through. We have practice starting in a minute."

"No worries. Talk to you later."

"Thanks, Caroline."

"Of course."

He ends the call. He did sound a little stressed about this whole situation, much more serious than he normally is. Now I'm questioning my decision to do this. Sofia is looking at me, waiting for me to say something.

"He said it was fine. He just didn't know his mom was sick."

"Now that he knows and is okay with it, I'd say you're in the clear. Let's have some fun with these peanuts. They're adorable."

She's right. I need to relax. Sofia is from a large family. She's accustomed to kids of all ages, which is part of the reason she's such a good dance teacher to the littles. She quickly plates some enchiladas for us, and the girls inhale their food. I'm slightly surprised they even still had an appetite after the ice cream. After dinner, we paint nails, and I notice Ellie yawning.

"All right, Sofia, we'll see you later. We've got to get home and into bed. Girls, tell Sofia thank you for dinner."

"Thanks, Miss Sofia!" they shout in unison.

I didn't expect to have so much fun tonight. I really love spending time with these two little girls. We get back to Jack's house, and I use the code Kathy gave me to enter. I park in the garage, and the girls leap out of the car. We head straight upstairs to do baths, pajamas, and bedtime stories. As I'm helping Ellie brush her teeth, she reaches for me and wraps her arms around me.

"Can you be our mommy, Miss Caroline?"

Oh my gosh, I'm going to cry. I think back to losing my own mom and that void that is forever in my chest. I want so badly for these girls to never experience that kind of pain. They were just babies when their mother died, and they're probably just now realizing that their family is different from a lot of their other friends. I need to hold it together and choose my words carefully. I hug her back and smile down at her.

"Right now, I can be your friend, Ellie. A really, really good friend. And I can help you learn to dance. And one day, I know you'll get the best mommy ever."

Satisfied with my answer, she spits the remaining toothpaste out and runs to her bed. Rosie is already waiting for us. After three stories, I sing a bedtime song, and the girls are both completely passed out. I carry Rosie to her room and sneak downstairs. I open my laptop and begin studying when my phone rings. I look down and see that it's Jack's mom.

"Hi, Kathy. How are you feeling?"

"Hi, honey. I just wanted to check in and see if you needed anything."

She starts coughing into the phone.

"We're all set. The girls are asleep, and I'm just studying. You should be resting too."

"I know, honey. I just felt bad leaving them with you. I talked to Jack. He should be home Friday. Do you mind picking the girls up so I can go to the doctor? I think I might need an antibiotic or something."

"That's not a problem at all."

"Great. Thank you so much. I'm going to go back to bed. Night, Caroline."

"Night, Kathy. I hope you get a good night's rest."

Chapter 20

Jack

We just got back to the hotel after team dinner following our meetings. My mind should be on tomorrow's game, but instead, I'm worried about what's going on at home. My mom sounded awful on the phone. I'm also worried about Caroline and the girls. I don't know if I should be relieved that she came to my rescue or slightly concerned about it. I've never brought a woman around Ellie and Rosie before. I really like Caroline, but I wasn't exactly planning on her spending a ton of time at my house without me being there. I don't want the girls getting too attached. This is all new and moving kind of fast for my liking. I really don't want a commitment right now or ever, and I wanted time to figure things out with this woman. Maybe I'm making a big deal out of nothing, but it doesn't feel like nothing to me. I should call her, but with the two-hour time zone difference, I don't want to wake her. I opt for a quick text.

Me: Hey. Are you awake?

Caroline: Hi handsome. I'm awake.

I decide to FaceTime her. Maybe if I see her, I won't be as worried. She pics up right away. It's dark in the room, and I know she most definitely wasn't awake. She leans to turn on the light by the nightstand. I see now that she's in the spare bedroom upstairs by the girls' rooms. That calms my nerves a bit. Her eyes are adjusting to the light, and she's squinting. Her blond hair is a mess, and she's wearing a thin little sleep tank that I can see her nipples pointing through. I'm trying to look at her face, but I can't seem to take my eyes off her chest.

"Hi, you."

Her voice is husky and thick from sleep. It's only nine o'clock here, but it's eleven in Chicago.

"I'm pretty sure you were asleep there, beautiful."

I wonder if she has any idea how sexy she looks right now.

"It's okay. I wanted to talk to you. How was your day?"

"It was okay. I'm looking forward to coming home. I feel bad."

"Don't worry about the girls. I promise I'll take good care of them."

"I know you will."

All of a sudden, I can hear one of the girls crying in the background.

"Rosie's been waking up with nightmares lately. I'm not sure why."

"I'll go get her. I'm going to let you go. Good night, Jack."

"Call me if you need anything."

"I will."

She disconnects the phone, and I'm not feeling any more relaxed about this situation than I was before the call. It's not that I don't trust her with my daughters. It's that I don't want to accept how perfectly she seems to fit into my life.

*****

Caroline's been at my house for three days without me now. When my mom was diagnosed with pneumonia, and my nanny was still recovering from her surgery, Caroline basically took over. She's taken the girls to and from preschool every day, had a picnic in the park, took the girls to a soccer game, and organized for her friends to watch the girls at night when she has classes to teach. She's even brought my mom homemade meals and get-well cards from the girls. Of course, she's downplayed all of it, but my mom has been keeping tabs and updating me. No matter how sick she is, she watches over us like the mother hen she is. I'm in complete awe of Caroline, and I'm pretty sure my mom is in love.

My car needed some work done, so I dropped it off before I left. Since I'm still without it, Jimmy's driving me back to my house now that we're back in town. I told Caroline I'd be home later tonight, but I am excited to surprise her and my daughters by showing up early. We pull up into my driveway, and there are multiple cars lined in front of my house. My heart starts racing. I have no idea what's going on at my house. Jimmy and I look at each other.

"Uh, is Caroline throwing a party at your place? I'll come in with you."

Jimmy throws the car in park, and we both get out.

"What the fuck?"

I'm trying not to get pissed before I go inside. As soon as we enter, we hear music blaring and a group of women laughing and chanting, "Go, Rosie, go, Rosie, go!" As I walk into the living room, I see Caroline with her four best friends and my beautiful daughters all standing in a circle. Rosie is in the middle doing some kind of dance routine that just ended with a series of somersaults. My daughters look like they're having the time of their lives, and I can't help but smile. Nerves instantly calmed.

"Hot chick party at Hannen's! I'm so glad I came in. I'm texting the guys."

I look at Jimmy and hold my finger to my lips, telling him to be quiet. I sneak up behind Caroline and wrap my arms around her. She jumps and screams. She then turns and wraps her arms around me.

"I'm home!"

"Oh my god, Jack! You scared me. I thought you wouldn't be home until later tonight."

"I wanted to surprise you."

"Daddy's home!"

Rosie comes running up to me, and as I bend down, she wraps her arms around my neck.

"Daddy, we love having Miss Caroline here. Can she stay?" Ellie asks as she tugs on my pants.

"Yeah, I think we'll keep her around. Now give me a hug."

I wink at Caroline.

"Daddy, will you dance with us?"

Rosie is dragging me into the circle full of women. I don't really dance without being inebriated so this should be humiliating, but I don't want to disappoint my daughters.

"All right, ladies, can I request a song? I really love Journey."

I look around and recognize the women from Caroline's dance recital and Club Indulgence. I'm about to make an ass out of myself. Jimmy laughs and makes his way over to the circle.

"This I've got to see."

He blatantly checks Sofia out. She literally laughs in his face and starts the music. My daughters begin chanting, "Go, Daddy, go, Daddy, go!" I'm immediately reminded of why I don't dance sober, and I realize that Journey's "Don't Stop Believin'" feels like an incredibly long song when you have a group of women staring at you. I pull Caroline in to dance with me and take some of the heat off me. She instantly comes to my rescue and somehow manages to make the whole thing fun instead of awkward. The doorbell rings, and Ari runs to answer it. She comes back with pizzas, and we all disperse to the kitchen.

Caroline grabs a stack of plates and silverware and starts dishing out slices. She serves my daughters first and even cuts Ellie's into strips just like she likes it. I stand back and watch her when Jimmy walks over.

"Close your mouth. You're drooling again, bro."

I punch him in the shoulder.

"Maybe you should be the one to close your mouth."

He laughs and ducks away. He reaches around Sofia and grabs a piece of pizza right out of her hand. He winks at her and stuffs it in his mouth.

Caroline laughs.

"Careful, Jimmy. Sofia doesn't mess around when it comes to food."

"Actually, Caroline, I'm going to need introductions of all your beautiful friends here. I didn't get a chance to talk to them all that much yet," I say.

The one who threw a beer in my face snorts and shakes her head.

Caroline introduces a petite Asian chick who is undoubtedly the center of some young boy's wet dreams. Her name's Ari, and I remember her leading a K-pop routine at the recital now. She's got thick, long, black hair almost to her waist. Then there's Sofia, the Latina with the killer curves, who Jimmy can't stop staring at, and Mel whom I think is biracial. She's got eyes the color of honey that draw you in. They remind me of a cat. She's stunningly beautiful. Victoria is the one who introduced herself the night of the recital. She's got ivory skin, auburn hair, and bright-green eyes. Needless to say, Caroline's friends are smoking hot. They've all got great figures, probably from dancing as much as they do, but none of them hold a candle to my gorgeous Caroline. She's perfect.

My door opens, and a group of my teammates enter. I look at Jimmy, and he gives me a sheepish grin.

"I figured we may as well all have a good time, Jack. It'll be fun after all of our traveling."

There are two groups of men on our team. There are those who rush home to their wives and children, the family men. They all hang together and so do their wives. I used to spend time with them when I was married, but after Bree died, I suddenly felt extremely uncomfortable around my own friends. So now I hang out with the second group, the immature, single playboys who are in no rush to go home and are always looking for a good time. To be honest, I don't really fit with either group at the moment, but this is the point I'm at in my life.

"Gentlemen, welcome! My daughters are attendees at this impromptu party, so let's all watch our language, eh?"

I look straight at Jones while I'm giving my warning because the guy might be incapable of anything but lewd language.

"Novotny, we're going to need some more pizzas."

"Already on it."

He holds up his phone. I head over to my daughters and set Rosie in my lap while I eat a slice of pizza. I look around for Caroline and notice Kelston talking on her. Caroline looks like she wants to punch him, and I immediately want to go to her. I don't know their exact history, but Cody did tell me that she hates the guy.

"Jimmy, take my spot for a minute."

Jimmy's like an uncle to my daughters, and he gives me a questioning look. I glance over at Caroline and Kelston, and he nods his head. I want to make sure I don't need to put Green in his place. Jimmy takes Rosie in his lap, and Ellie's seated to his right. Caroline's back is to me, so I walk over and slide my arms around her waist. I lean in and smell her hair, kissing her neck.

"Hi."

Green looks straight at me with an annoyed look on his face.

"Hey. I was just getting juice for the girls."

She sounds flustered. I look in her hands, and she's carrying two glasses with watered-down juice.

"Green, you think you could give these to my daughters? I need Caroline for a minute."

"Yeah, sure. We'll talk more later, Caroline. Nice to see you again."

Green gives me a "fuck-you look" and takes the juice from Caroline's hands. She turns toward me.

"You okay?" I ask.

"I'm fine. Thanks for checking. I think you missed me though."

She wraps her arms around my neck and looks up at me. I put my hands back on her waist but start moving them toward her ass. I cup one cheek in each hand.

"What gave me a way?"

"I don't know. Maybe the boner that was just rubbing against my back?"

"You felt that, huh? It wasn't there when I originally came over here, but as soon as I put my hands on you and smelled you, well, shit, it was game on."

"We have company, handsome."

"Jimmy agreed to keep an eye on the girls for me. Come with me for a minute."

I grab her hand and lead her toward my bedroom. As soon as we enter, I shut and lock the door. Our lips immediately meet, tongues licking, teeth nipping, and hands everywhere. Neither one of us can control ourselves.

"This can't take long. I'll treat you right tonight, but this right here is a quick fuck so that I'm not walking around with a hard on for the next two hours."

"Hard and fast. Yes, please."

She's already stripping out of her clothes. Man, this chick does it for me. I pull my shirt off and grab a condom from the nightstand. She's unbuttoning my pants and starts pushing them down once I have the condom in my hands. I pick her up, and she wraps her legs around my waist. I push her up against the bedroom door and enter her in one hard thrust. We both moan. We find our rhythm, and I know I'm going to come almost immediately. She's so tight and wet. I take my right hand and rub her clit with my thumb while I hold her up with my left hand. I then put my mouth around her tit. I suck hard and keep rubbing her clit until she's quivering around me. She screams my name as she comes, and I follow, coming hard. When I open my eyes, she's looking at me with a huge smile on her face.

"That. Was. Awesome. Let's go join our friends now."

She unwraps her legs from around my waist, and I pull out and set her down. She runs into my bathroom to clean up, and I grab our clothes, following her. We dress quickly and head back out to the party. This woman is everything—everything I want and everything I can't have.

Chapter 21

Caroline

Jack basically kicked all our friends out once it was time for Ellie and Rosie's bath. I was ready to have them gone. I'd been avoiding Kelston Green all afternoon and wanted Jack to myself. Jack got the girls ready for bed while I finished cleaning up. I started gathering my things so that they could have a daddy-daughter night when Ellie came running down the stairs.

"Ellie, honey, I think you're supposed to be upstairs reading stories with your daddy."

"I asked Daddy if you could come cuddle with us before bedtime. You do a really good job with the voices, and we like your songs."

"Oh, sweetheart, that's so nice of you, but your daddy has really missed you, and I know he wants some time with you too."

I hear footsteps coming down the stairs, and I know it's him before I even look up.

"Well, Caroline, it looks like they want us both tonight. Do you want to come upstairs and read bedtime stories with us?"

Jack has a sheepish grin on his face, and I want to jump into his arms.

"Are you sure I'm not imposing? I know how much you've missed them."

"I've missed *all* my girls. Come join us."

He pulls me in and gives me a quick kiss on the cheek. I can feel myself blushing. This is so much more than some friend with benefits arrangement. I don't know why he can't see that.

"Well, all right then."

I grab Ellie's hand, and we walk up the stairs. Rosie is already in bed with a mound of books on her lap, and she's set up pillows for each of us to lie on. Jack and I lie on her queen-sized bed with both girls sandwiched between us. I have my arms around Rosie, and she snuggles right into me. Ellie is lying on the crook of Jack's arm while he reads us stories. I think this is the moment I needed for it all to hit me. I'm falling deeper in love with this man and his family every single minute we're together. Jack reads until both girls have fallen asleep, and I'm well on my way. The bed is so cozy and warm. He sneaks out of his side and tucks the blankets around his daughters. He comes over to me and picks me up.

"Do we need to move them?"

"No, they can sleep together tonight, and you can sleep with me."

He presses a kiss to my forehead and carries me down the stairs and into his bedroom. He lays me on the bed and looks at me with such adoration that my heart skips a beat.

"Thank you for taking such good care of everyone while I was gone."

He lies down next to me and brushes his lips to mine ever so softly. It feels so intimate that if I'm not careful, I'm going to lay all my cards on the table before he's ready.

"It was no problem at all, Jack. What are friends for, right?"

He tenses slightly at the term "friends," and I instantly know I screwed up. Then he lets his boyish smile out, and I can see that he's already switched gears and shut off some of himself from me.

"I'm going to be the best damn friend you've ever had, Caroline."

With that, his lips come crashing down on me, and I know that he's trying to separate the emotional from the physical. I kiss him back with all the emotions I'm feeling bottled up. I kiss him like I'll never get enough of him. I kiss him like I never want to let him go. He makes his way down and buries himself in between my legs. He laps, licks, sucks, and nibbles with such intensity that it feels as if I'm soaring through the sky looking down at us. He slips two fingers in, and I'm gone, cascading though the heavens and flying higher and higher into the sky. When I come down, I'm trembling. He wraps himself around me and covers us both with a blanket.

"I could spend the rest of my life making you come like that."

I put my hands on his face, outlining his jaw with my fingers.

"Jack, I want you inside me."

He reaches for a condom, and I stop him.

"I'm on birth control for my periods, and I'm clean so if you want to forego the condoms, I'm okay with that."

He sets the condom back in the drawer.

"I get screened all the time for our routine health checks. I'm clean too. I haven't had sex without a condom since I was married. Are you sure you're okay with this? I don't want you to feel pressured."

I nod, but I know he needs to hear the words.

"Please, Jack. Let me feel you inside of me with no barrier."

I must have unleashed a beast because he centers himself over me, gives me one more final look, and then enters in one long thrust. I'm ready and wet for him. We both groan, and this feels so much better than I expected it to. He's relentless and hammering into me over and over and harder and faster than he ever has before. He's so deep inside of me that I don't know where I end and he begins. I feel so full, and with every thrust, I swear he's finding new areas of pleasure. I cry out at the combination of pain meeting pleasure and pull him closer. My nails are digging into his back. He's kissing and nipping at my neck. I feel his body stiffen, and I know he's about to lose himself inside of me. He grunts, and I lose it. I start quivering around him, tightening so much. I can feel his shaft twitching inside of me. We explode together and just stare at each other in awe, panting.

"Holy shit," he says as he brushes my hair from my face.

"I know."

"That was amazing."

He's looking at me like I'm an enigma that he just can't figure out. Welcome to my world, honey.

"I know."

I lean up and kiss him. His lips meet mine, soft and gentle. It's the complete antithesis of the hard, fast pounding he just gave me.

"Did I hurt you?" he whispers as he gently caresses my arm.

"No. You felt unbelievable."

He kisses my neck and works his way down to my breast. He gently kisses me over my heart and then stops and looks up at me.

"So much for taking our time tonight. We'll just have to do that again. Let's go get cleaned up first."

He grabs my hand and walks me over to his attached bathroom. He starts the shower and holds his free hand under it until he's satisfied with the temperature. He pulls me in with him. It's one of those huge walk-in showers that could probably fit a dozen people, and there's water shooting from every direction. He's gentle and sweet. He lathers bodywash in his hands and starts rubbing it all over my body. He's taking his time over my shoulders, rubbing out any tension he can. He rubs every inch of my body until I feel like jelly, and then he rinses me off with one of the attachments and holds me close to him. He washes himself in a minute flat and then turns the water off. We still don't speak as he wraps me in a warm, fluffy towel. I watch him dry himself off, and I run my fingers through my hair. He opens a drawer, and I see several different brushes and colorful hair ties. No doubt, these are Ellie and Rosie's.

"Will one of these work in your hair?"

I smile and grab one off the top. I start brushing through my wet hair.

"It's perfect. Thanks."

"I told you I was the best damn friend you'd ever have."

Even after all of that, he's still playing his games. It hurts, and it shouldn't. I agreed to be nothing more than a fuck buddy, so I can't get all bent out of shape when he treats me as such. I try not to let my smile waver, but I'm not as good as I think I am, and I'm sure he can see he's hurt me. He kisses my cheek and watches me brush my hair. His towel is wrapped around his waist, and I stare at his beautiful body while I work the brush through my hair. Neither one of us speaks.

*****

Jack

I'm such a dick. I hurt her. I don't want to hurt her. I want to make her feel as complete as she makes me feel.

"Will you stay the night with me?"

I can see her contemplating.

"I should get home. This will be the fourth night I've slept here, and I'm sure you're exhausted anyways."

"I really want you to stay. Please, just one more night?"

I still can't believe I always want her here. I've never had a woman stay here until her, let alone for an extended period of time, and yet, I can't stand the idea of her leaving. I'm going to try and get us back on track so she wants to stay.

"I'll stay for a little bit, but I'm going to go home pretty soon."

Why the fuck did I have to make the friend comment? Now she just wants to get the hell out of here.

"Okay. I'll take any time with you I can get. I'm going to go get us a snack. Go lie down in bed, and I'll be right back."

I run into the kitchen. I grab some fruit and cheese and slice it up as fast as I can. I throw everything on a large tray, grab two bottles of water, and head back to my room. When I get there, Caroline's dressed and sitting on the edge of the bed.

"I was kind of hoping you'd still be naked."

"Jack, I told you I have to leave soon."

"I know you did. Here. Let's sit back and eat a little something first. Do you have stuff to do for school tonight?"

She scoots back and leans against the headboard. Her legs are crossed at the ankle, and her wet hair is all draped over her left shoulder. She opens her water, takes a sip, then grabs a strawberry, and bites into it. I walk over to my dresser and grab a pair of plaid pajama pants. I slide them on and join her on the bed. I can see her guard is up.

"I always have stuff to do for school. One of the joys of a master's program, I guess."

"Care, I've been meaning to ask you this for a while now, but I get the vibe that you aren't too stoked about graduating soon."

"I guess it's hard to get excited about a degree I'm not going to use."

"What do you mean? I thought you loved teaching. The girls can't wait for their time with you each week."

"Teaching dance is a lot different than teaching in the classroom."

"So you don't like the classroom?"

She lets out a long sigh and looks at me. I don't break eye contact. I'm waiting to see why she's doing something she doesn't like.

"I always thought I wanted to be a teacher. When I was at the University of Michigan, it was an easy decision to pursue a bachelor's in elementary education. I double minored in dance and psychology because my father would never pay for my education if I wanted to pursue dance. He looked at it as nothing more than a hobby even though my mom was in a ballet company when they met. I hated my student-teaching experience. I thought it was because it wasn't my classroom, but I was frustrated. I felt like I didn't have enough time to dedicate to the kids who needed extra help. I didn't have my student's family support that I wanted to so badly, and to be completely honest, I knew the first day I walked into the classroom that I had made a huge mistake."

"What about having your own classroom?" I ask as I grab a handful of grapes.

"When Brandon and I moved to Dallas, I found a teaching job at one of the schools in a rougher area of town. It worked well because all my cheerleading stuff was at night or on the weekends. I could do both. I loved being on the cheer team. It was one of the greatest things I've ever done for myself. But I hated my job. Working in the inner city was rough. I never felt safe during my commute. Kids were coming to school hungry and dirty. They weren't where they were expected to be for third grade. I had kids who couldn't even read. The more I tried, the more pushback I got. I was miserable at work. Once Brandon and I split, I knew I couldn't stay there anymore. I finished the school year and submitted my letter of resignation."

"So why did you get a master's degree in something you didn't enjoy?" I ask as I grab another handful of grapes.

"My father values education above all else. He told me to get a master's degree and then even a doctorate, and then I could work in an administrative position where I could make policy changes to make things better for teachers. He talked about becoming a superintendent or becoming a teacher at the collegiate level. I was so distraught at the time. I kind of just let him talk me into it."

"That doesn't sound like you, Caroline. You're always so passionate about everything you do."

"Well, my fiancé had just crushed me. I was questioning my worth and trying to figure out why I wasn't enough for him. I was in a job I hated, in a city where I didn't know anyone except my fellow cheerleaders, and I was cheering for the same guy who just crushed me week after week. I needed a fresh start. Chicago was my mom's city. She was born and raised here. She loved it so much, and I loved her so much that I just wanted to be near her in some way. I thought moving to Chicago might give me the strength I needed to move forward."

"I would say it did. You don't come across as unhappy. You have friends, volunteer work, a job you love. You seem pretty happy here. Am I wrong?"

"No, you're not wrong at all. I decided not to teach in the classroom when I moved, but I had already applied and been accepted to the master's program here, and I didn't have any other options at the time, so I figured I'd pursue it. My dad was not happy that I was teaching dance and not school, but I needed to make some changes for me. I started teaching dance and working with a dance movement therapist at the academy. I had never thought of becoming a dance movement therapist before, but the more time I spend with her, I know, without a shadow of a doubt, it's what I want to do."

"What exactly is dance movement therapy?"

"It's the use of movement to improve one's overall health and well-being. It can be used for people of all ages. I've been doing a lot of exercises at the nursing home I work at even though I'm not certified in it yet. My colleague does it at a group home for young adults with special needs, but it can be used in a variety of settings for all different types of people. Your dad really seemed to enjoy the class I do geared toward kids with Down syndrome."

"Yes, my dad's brother has Down syndrome, and my dad has been really big in the Special Olympics. I bet he knows all about dance movement therapy. I think you'd be great at it."

"Thanks. Yeah, your dad and I actually talked about it quite a bit. It will require some additional training. I need a master's degree and will need to take some more classes, but I think I could do the most good and use my skills to help people."

"I love watching you work with your students. You glow."

"Thanks, Jack. I think the same thing when I watch you play hockey."

"Yeah, I'm lucky that I get to do what I love every single day. It doesn't feel like a job, but a gift most of the time."

"Even when you come home with black eyes?"

She smiles at me and pops another strawberry in her mouth.

"Even then."

I put the tray on the nightstand and reach over to pull her into my arms. She comes willingly. We're lying next to one another with my arms wrapped tightly around her. I kiss her forehead.

"Tell me about your mom."

"Jeez, Jack, for just wanting to be friends and keep this casual, you sure do want to know a lot about me."

"I know, and I'm not trying to be an ass. I just really like you. You make me want things I can't have."

She looks at me for a minute, and I'm wondering if I said too much.

"I'm not going to ask you why you think you can't have the things you want. We all have our own demons, and maybe one day you'll be ready to talk to me more about that."

She pauses for a minute and then continues on.

"My mom died when I was fourteen. She was my best friend. She had me in ballet slippers before I could walk, and I was in recitals by the time I was two. Dance was something we always did together. It didn't matter the genre. She loved it, and so did I. Our house was always filled with music. She had the biggest smile and gave the best hugs. She always smelled like lilacs, and she loved anything chocolate. She and my dad loved each other so deeply that they set the bar for love high. Dad was never the same after her death. He became aloof, hard, unapproachable. He had a series of failed marriages after Mom and fully admitted to me that he could never love someone the way he loved her. I just want him to be happy, but somedays, it seems impossible. Cody and I were always close, but Mom's death and Dad's absence brought us closer."

"I can't imagine losing a parent, Caroline. I'm so sorry."

She looks down at our hands, and I didn't realize that I had grabbed hers while she was talking. Our fingers are interlaced, and she kisses my knuckle. She's easy to open up to.

"My dad played hockey in college. He loved the game. He had me in skates early too, and by the time I was three, I was skating circles around pretty much everyone in the rink. My entire hockey career is because he believed in my abilities and always pushed me to be better. I owe it all to him. I don't think I let him know how much I appreciate everything he's done for me and continues to do for me."

"It's never too late, Jack. Let him know."

"I will. Thanks, beautiful. Now let's go to sleep."

I'm afraid to let go of her hand, so I squeeze it tighter and give her a kiss on the back of it. I reach over with my other hand and turn off the light on the nightstand.

"You planned to have me spend the night all along, didn't you?"

"Of course, beautiful. I'm not letting you go. Now let's cuddle."

"You want to cuddle with our clothes on?"

"Yep, and sleep with you."

"Just sleep?"

"We've had sex twice today, babe. I know you want me, so if you want more, I'll give it to you. You know I can't deny you, but I'd also be perfectly happy just sleeping with you in my arms."

She starts laughing.

"Cocky much? Gosh, Jack. You're killing me."

"Shhh. Let's go to sleep, beautiful."

I kiss her lips softly and pull the blankets up and over us. She reaches into my pants and starts stroking me gently with her tiny, soft hands. Game on, babe.

Chapter 22

Caroline

It's been one month since Jack's mom got sick, and I stepped in for those few days, one month since everything changed between us in my eyes, and one month since I fell head over heels in love with him. Since then, I've spent every night Jack's in town at his house, and even a few of the nights he wasn't, just to have a movie night with the girls or give his parents or the nanny a night off. Jack and I haven't discussed our relationship status except for in the beginning when he told me he couldn't give me more than a glorified friend with benefits package. I've opened up and shared so much of who I am with him. I honestly think he knows me better than anyone, maybe even my closest friends. I never felt like this with Brandon, maybe because it was that young, first love, but everything with Jack seems so much better.

    I kept thinking that once we got passed the sexual attraction and infatuation we have with one another's bodies, we wouldn't have much else in common. The truth is when he's traveling for his away games, we talk about anything and everything. Even when we remove the physical, the emotional bond is there. Our conversations flow effortlessly, and it doesn't matter if they're serious or silly. I enjoy every minute I'm talking to him. However, I still feel like he's holding back. He's never told me anything about his marriage, nothing about Bree's death, or nothing about why he's so afraid to commit again. I've asked, but he always dodges the questions. I assume it's because he lost the love of his life, and I'm not sure I'll ever be able to fill that monstrous hole in his heart that is so clearly there. I guess that's what scares me the most about all of this. Maybe he's like my dad and will never be able to love someone the way he loved his first wife. All my fears surface, and once again, I'm not enough.

    I can't believe I'm jealous of a dead woman. Is the pain still so fresh that he isn't ready to move on yet? Am I just being too inpatient? Will he ever be able to love me? The more time I spend with him and his daughters, the more I want to be a fixed part of their family. Watching him as a father has shown me just how deeply he loves. Ellie and Rosie couldn't be luckier. He's so patient, sweet, and nurturing toward them and toward me. He's so giving in the bedroom, always putting my needs first, and I've never had better sex. But it's more than that. It's him remembering all my favorite foods and making them for me. He knows I like fresh lemon in my water, so now there's a bowl of lemons on his kitchen counter. He wakes me with kisses every morning and texts me throughout the day just to let me know he's thinking about me. It makes me wonder if that's how he was with Bree. Did he always put her first? Did he make her feel like the luckiest woman in the world? My old insecurities keep returning, flying back front and center. Maybe it's me. Maybe I'm just not enough for him to try at love again. Maybe he thinks I'm not worth the heartache. Maybe I won't be able to keep his interest in the long run, and just like Brandon, he'll crush me.

    It's hard not to think of my father when I think of the walls Jack has erected so high around himself that I don't know if I'll ever break them down. I watched my father struggle to form new relationships after my mother's death. He was never the same. He never laughed quite as hard or smiled quite as bright. His second wife ultimately left because she got tired of trying to make him happy and loving him without having his love in return. His third wife, as sweet as she was, seemed to be more of a friend than someone he loved down to his core. Am I destined for the same fate if I stick it out with Jack? I can't vocalize my fears to my friends because they keep stressing to me that until Jack and I agree to more, he's simply my friend with benefits and nothing more. I realize that a man who was married and with a woman for nearly a decade may need more than a month to fall in love. I realize that being a parent will make you more cautious about relationships in general. But as far as I'm concerned, we're in a loving, committed relationship. He's my one and only.

Whenever I have these kinds of days, I go and talk to Mom. If she were here, I know that we'd go and get coffee or sit and chat at the park. But since she's been gone for years, I find myself walking the cemetery, lost deep in thought. When I get to her grave, I no longer cry like I used to. Instead, I talk to her. I tell her how I am. I share all my deepest, darkest secrets with her, and I ask for guidance. It probably sounds crazy asking your dead mother for advice, but I always feel like I walk away from these discussions with clarity. Her birthday is next week, and I'll be here again with Cody to celebrate her on her special day. But today, I'm a mess, and I want her to myself. Jack just left for another stretch of away games, and I'm hoping that the time apart will help me clear my head. Right now, I feel like a fool grasping onto something that's out of my reach.

I clean off her grave and lay the flowers I've chosen for this week, orange and pink Gerber daisies. I sit for a long time, asking for a sign, an indication of what I should do. I don't know if I spend minutes or hours, but as the cold November wind starts to pick up, I know it's time to leave. For some reason, I choose to take the long way back to my car. As I'm wrapping my coat tighter around me, I'm not paying attention and stumble. I try to quickly regain my balance but something catches the corner of my eye. Freezing rain starts to fall from the dark gray skies, and yet I find myself walking further away from my car. I look down, and I'm staring at the grave of Aubree Hannen, loving wife and mother. My tears begin to fall, and I'm wondering why my mom would have guided me here.

*****

Jack

I'm having the best season of my career. I don't know if it's the amazing sex I'm having daily that's pumping me full of endorphins or if it's that I'm happy for maybe the first time ever in my life, but I'm feeling on top of the world. My parents have noticed a difference in me, Jimmy commented on it the other day, and tonight, after the game, even my coach told me he wanted to meet the woman who's put a smile on my face. I do have Caroline to thank for it. She makes me feel alive again. I've been living under a rock of guilt and grief for years. But when I'm with her, I want to believe I'm worthy of something better, worthy of her. I know she deserves better than some fucked-up asshole who's responsible for his wife's death and all the unhappiness she endured during her short life. But I'm a selfish prick, and I can't bring myself to end it. To be honest, I love Caroline, and I have for a long time now. I just can't figure out what that means for us.

"Great game tonight, man."

Jimmy sits down next to me in the locker room. I've already showered and dressed but sat down to check my phone really quick.

"You too. We were unstoppable tonight."

"It felt good. If we keep playing like that, we're going to be a force during playoffs. Hey, are you bringing Caroline to the holiday party in a few weeks?"

"I haven't asked her yet, but I was thinking about it."

"What's there to think about? You two are basically inseparable. I've never seen you so happy, Jack, and I've known you for years."

"Yeah, but nothing can come of this thing with Caroline."

"Why not?"

"Come on, man. You know why."

Jimmy looks around the locker room to make sure everyone else has left.

"Look, Jack. It's just me and you in here. You're like a brother to me. I'm going to give it to you straight, and I don't care if you get pissed at me because you need to hear this. Bree was a selfish, manipulative, unfaithful bitch. You deserved so much better than her, and no one understands why you put up with her abuse for years. Caroline is an angel, man. Don't hurt her because of the shit that went down with Bree."

"If I hadn't kicked Bree out of the house that night, she'd still be here, Jimmy. She wouldn't have jumped into a drunk man's car, and the accident would have never happened."

"Jack, you walked in to find your wife fucking another man on your couch, with your kids sleeping down the hall. I honestly can't believe you didn't beat that asshole to a pulp. I wouldn't have been able to stop at one punch. You have more self-control than I ever would have had. But honestly, like you knew his blood alcohol level when you told them both to get the fuck out of your house? Come on, man. You couldn't have known."

"It still doesn't excuse my actions. I knew how bad the roads were."

"Jack, no one would have been thinking about the driving conditions at that moment."

"I had hoped motherhood would change Bree. Instead, things went from bad to worse."

"It's time to move on, Jack."

"I don't think I can."

"Hey, assholes! Everyone's waiting on the bus. Hurry up!"

Jones comes running into the locker room.

"What's taking you so long?"

"We'll be right there," Jimmy says as he swings his bag over his shoulder. "Come on, Jack."

I stand, and he hugs me.

"It's going to be all right. Trust me."

I feel like a pussy choking up.

"Yeah. Let's go."

As we head back to the hotel, I put my headphones on. I really don't want to talk to anyone right now. I make my way to my room and collapse on my bed. Less than a second later, my phone starts vibrating in my pocket. I reach for it and see Caroline's beautiful face pop up on the screen. It's a picture I took of her in my front yard. She's lying in a pile of leaves with a blue winter hat that matches her eyes, and she's smiling up at me. That was a fun day. I came home from practice, and she and the girls had raked the whole yard and were laughing hysterically when I found them, rolling and jumping in the leaves. Caroline just has this light about her that makes everything so much better. I don't know how to be the man she deserves.

I decide to let it go to voice mail. I can't talk to her right now. All of a sudden, a text comes through on my phone.

> Caroline: Hi handsome. Great game. That goal in the third almost made me pee my pants I was so excited. I'm so happy for you. I love seeing you succeed. I tried to call but it went to voicemail. I'm going to go to bed soon and wanted to talk to you about something. If you're free in the next 20 minutes or so, give me a call, otherwise, we can talk tomorrow. XO

Despite the tornado of emotions spinning in my brain, I have to smile. She really couldn't be any more amazing. She is funny, supportive, and sweet all in one text. I immediately call her back.

"Hi. I'm sorry I missed your call."

"Hey, you. Don't be sorry. It's nice to hear your voice, handsome. You played great tonight."

"Thanks. I think I'm playing so well because I have this really great woman in my life who's managing to make me smile all the time."

"Ohhh! Do I know her?"

She teases me, and I can hear the smile in her voice.

"I think you do. She's gorgeous inside and out. Blond hair, blue eyes, beautiful breasts, and a heart of gold."

"Oh my god, is that how you describe me to your friends?"

"Absolutely."

Man, she makes me happy. The phone lights up requesting FaceTime. I click on the accept button.

"So much better. You should have told me you weren't wearing a shirt. A girl needs to prepare herself for your hotness."

Seeing her changes something. I can't hide my emotions because she sees right through me. I suddenly feel guilty, guilty for not being able to get past Bree's death, guilty for stringing this perfect woman along when I clearly am not in the right headspace to give her more, and guilty for getting myself in this position in the first place.

"Sorry, beautiful. I'll give you a fair warning next time. But it's been a long day, babe, and I need to get to sleep."

"Oh, okay. I'm sorry, honey. Are you all right?"

"Just tired."

I hate lying to her.

"Of course, you are. Get some rest. We can talk tomorrow."

I can see the disappointment on her face. I should have taken the opportunity to get her off. I'm so fucked up in the head right now that I don't think I could even get the words out. I give her a small smile, blow her a kiss, and disconnect the call.

Chapter 23

Caroline

I'm in the dance studio of the community center first thing in the morning. The sun hasn't even risen yet, and I'm looking for an outlet. Last night was weird. After spending time at the cemetery, I came home and took a long shower. I had no more clarity than before but spent way too much time online trying to find out more about Aubree Hannen. It took me forever to build up the strength to call Jack after the game, and then once I did, he was the one who obviously was too upset to talk. I need answers.

I try to focus on the present. It's my second season volunteering with Dance It Off, the program geared toward helping troubled inner-city youth through dance. Today is our first day with a new group of kids. We'll have some returning dancers, but today is all about connecting with the newcomers. I'm trying to escape the storm raging in my mind, but my thoughts keep drifting off to Jack. It's hard to believe that I first met him during one of these recitals a few short months ago. This morning, I have the studio to myself. I start the music and lose myself in it. I allow my body to lead and turn off my brain entirely. All I've done is think lately, and I'm tired. I want to let everything go. This is my therapy. This is my safe haven, my place where I can escape everything the world throws at me and just be.

*****

After my morning at the community center, I'm feeling better. Most of the instructors met this morning, and I'm going to have to see if I can talk my girlfriends into volunteering for another season. We have some gaps in our caching staff that they could fill perfectly. Meeting the kids, talking with them, and being reminded that the world is bigger than me and my unrequited love were exactly what I needed. When I get to my place, I see Sofia has most of her boxes packed and is folding a load of laundry. I sit down next to her and begin folding.

"I'm sad to see you go. I liked having a roomie!"

Our weeks of being temporary roommates has come to an end, and even though I was hardly ever here, I liked having Sofia at my place. She starts laughing at me.

"Caroline, I think you already have a roomie, and his name is Jack. You hardly even sleep here!"

"I know. I'm sorry. I hope I didn't hurt your feelings."

"Not at all. I like you with him. You two fit better than you and Brandon ever did."

"I like me with him too."

"Then why do you seem so down these past few days? I know you miss him when he's gone, but you get to see him today."

Of course, she sees right through me. I was trying so hard to hide my insecurities, but Sofia is too good of a friend to let me get away with it.

"I love him, Sofia."

"Yeah, we all know you do, honey."

"I broke the whole sex-with-no-strings-attached rule that you all warned me about."

"Care, it's not a bad thing that you developed feelings for him."

"But I'm afraid if I tell him, I'll lose him."

"Babe, have you seen the way he looks at you? He's head over heels in love with you. Anyone can see that a mile away. You need to talk to him."

"And say what? Oh, sorry, I fell in love with you?"

"Yes. Exactly that."

We've finished folding the laundry, and she starts placing it in the basket.

"I wish your new place wasn't ready."

"I just appreciate you letting me stay here after the breakup from hell."

"Why don't you ever want to talk about it?"

"Because it's stupid. I thought I was in love, I moved in with an asshole, and now it's over. Nothing more to say except I'm moving into my own place and starting over."

"Have you talked to him?"

"I blocked his number and asked all of you to keep my current living situation a secret. I've just been fortunate that I haven't seen him."

"If you ever want to talk about it, I'm here for you."

"I know, but I don't want to talk about it. Would you mind helping me load some of the lighter stuff into the U-Haul?"

I don't comment on her changing the subject. I'm not sure what went down between Sofia and her ex-boyfriend, Andrew, but I know that it was bad.

"Of course."

Sofia rented a U-Haul trailer to tow with her jeep. Most of her larger items have been in storage since she moved in with Andrew, and her brothers are supposed to help her move that next weekend.

"Hey! You started without us?"

I look up to see Jack and Jimmy walking up my drive with deli sandwiches and lemonade in hand.

"What are you two doing here? You got back so late last night. I figured you'd be sleeping all day!"

My insecurities leave me at the sight of him, and I run over to Jack. I throw my arms around him and kiss him. He's all smiles, and all the demons of last night seem to be in hiding for the time being.

"I like surprising you. Plus I slept all morning."

"Aren't you still exhausted?"

"Not too exhausted to help you ladies with the heavy lifting. Plus I brought more muscles with me."

Jack points to Jimmy who is shamelessly checking Sofia out. They definitely have chemistry, but I can see Sofia pushing him away before he even has a chance. Poor guy.

"Hi, Jimmy. Thanks for coming."

I leave Jack and give Jimmy a big hug and a kiss on the cheek.

"Hey, Caroline."

He smiles at me and turns to Sofia.

"Sofia, Caroline gave me a kiss. You think I can get one from you too? I mean, I am here helping you out. One little kiss won't hurt."

He looks back at me and winks.

"Thanks for coming, Jimmy. Are one of those drinks for me?"

She totally ignores the question, and Jimmy hands her a lemonade. The guys have everything loaded within twenty minutes. I'm sure it would have taken us about two hours alone. We head over to her place, unload, and are done before dinner. After Sofia thanks us repeatedly, I'm heading out the door with the guys.

"Hey, Caroline. I almost forgot! What time is Cody getting here tomorrow?" Sofia asks me, stopping me in my tracks.

"Noon. He's taking your bedroom over, but I'll gladly throw his ass on the couch if you want to stay until your brothers move the rest of your stuff over here."

I feel Jack tense next to me. I still haven't told him that my mom's birthday is tomorrow. I had been putting it off, and when I tried last night, he wasn't up for talking. I don't want to freak him out and invite him to dinner to celebrate my dead mother. But now that he's here, I'm realizing how much I want him there with me tomorrow night.

"Nonsense. I'm all set over here, but let me know how your fancy dinner goes."

"Will do. I love you, and for real, call if you need anything at all."

"I love you too. Ari should be here in a few minutes. She's just getting out of work, and Victoria said she'd come by after her shift at the hospital tonight. I'm good. I promise. I'm going to head to the grocery store now. Jack and Jimmy, thank you so much for helping us. I really appreciate it."

After everyone is done with hugs and goodbyes, I grab Jack's hand. We start heading for his SUV. I'm going to ride back to my place with him and Jimmy since I rode with Sofia on the way here.

"You can have shotgun, Jimmy. You have longer legs."

"Aww, Caroline. Are you always this thoughtful?"

He smiles his adorable smile at me. He is such a charmer.

"I try. Are you going to tell me your intentions with my best friend?"

He chuckles.

"Is it that obvious I've got a crush?"

"Oh my gosh. I love it!"

I start clapping my hands like a giddy little schoolgirl.

"Is she over her ex?"

"Honestly, I don't know what went down there. She's been very quiet about the breakup, but I'll put in a good word for you, Jimmy."

"Thanks, but don't build me up too much. I don't want to disappoint," Jimmy says with his usual little boy grin.

He shifts in his seat, and we start talking about the guys' game last night when Jack pulls into my driveway.

"Thanks for bringing me home, handsome. I'll see you later."

I lean over to give him a quick kiss. He looks surprised.

"You're not coming home with me?"

"You brought me here."

"Yeah, to grab a bag so you can spend the night, and I can ravish you."

I can feel my cheeks redden. I want that so badly too. Jimmy chuckles, shakes his head, and looks out the window.

"Oh. Okay then. I thought you might be tired or something. I'm going to take my car though. I need to get some groceries before my brother gets here, and I have some schoolwork I need to finish."

"Caroline, I literally cannot wait another minute. I'll be your gopher boy, get your groceries, and cart you around all day. You can do your work at my place, but I need you to come home with me right now. Mom still has the girls at some petting zoo thing for another hour, and I intend to spend that hour naked with you. Bringing you here to grab a few things was really me just trying not to be a total caveman."

I bust out laughing.

"And this is only one of the reasons why I love you so much!"

Before I've even realized what I just said, both he and Jimmy have turned around in their seats and are looking at me. Jimmy has a huge smile on his face, but Jack looks terrified. I swallow.

"I'll be right back."

I literally run into the house as fast as I can and close the front door behind me. I lean back against the door and try to just breathe. His face after my slip says it all. He's not ready, and he's definitely not where I am emotionally. He's just another guy I've fallen in love with who doesn't feel as deeply for me as I do for him. Why didn't I learn after Brandon? Obviously, if he felt an ounce of what I felt for him, he would have never cheated. I can't do this. I can't go to his house and pretend everything is all right. I've set myself up for heartbreak, and I have no one to blame but myself.

*****

Jack

I look up to the sky and close my eyes. I let out a huge exhale and try to calm my nerves. She was joking, except I know she wasn't. Shit. I knew I let this go too far. Why can't I just be normal and be excited that this amazing woman just said she loves me? Why can't I say it back or tell her how much she means to me? Because deep down, I don't believe I deserve that kind of happiness. She deserves everything this world has to offer and more. I look over at Jimmy who has the biggest smile I've ever seen on his face.

"Don't say a fucking word."

"Are you kidding me right now? I knew she loved you, but that little scene right there was kind of adorable. You're a lucky bastard, and I'm jealous. I'm guessing that's the first time she's told you?"

"Jimmy, I'm serious. We're going to pretend that didn't just happen, and we're not going to talk about it."

"Jack, are you for real right now? Don't screw this up."

"I'm flipping the fuck out and am just trying to keep it together, okay?"

How does he not get how bad this scares me? He's been there for all the shit that's went down in my life. He's one of the only ones who knows all my past, and I've come clean to about my demons. He should see why this is a problem for me. I know I love Caroline, and I thought she might love me, but I never expected her to say it so soon. I've barely spoken to her since Jimmy and I had our talk in the locker room. I was trying to distance myself and figure out what I need to do to give us a fighting chance. Showing up at her place for moving day did nothing but send mixed signals.

"Don't even tell me you don't love her. I know you too well."

Just then, Caroline comes out of her place empty-handed. I get out to open her car door.

"Actually, Jack, I'm going to stay home for a bit. I'll see you tonight."

She kisses my cheek and turns around to walk up the driveway.

"Caroline, wait! Where are you going?"

"I just told you. I'm going to take care of some stuff here for a bit."

Fuck this. She's going to talk to me. I turn to Jimmy.

"Jimmy! Drive my car to my house for me, will you?"

He gives me a warning glance and gets out of the passenger side. He walks over to Caroline, gently squeezes her arm, and whispers something in her ear. She bites her bottom lip like she's trying to hold back tears and nods her head at him. He gives me one final look, then jumps in my car, and backs out of the driveway. I walk over to Caroline and wrap my arms around her.

"What's wrong, beautiful?"

"I don't want to talk about it yet, okay?"

She looks like she's hanging on by a thread, and the dam is going to burst any second.

"Okay, will you tell me why Cody's coming in town? Is he here for business again?"

I push because I'm hurt that she didn't tell me. She and her brother seem to have a great relationship. I know he doesn't think I'm the right man for her, and I have to agree, but I wish to God I was. She deserves so much better than me.

"Not exactly, but knowing Cody, he'll find a way to make some business connection while he's here."

She has a small smile on her face when she talks about her brother. I grab her hand and lead her inside. As we enter the threshold, I hold her in my arms again. It takes a second for her to return the embrace, and then she holds on to me tight.

"You're avoiding talking to me."

I nuzzle into her neck. Maybe she'll talk more if I'm not looking right at her.

"You're perceptive."

She sighs as she opens her neck to me. I pull her hair back and kiss my way along her jaw. This, I know how to do. I know how to make her physically feel good.

"Why?"

I already know the answer, but I need to hear her say it.

"You were so tired last night, and then with the whole moving thing this morning, I didn't want to add more to your plate."

I pull her closer to me and lean into her. I rest my forehead on hers.

"You can tell me anything."

"I'm scared to tell you everything, but I did try to tell you about Cody last night. I guess I didn't want to freak you out. Tomorrow is my mom's birthday, and he's coming to celebrate with me. It's kind of weird celebrating my dead mother's birthday, isn't it?"

She's drawing little circles on my biceps with her thumbs, but I can see the vulnerability in her eyes. She looks like she's about to cry, and then she looks down, breaking our eye contact.

"It's not weird at all, and I'm sorry for last night. I never want you to feel like you can't talk to me. I'm also sorry for how I reacted in the car. You caught me by surprise, but that doesn't mean I don't have feelings for you."

I lean in to kiss her. This kiss is different from our others. It's all the things I can't say. It's the love I feel for her, the gratitude that she's even given me the time of day. I gently pick her up and carry her to her bedroom. We don't speak again. I undress her and take reverence in her beauty. I kiss every inch of her body before I center in on her sweet pussy. I lick, suck, and nibble. I've learned what she likes over these past few months, and I want to give her everything, right here, right now, in this moment.

After we're both sated and lying in bed, she's curled into me with her thigh over me and my arms around her. I think we both know that what we just did was so much more than fucking. As cliché as it sounds, we made love, and I know I just crossed some major boundaries I shouldn't have, which is probably even more of a reason for me to put a little distance between us again. But I can't. Instead, I'm an idiot and decide to ask her what I've been thinking about since she mentioned her brother.

"Would I be imposing if I went with you and Cody? I don't know how he would feel about it, but I want to be there for you. I know how important this is to you."

I kiss the top of her head, hoping she'll let me come with them. This woman deserves it all. I want to be there for her.

She looks up at me through her lashes, and a single tear comes down her cheek.

"I would love it if you came with us."

I kiss her again, wishing our little bubble didn't have to eventually pop.

Chapter 24

Caroline

"Short stack!" Cody calls into my town house through the front door.

I'm always happy to see him, but on Mom's birthday, it's always a little bit emotional for me. We lived in Boston when Mom died, but since her parents were buried in Chicago, and this was the city she loved and called home, she wanted to be buried here. We haven't always celebrated in Chicago, but we have always gotten together. Last year was the first year Cody included his girlfriend, Lauren. They dated for two years, and I honestly thought they'd get married. They broke up a few months ago, and Cody never really got into the specifics. We don't talk much about our love lives with each other, which is why this Jack conversation is going to be a little weird. Honestly, the most we ever discussed was probably our talk about Jack when we were at Giovanni's after the nightclub. Cody and I have talked a little about Jack over the last few months, but he doesn't have the whole picture. I'm going to need to fill him in before dinner. I'm not sure how he's going to react, but I was able to get the restaurant to add a third-place setting, and he needs to know Jack's going to be there.

Even though Jack may not be able to tell me he loves me, his actions have shown me that love. He's been different since he came home, but last night seemed to put me at ease some. I know he made love to me. It's as if he's in an internal war with himself and doesn't know how to proceed with me. I don't know if he loves me but doesn't want to or feels guilty "replacing" Bree although I know I could never do that. I'm utterly confused at where we stand, but it's so much more than fuck buddies. My confusion isn't going to make this conversation any easier with my brother. All I know is that if Jack didn't love me, he wouldn't be coming to dinner tonight.

"Hi, Big Bro!"

I squeeze him as tight as I can.

"I'm starving. Too bad Sofia isn't still staying here. She makes the world's best enchiladas."

"And spoil our appetite for tonight? No thanks."

"We still need lunch."

He starts rummaging through my cabinets. I reach into the fridge and start pulling out cold cuts for sandwiches. We talk about his flight and his plans for his short trip to Chicago as we make our sandwiches. After lunch, we'll head to the cemetery to see Mom, but right now, we need some time to catch up first. We've gotten comfy on opposite ends of the couch, sandwiches in hand. Cody turns on the TV to catch the game. The Wolves are at home today, and it's one of the first games I haven't attended in person in a while. On weekends, Jack often plays during the day, which is perfect since we have plans for tonight.

Jack had wanted me and Cody at the game today, but I wanted some time with him alone. In all honesty, Cody would have loved to go to the game, and we should have. Jack is in the zone and playing extremely aggressive. He's making me a little nervous. He just got a penalty and is being sent to the sin bin. His picture pops up on the TV screen, and I figure it's a sign to talk about him.

"I hope you don't mind, but I've invited Jack to join us for dinner tonight."

I take a sip of my water, trying to gauge his response.

"What? Are you guys together?"

He's looking at me like I've grown a second head.

"Kind of?"

"What's that mean? I know he apologized for being a douchebag after the whole nightclub hookup and that you watch his kids sometimes, but I didn't think that would equate to inviting him to this dinner."

I notice immediately how he says *this* dinner, inferring how special it is. I may as well rip off the Band-Aid and come clean.

"We've been sleeping together for a few months."

He spits his iced tea all over, splashing the amber liquid all over my face. I grab a napkin to wipe it off.

"Jesus, Caroline! What the fuck?"

"After he apologized, we kind of came up with a friend with benefits arrangement. It's working," I say as I set the napkin back down.

"Playboy offered you friends with benefits and you accepted?"

"He's not a playboy anymore."

"Yeah, okay. What I can't believe is that my sweet, wholesome sister is fucking a guy with no commitment."

"We're committed, and we agreed to not sleep with anyone else while we're doing this."

"Wow. Care, what is it about this guy? Everything with him is out of character for you. The Caroline I know would never have sex in a nightclub and agree to be fuck buddies with a professional hockey player."

He takes another sip of his iced tea.

"I know. I can't explain it. Cody, you have to just trust me on this. I really care about him."

"And I care about you. This has bad idea written all over it."

"He asked to come tonight. He knows what this dinner is and how important it is. He wanted to be there for me. It means a lot to me to know that he cares that much."

Cody's quiet for what feels like forever, and I wish I knew what he was thinking. He studies me for a minute.

"Caroline, you love him, don't you?"

It's more of a statement than a question. I can tell he already knows. Of course, he knows. It's been me and Cody for so long that we have each other figured out.

"I really do," I say it quietly, not able to meet his gaze.

"Does he love you?"

I don't even know how to answer this question, so I try my best to be as honest as I can be.

"In his own way, I think he does. Sometimes, I don't think I'll ever live up to his dead wife. He was with her for nine years. She's the mother of his children. What they had was special. I'm just trying to figure out how I fit into his life. Sometimes, I think he loves me, and sometimes, I think I'm just the chick he's banging."

"Why are you doing this to yourself? You saw how hard it was for Dad to move on. One failed relationship after the next. Care, I wasn't kidding when I said you deserve the best. This isn't it."

"Just be nice to him tonight, okay?" I ask, pleading.

"Anything for you, Sis."

He's finished his sandwich. He stands up and turns the TV off. "Let's go to the cemetery."

*****

Jack

I played my ass off. I keep trying to channel all this confusion I have over my relationship with Caroline and the frustration I have with myself into my game. I guess I thought getting into a fight or two would get rid of some of the angst I was feeling. Not so much. Now I'm walking into a classy ass restaurant with a split lip and a black eye. I was lucky we had an earlier game today, but I still scrambled to get to here on time. I'm not sure what her brother knows about us, but I know how important he is to her. I immediately spot them when I enter the restaurant. Caroline looks beautiful. She takes my breath away. She has a royal-blue dress on that matches her eyes, and her long legs are on display. I can't believe she's mine. Her brother must see me staring at her because he looks up from their conversation and catches my eye. I smile and head over. Caroline wraps me in a big hug and kisses my cheek. She smells like vanilla and feels like heaven in my arms. I shake Cody's hand, and we all sit down.

I look straight at Cody.

"Thanks for letting me join you tonight. I know what a special occasion it is for you, and I'm honored to be a part of it."

Cody takes a sip of his wine and studies me for a second too long before responding.

"Anything to make my little sister happy."

Yeah, I should have figured he wouldn't want me here. I wonder what she's told him. Caroline breaks the tension. As always, she's my saving grace.

"You played pretty rough out there, handsome."

I smile at her. I didn't expect her to use my nickname in front of her brother.

"Nah. That guy deserved it. Plus we won, so everyone's happy."

I take a sip of my water before going on.

"Hey, Cody, Caroline told me you played in the minor league and at U of M. I looked you up. You've got some skills."

"Yeah. I love the game."

"Me too. There's something about being on the ice that makes me feel alive."

Just then, the waiter comes out with our appetizers. They must have ordered these while they were waiting for me. He asks if we're ready to order. I can tell they're ready, so I decide to order a steak without looking at the menu. While we're eating the delicious mussels and broth, Caroline moans. I can feel myself getting a semi just from the sound and have to reign it in. Her brother's studying me. I feel like I'm under a microscope. I don't know why I thought coming to this dinner was a good idea. I should have never invited myself into their traditions. I wish I had a stiff drink, and even though I don't drink during the season, I make a mental note to track the waiter down and get one ASAP.

Once the initial awkwardness fades, I'm actually having a really good time. I like Cody. He seems like a solid dude. We have a lot in common, and I plan to invite him to play in some pickup games with my teammates when he's in town over the summer. I can tell he's really protective of Caroline, and I'm grateful for that. She deserves to have people looking out for her. Caroline excuses herself to the bathroom after we've all stuffed our faces full and even eaten a delicious chocolate lava cake with vanilla ice cream. This meal definitely wasn't part of my meal plan for the week, but damn was it good. As soon as Caroline is out of earshot, Cody speaks to me.

"Look, Jack, we only have a minute before she comes back to the table, so I'm going to be direct. I'm confused. How in the actual fuck do you expect me to feel about you using my sister for sex?"

Well, shit. He's not messing around, and I'll have to be careful with my words, or I'll end up in another fist fight today.

"I'm not using her for sex. It might have started off as just sex, but I think any guy with half a brain would want to call her his."

"I agree."

I sigh. I should have known she told him that much.

"Look, Cody, I'm a little fucked up."

I really don't want to mention Bree, but I don't think I have a choice here.

"I've been a widower and single dad since I was twenty-four. I've done some shit I'm not proud of, but when it comes to your sister, I wish I could do everything right."

"You wish, but you're not going to. Is this some sort of game to you? Because you're going to break her fucking heart. She's in love with you, man."

And there it is again, that four little word that haunts me. I don't deserve her love, but what I wouldn't give to be able to love her with every fiber in my body. I let out another long sigh.

"It's not a game."

I can't comment on her love for me. I can't tell him how much I love her. I'm a fucking mess. Goddamn it. Why can't I just be normal? Fucking Bree. I wish I didn't hate her so much.

"That's all you're going to say?" He laughs manically. "Look, she's comparing herself to your dead wife, saying that she's never going to live up to her. So if you can't get over your shit, at least let my sister go. She deserves a guy who's capable of love."

"You're right. She deserves everything."

I'm about to say more, but Caroline is approaching the table, and I know our window of opportunity is gone. I can't believe Caroline would ever compare herself to Bree. There's no comparison. Caroline is light and life and the future. Bree is my dark, depressing past. How could she ever think that I can't love her because I'm still in love with Bree? I guess I really haven't let her in enough to protect her from being hurt after all.

I just wish I could go back in time and change all the shitty decisions I made when it came to Bree. I would start with not kicking her and her drunk-ass lover out of my house in a fucking blizzard. I should have just walked out. I should have been the one to drive away. I should have been the bigger person. Instead, I send a drunk, naked asshole with a broken jaw out the door, dragging my wife with him. I wouldn't have had to go to the morgue and identify her dead body after the accident. He wouldn't be dead as well. Even before all of that, I wouldn't have taken her back after I found her cheating on me the first time. I would have never married her. I would have never left Minnesota for college, putting her above my own family. I would have never pretended she was a nice person. I would have never spent nearly a decade of my life trying to make her happy when there was absolutely nothing I could have done to be enough for her. And now I can't fucking forgive her for making me responsible for her death, making me feel like garbage day in and day out.

I try so hard to fight these demons that weigh me down. I've been a shell of a man for years, but I finally felt alive with Caroline. Now I know I have to end it. She deserves the moon, and I can't give her a damn thing. I just pray that I can survive the heartache that follows.

Chapter 25

Caroline

I come back from the bathroom, and I'm shocked punches aren't being thrown. My brother looks like he's using every ounce of self-control to not lunge himself across the table at Jack. Jack, on the other hand, looks like he's in physical pain. The anguish on his face is like nothing I've ever seen on him before. When I left the table, they had at least been cordial with one another. What the hell happened? I'm not able to ask because as soon as I'm about to sit down, Jack's phone rings with his mother's ringtone.

"I'm sorry. I have to get this. It's my mom, and she has my daughters. She wouldn't interrupt if it weren't important."

He answers the phone and immediately pales. If I thought he looked upset a minute ago, he looks absolutely awful right now. I hear enough of the conversation to know something is terribly wrong.

"Jack, talk to me. What' going on?"

He's got me really worried.

"It's Ellie. Mom said she was complaining her stomach hurt all day. She wouldn't eat anything at the game or for dinner once they got home. Then I guess the pain got worse, and she curled herself up in a ball crying. My dad had my mom bring her to the ER while he stayed home with Rosie. I guess its appendicitis, and they're taking her to surgery. I have to get to the hospital."

"I'm coming with you."

I don't hesitate. I need to be there with them.

"Caroline, no, tonight's about your family. I'm sorry, but I have to go."

He gets up and throws some cash on the table.

"Dinner's on me."

He nods at my brother, kisses me on the cheek, and runs out the door.

"Go, Caroline. It's fine. I'll meet you at your place after. I think he needs you there," Cody says.

"Thank you, Cody."

I grab my coat and run out the door after Jack. The valet has just brought his car around, and I jump in the passenger side as he slides into the driver's seat. He looks at me, and the smallest curve of a smile crosses his lips. We don't speak. He pulls out, and we are at the children's hospital in record time. We stop at the information desk to find out where Ellie is and are ushered over to the preoperative area. She looks so tiny on the big hospital bed. She's as white as the sheets that cover her, and she's sleeping. Kathy is at her side holding her hand and rubbing her head.

"Ellie, sweetheart. I'm so sorry I wasn't here."

Jack rushes over to her and kisses her forehead. Ellie opens her eyes and smiles at her daddy.

"Are you hurting?" he asks.

She shakes her head.

"They just gave her some morphine for the pain, and she passed out almost right after they put it in her IV," Kathy says, looking up at Jack.

"Mom, thank you so much for taking care of her," he says as he kisses his mom on the cheek.

I slowly walk over and sit on the edge of Ellie's bed. Seeing her like this is torture. I just want to take her place so badly so she never has to feel the hurt. I start to rub Ellie's back.

"Miss Caroline, it's okay. Please don't cry."

Ellie looks at me with her big, beautiful blue eyes, and I realize that I am crying.

"I'm sorry, honey. I just don't like seeing you hurt," I say as I try to stop the tears and be strong for her.

"Will you sing to me like you do at home?" she asks, her voice only a whisper.

In this moment, she looks so much like her father.

"Of course."

I crawl into the bed next to her, pull her into my arms, and start to sing the song my mother always sang to me. She hums along and plays with my hair. When I finish the song, I smile at her.

"I love you, Care Bear."

My heart stops. New tears fall from my eyes. I've loved these two little girls from the first moment I met them, but I never in a million years imagined how good it would feel to have them tell me they loved me. Ellie's admission seeps deep into my very existence, and I feel whole for maybe the first time in my adult life.

"I love you too, Jelly Bean."

She grins at me. Jack clears his throat, and I see tears in his eyes. He tries to quickly wipe them away, but in that brief moment, I see all the love I've felt for him directed right back at me. We're interrupted by a nurse coming into the room.

"All right, Ellie. They're ready for you," she says as she enters the room. "Oh, great! Mom and Dad made it. I'm sure this wasn't the way you expected date night to go, huh?"

She addresses Jack and me. Her calling me mom just seconds after Ellie told me she loves me tugs at my heartstrings. I'm a ball of emotions right now. Neither Jack nor I correct her. Jack speaks first.

"She's going to be okay, right?"

The nurse gives a reassuring smile.

"I promise you, she's in good hands. Dr. Selzar is the best. Okay, Ellie. Give everyone one last hug."

She wraps her little arms around me once more. She then embraces Kathy and Jack, and I scoot off the hospital bed.

"Love you, Daddy," she says, and with that, they begin to wheel her away.

The nurse tech shows us to the family waiting area.

"I'm sorry, but hospital policy is only two family members visiting at a time. One of you will have to step out."

I immediately grab for my phone out of my purse so I can text Cody and ask him to come pick me up. Kathy puts her hand on my arm.

"You stay with Jack, honey. I'll go."
She gives me a squeeze and looks at me.
"I'm so glad you've come into our lives."
It's as if my heart could take any more tonight.
"Jack, call me with updates."
He gives her a hug.
"Of course, Mom. Thank you."

Suddenly, it's just the two of us. The air feels heavy, and reality sinks in. He pulls me in for a hug, and we just stand there, arms wrapped around one another and my head flat against his chest listening to the steady lubb-dubb of his heartbeat. He leans down and kisses my forehead.

"Thank you for being here."

"There's nowhere else I'd rather be right now."

I lean out of his embrace, take his hand, and bring him over to the seating area. There's a large bench that almost looks like a love seat. I pull him toward it. We both sit. He leans forward, elbows on knees, resting his head in his hands. I see tears streaming down his cheeks as he silently cries. I put my arms around him and hold his massive frame the best I can. Eventually, he puts his arms around me and holds me close. Neither one of us dares to speak. It feels like eternity before the surgeon comes out to update us. He tells us Ellie did well. Her appendix wasn't ruptured, and it was caught early. He lets us know that she'll have to stay in the hospital for a few days for IV antibiotics and pain control. I'm not sure how much Jack is hearing. He keeps nodding his head but looks like he's covered in a fog. I ask the doctor questions about what to expect postoperatively and how we can help Ellie get back to herself as soon as possible. He answers my questions and then heads back toward the operating rooms. He tells us we'll be able to see her soon in the recovery room.

"She's okay, Jack. You can breathe."

I squeeze his hand.

"I haven't truly taken a breath in years until you."

Before I can answer, he walks away from me, down the hall, with his shoulders slouched forward, his hands in his pockets, and his head hanging low in defeat. He looks like he has the weight of the world on his shoulders. I can't help but wonder if he stopped breathing during his grief and am again reminded that I'm never going to be his first wife or the mother of his children. It's like a punch in the gut that I'm more in love with this man than I thought was humanly possible, and he's waging war with himself, stuck in some internal battle in hell.

*****

Jack

After two days in the hospital on IV antibiotics, it's time to go home. Ellie's doing well, checking all the boxes necessary for discharge. I haven't left the hospital. I called Coach as soon as Ellie was admitted, and the entire team has been sending me texts and blowing up my phone with support. My teammates sent Ellie the hugest teddy bear I've ever seen, along with balloons and flowers. Sometimes, I forget how lucky I am to have them as my second family. I feel bad for abandoning them during these last few games, and we lost both of them. I'm eager to get our lives back on track with my beautiful little girl all healthy and better.

That leaves one variable that I still need to address. It's time to be real with Caroline. Maybe I can tell her my truths, and she'd accept me with all my faults, or maybe she'll hit the ground running. Either way, I don't honestly know if I'm capable of loving her the way she deserves. If I could tell her how I feel without worrying that I'd be holding her back, I would. I couldn't make Bree happy, and I'll be damned if I drive Caroline to the same misery I drove my wife to. Maybe, deep down, I really am just a selfish prick. Watching her with Ellie, broke me. Foolishly, I didn't realize the level of attachment they would feel toward her, like any of us are capable of not falling in love with her. Over the last few months, she's seen them more than I have. If I'm home, she's at my house. If I'm away, she still stops by to take them places or watch them for a bit. I don't know if she's missed a day of their lives since the first time she spent the night.

Before I can figure out a future with her, I have to talk to her about Bree. Her brother told me that she's distraught because she thinks I'll never be able to love her the way I loved my wife. I love Caroline so much more than I ever loved Bree. In some ways, leaving Bree out of our relationship has hurt Caroline. My intentions were to protect her from my wicked demons, and in doing so, I never stopped to think about how she would interpret that, especially after she told me about her father never being able to get over her mother. I plan to talk to her tonight when we're finally sleeping in our bed again. I realize I called it *our* bed and not *my* bed, but once again, I'm going to ignore that blaring siren for the time being.

We were discharged late in the afternoon. By the time we got Ellie settled, dinner made, and laundry going, it was late. I was exhausted from the restless nights trying to fit my six-foot-four frame on a pullout chair. Caroline was tiny enough to fit on the hospital bed with Ellie, and the two had spooned most of the time we were there. Caroline only left once for a few hours to wish her brother farewell before he boarded his plane. She had given him my number, and he had shot me a text wishing Ellie a speedy recovery and apologizing if he came on too strong in his big brother protector act. To be honest, I would have done the same damn thing if I were him.

I start the shower to rinse off the hospital grime before I sink into my inviting bed. Caroline showered while I was cleaning up the dinner mess and is sorting through her overnight bag. I'm left to think about what it would be like if she had her own space here for her clothes—dangerous, fucking thoughts. I start stripping out of my clothes as the water heats up. When I look up, I see her standing in the doorway, leaning against the frame staring at me with reverence.

"I do love that body," she says with a coy smile.

Completely naked now, I take the two steps it takes to close the space between us and pull her into me. I kiss her softly. Then I rest my forehead on hers.

"I'll meet you in bed in two minutes."

I grab her ass, and she moans. Normally, she would join me, but I want to talk to her about Bree before I clam up and take the coward's way out. I shower quickly, throw on a pair of pajama pants, and join her in the bed.

"Hi."

"Hi."

She smiles coquettishly. She's wearing a pair of pajama shorts and a tiny sleep shirt that leaves little to the imagination. I'm starting to think maybe I should try to fuck her before we have this conversation but decide against it. Right now is not the time to be selfish.

"I've never told you about Bree," I start.

I know that I physically can't talk about Bree's death. I've never talked to anyone about it other than Jimmy and my parents. I hope I can let Caroline in on a little bit of my relationship with my late wife. Maybe then she'll realize that I'm not still in love with Bree. I guess I don't know if I really knew what love even was with Bree. Caroline's body tenses, and her eyes go wide. I know she's got to have mixed emotions about having this conversation.

"Is it okay if we talk about her?"

I want to make sure she's comfortable before I start.

"Of course, Jack. She was a huge part of your life."

We're lying in bed, looking at one another, and I pull her closer to me. She puts her hand on my chest. It seems like such a small movement, but in this moment, it's everything. It's her telling me that it's okay and she's here for me.

"I met her when I was a freshman in high school. We hadn't gone to the same middle school, so I saw her for the first time in algebra. I thought she was so pretty. It took me a full month to find the courage to talk to her."

Caroline smiles, her doe eyes looking up at me and encouraging me to say more.

"Once I made that initial move, we were inseparable. My entire life was hockey up until that point, and she was my first real girlfriend. I spent every weekend at some tournament or training camp. My parents would drive all over the state, sometimes all over the country. I'd be on the ice three hours each night after school doing drills, and I loved it. Bree came to every practice after school. She'd bring her homework and work on it. She'd beg me to come with me and my family on weekends, even if it was just a training camp, and she wouldn't even see me play in a game. I thought it was because she wanted to be with me and spend time with me."

I pause, unsure of how much I should disclose, and then decide to just let it all flow out.

"It was months before I realized why Bree never wanted to be at home. She was told her father was an abusive drunk who couldn't keep a job. He bolted when Bree was in diapers, and she didn't have any memories of him. Her mother, Rhonda, had a drug problem. She had random men in and out of the trailer they lived in all the time. She used all her money on her next fix. It didn't take long before Bree was in the foster care system. Her mom would clean up just long enough to get her back, and then the cycle would continue. Bree suffered some sexual abuse early on in her life. She had no stability. Her mom would get her back, and then she'd fuck up again."

"Oh my gosh. That must have been so hard. I can't even imagine growing up like that."

Caroline looks at me, urging me to speak more.

"It was. I think my parents felt sorry for her, so they didn't complain about taking her with them on the weekends. She just became a part of the family. We started having sex pretty shortly after we both turned sixteen, and I thought I was in love. I had this girl who wanted to have sex with me all the time, came to my games, and never complained. My parents started to worry that we were getting too serious for how young we were. They thought Bree was clinging on to me and was looking to me to solve all her problems. In a way, she was."

Caroline nods, no judgment, just understanding.

"I didn't look at it like that. I thought she just loved me. It's pretty easy for a young boy to fall in love when he's getting laid all the time. Lust and love blend together at some point."

Caroline smiles and rubs her hand over my heart.

"But as time went on, Bree would say things about all the sacrifices she was making by dating me since she always thought I loved hockey more than her. We'd miss dances, time with friends, football games, all the stuff normal high school kids do. For me, it was always hockey. My dad had played in college and lived for the game. He was just lucky that his son loved it as much as he did."

I pause but decide to trudge on.

"I'd encourage Bree to do stuff with friends, skip some of my practices or games to do things she wanted, and develop her own hobbies. She never did. When I started having college recruiters coming at me from all angles, she became immensely interested in our future together. I had always envisioned playing in Minnesota like my dad had. It was home, and I basically had an automatic in since my dad was still good friends with so many of the coaches. But Bree had no desire to stay in Minnesota. It pissed my dad off. My parents thought she was trying to control my future. She talked me into Norte Dame. She had always wanted to go to a big-name school, and even though she had no money or family support, she was positive she'd be able to get accepted and get some sort of scholarship money."

"I can only imagine your parents' frustration with all of this. Jack Sr. had to be on fire," Caroline says.

"On fire is putting it nicely. They were proud of me for getting to that level, proud that I got multiple offers from great programs, proud that I'd have a full ride wherever I chose to go but not happy for my reasoning to leave Minnesota."

"Anyone who sees you play can see your love for the game. It's like you were born to play hockey. Your parents knew you'd be okay wherever you were. They just wanted you near," she says as she continues to run her hands over my chest.

"Yeah, exactly. Hockey is a part of me. Anyways, Bree didn't get the amount of scholarship money she needed to offset the out-of-state tuition. She moved with me and enrolled in a nearby community college. She had wanted for us to live together, but there were strict rules for team housing among the athletes. She ended up in a small apartment with a roommate she hated. She was working as a waitress and wanted to be a nurse. She was taking the prerequisites but would tell everyone that she was a student at Norte Dame. She didn't like the girlfriends of my teammates, who were mostly students at Norte Dame because she said they all acted like they were better than her. She couldn't watch my practices because the athletic complex required badging in, and I couldn't get her into the building every time. She despised away games. She was miserable. We were miserable together."

"I'm sorry, honey."

I can see the pain in Caroline's eyes. I keep going.

"Despite my messy personal life, I was playing really well. We somehow stayed together during college, but it wasn't easy, and I have a lot of regrets about it. I should have ended it multiple times. I was always playing hockey. She didn't have any support while we were at Norte Dame. She felt alone and empty. I was hoping once we moved somewhere new, she'd be in a better spot mentally."

"It wasn't your job to make her happy, Jack. I've moved to so many cities over the last few years, and each one brought about new challenges. It wasn't Brandon's job to make me happy in Dallas when he got drafted, just like it wasn't Cody's job to make sure I was okay in Ann Arbor. I had to find my own people, my own life, outside of my relationships. Bree being unhappy wasn't your fault. She likely just had issues coping with things after her messy childhood. She should have been seeing a counselor and not waiting on you to fix her life for her."

"No one has ever said it to me like that before. Caroline, I love that you want to stand up for me. However, I can't help but take some credit. I'm the one she followed. She left everything, and maybe she didn't have much to leave, but I felt like her happiness was my responsibility. Before I knew it, college was over. I graduated with honors with a degree in business. Bree had only been going to school part-time, and got her associates degree, but hadn't gotten into the nursing program. I was twenty-two and got drafted to play in Seattle. She was so excited to leave Indiana. I remember her constantly saying how she never would have chosen to move there if it hadn't been for me when in reality, it was the opposite."

I pause and look at Caroline. There's no judgment on her face, just listening intently. She continues to rub small circles along my chest. I continue on.

"I only had a one-year contract my first year in Seattle. My dad urged me to rent a house until I had more experience in the league. Bree was irate. She wanted us to buy a huge house. We did rent but a bigger house than I wanted. At first, things were really great. I think she just loved being with an NHL player. We had a lot of sex. That might have been the only thing keeping us together. I was busy trying to prove myself in the league. I wasn't home much, and when I was, I got laid, so I really wasn't complaining. But then the pressure to propose started. She kept talking about how long we'd been together, how the other players' wives hadn't been together as long as us, how it was the next step. I guess I thought that it was what was expected of me, but I really didn't want to get married. But then she got pregnant, and I guess I figured it was time to man up. She continued to push, and I eventually caved. I proposed, and we got married in Vegas the following weekend. It felt rushed and was definitely stupid. My parents were so pissed. Mom tried to pretend she was happy for us, but it was crystal clear to me that she wasn't. Dad didn't even try to hide it. Bree had a miscarriage a few weeks after we got married. To be honest, I don't think she was ever pregnant. It feels wrong to say that it was a trick to get me to marry her, but she was so manipulative that I honestly believe it. My dad still thinks that was the case. Either way, we were married, and I was still a twenty-two-year-old baby myself."

"Jack, I'm so sorry."

She stops rubbing the circles on my chest and kisses me there instead. I must have diarrhea of the mouth at this point because I push on, feeling a sense of relief at getting it all out. Sharing it with Caroline feels right.

"After that, she fixated on wanting to start a family. She was so upset about the questionable miscarriage, and I felt guilty to admit I was relieved. I told her I thought the miscarriage might have been God's way of telling us to take a step back and to just live in the present. We were still young and had a lot of time. I encouraged her to go back to school and see if she could get into a nursing program if she applied again. She let the baby stuff go after that. We continued to have a lot of sex. Really, that's all our relationship was. She went on as a housewife with no drive to finish her schooling or to work outside of the home. I got drafted to Chicago. Things went from bad to worse. I found out she was cheating on me. I was devastated. I kicked her out and filed for divorce. A few weeks later, I found out she was pregnant and didn't know who the father was. I spent a shit ton of money to get paternity testing done through amniocentesis. When I found out I was the father, I was in a state of shock. I just couldn't escape her."

"I don't have words, Jack. That kind of betrayal would have killed me. You're so much stronger than me."

I can't help but laugh.

"No, babe. I fucked up a lot. I tried to make my marriage work. We went through a lot of counseling. In the end, it didn't matter."

Caroline doesn't speak. She simply leans in and kisses me softly. I hold her close, feeling the tension roll off me as I settle into her embrace. Her kiss is sweet and nurturing. I break it and trudge on.

"She may have been the world's worst partner and wife, but she gave me twin girls we named after our grandmothers, Eleanor and Rosemary. The moment I became a father, I learned what unconditional love was."

"They're amazing little girls, Jack, and you are an incredible father."

"Thank you. They've been my everything for a long time now." I swallow. "Just know that I could never compare you to Bree because there is no comparison. You're so much better for me than she ever was."

There's so much more I want to say. Instead, I know it's time to end this conversation before I say too much.

"But I don't want to talk about her anymore tonight, okay?"

I have to stop here because the rest of this story doesn't end well. It ends with my wife dead and me at fault. It ends with the reason I can't give this amazing woman lying in my arms everything she deserves and more. Instead, I just hold her, smelling her hair and wishing I were another man. We're quiet for a few minutes.

"Thank you for opening up to me. It means a lot."

She looks tormented over what I just told her, and I was hoping to give her clarity.

"Thanks for listening. I hope it wasn't too much."

"Not at all. I needed to hear it. Just like you need to hear this. I love you, Jack, and I think I fell a little more in love with you tonight."

I reach down and kiss her. I hold her tight until we both fall asleep.

Chapter 26

Caroline

I woke up in Jack's arms fully clothed. That never happens. We didn't have sex last night. After listening to Jack's story, I feel closer to him and more confused than ever. I'm no longer worried that I can't compete with his dead wife. To be honest, that may have been easier. It's still not clear to me why he's so against a relationship unless he's still hung up on how awful she was. But she passed away four years ago, and I feel like there has to be some part of their story that I don't understand. He didn't mention her death. I want to ask his mom about Bree now that I have some background information, but getting together one-on-one isn't in the plans for the day, and this isn't a phone call kind of conversation. If he's not still in love with her, why can't he love me? After I told him again last night and was met with silence, I pretended to fall asleep because it hurt too badly to look at him.

I have my finals this week and then will be graduating with my master's degree. I have a lot of studying to do since I didn't get much done during Ellie's hospital stay. I still haven't told my father my plans to pursue dance movement therapy, and I'm hoping the conversation goes better than anticipated. This morning, I left Jack's early to get to the library and put some much-needed hours into my studies. I've already been studying for several hours and needed a break. I'm standing in line at Coffee! Coffee! Coffee! completely lost in thought when I hear someone call my name. I turn around and see Jimmy waving at me. He's holding a coffee and a muffin and has a huge smile on his face. I walk over and give him a hug.

"Hi, Jimmy! What a nice surprise. How are you?"

"I'm great. Just finished practice and wanted to grab a coffee before we have to be back for afternoon meetings. We're reviewing films in an hour, but I needed to get out for a little bit. What about you?" he asks as he stuffs some muffin in his face.

"I'm studying for finals all day, and then I finally graduate."

"Good for you. Jack told me about your plans to do dance movement therapy. It sounds pretty cool."

"He told you about that?"

"Yeah, Caroline. If you didn't notice, he's a lovesick puppy and talks about you incessantly."

I laugh but realize that Jimmy may have some insight on Jack since he's his oldest friend. Jack sure as hell hasn't told me he loves me. Maybe I can ask a few questions casually and not give away that I'm digging for information.

"Are you in a hurry, or do you want to drink our coffees together?"

"I'd love to have a coffee with you, Caroline. I'll grab a table while you wait for your order."

I smile at him as he heads to a high-top near the windows. My order's ready within a minute, and I head over to join him.

"This is nice, Jimmy. There are normally always a ton of other people around when we hang out. I'm glad we're doing this."

I set my coffee on the table. I take off my warm winter coat, scarf, and hat. Winter is sneaking up on me this year.

"Me too. I've been wanting to thank you for getting Jack out of his funk. It's like he's the guy I met years ago. I'm pretty sure you're the reason for that."

I don't respond right away.

"I don't know about that. Did he tell you he finally talked to me about Bree last night?"

Jimmy looks shocked.

"He did?"

I nod.

"Yeah, I've been worried this whole time that he can't fall in love with me because he's hung up on his dead wife, but it sounds like their relationship was kind of awful."

"Awful is putting it lightly. Bree was the worst. No one could stand her. She slowly sucked the life out of Jack. That bitch put him through hell."

I don't know what to say about a dead woman whose grave I've been visiting when I go to see my mom. What would he think if he knew I'd been leaving her flowers and telling her about her daughters? Instead, I wait and let him keep talking. It's quiet for a minute. Then he lets out a loud sigh.

"Caroline, Jack's my best friend. I know he loves you, but he can't accept that he's not responsible for her death. He's been torturing himself for years. He thinks he doesn't deserve to be happy, which is why he won't move forward with you. The whole thing is fucked up."

"Why do you think he blames himself?"

I didn't realize that he blamed himself for her death. She was killed by a drunk driver. Jack wasn't even with her. I'm not sure I understand how he could have been responsible.

"Well, shit. He didn't mention that part of the story when he talked about her, huh? Damn, Caroline. He's going to be pissed. I shouldn't have assumed he went there."

"I won't say anything, Jimmy. It's just hard to love someone who's closed himself off. Last night was the first time I thought he was letting me in. He told me so much about their relationship but stopped before he got to her death."

He nods his head as if he understands.

"There was a blizzard. We weren't supposed to get home, but somehow, the plane made it that night. Jack and Bree had been going to counseling since he last caught her being unfaithful. The twins were only a few months old when it happened."

"I can't imagine what he went through."

I want to say it makes me love him even more.

"Caroline, he walked in to find her fucking some guy on the couch that night. He lost his shit, punched the guy, kicked them out, said some shit he regrets to Bree. They left in that snowstorm and died a mile from his house. He didn't even know they had been drinking until later."

My hand flies up to cover my mouth. Tears sting my eyes, threatening to erupt. My poor, strong man, he's been through so much, and he's been holding the weight of their deaths on his shoulders. How could he blame himself for their deaths? I suddenly feel sick. It's like the ground is coming out from beneath me.

"It wasn't his fault," I whisper.

I need to be with him. I need him to know that it's okay.

"I've been telling him that for years, Caroline. He doesn't believe it. He feels like he's relinquished his rights to happiness and has created his own sort of hell in his mind. That's why he can't tell you he loves you. He doesn't think he deserves you."

"I love him so much. I broke all his rules. He told me no relationship, no strings attached, just friends who have sex. I wanted so badly to be more, but I agreed because it meant more time with him. But, Jimmy, he has to know that this only makes me love him more."

"Caroline, you can't tell him you know any of this. He'll lose his shit on me. He needs to tell you this on his own timeline when he's ready. I'm only telling you because I'm asking you to be patient with him. You're good for him. But the guy's fragile. The fact that he even talked about Bree to you at all tells me he's finally letting you in."

"Thank you for telling me. To be honest, I was crushed last night when I told him again that I loved him, and he didn't respond. At least now I know why he won't say it."

"He loves you. There's no doubt about that. Just be patient."

I'm about to say more when my phone dings.

> Jack: Beautiful, I'm so sorry but I forgot about the holiday ball is this weekend. Did you still want to go?

"It's Jack. He's asking me if I still want to go to your team's holiday party this weekend. I think we both forgot about it with Ellie being in the hospital."

Jimmy nods.

"You should definitely go. It's a great time. Just make sure you have something fancy. Everyone gets real dolled up. The guys all wear tuxedos. I'll be in my kilt."

He smirks. Jimmy is from Scotland, and every time the guys have to dress up, he's in his kilt. I smile back at him.

"Sounds like I need to plan a shopping trip."

I look down at my watch.

"Jimmy, thanks so much for everything. I have to get back to studying, but honestly, you have no idea how badly I needed to hear this."

"You didn't hear anything from me, remember?"

He winks, and I give him a quick kiss on the cheek. I head to the library with a clear head. Jack Hannen better watch out because I'm not letting him go.

Chapter 27

Caroline

I just finished the last final exam of my master's program. I feel freer than I have in years. I've signed up for my requirements for my certification in dance movement therapy, I have a clear vision for my future, and my father actually handled the news very well. Plus I'm in love. Everything feels like it's falling into place, and I'm so happy I chose to move to Chicago. I've felt my mother's guidance every step of the way. Now that I know Bree's story, I've made it a point to visit her grave when I go to see my mother. I've only stopped there twice, but I plan to make it part of my routine. I brought her flowers and told her about her daughters. No matter what, she's Ellie and Rosie's mom, and I know she's looking down on them. I feel at peace with her history with the man I love, and I'm hoping that one day, he'll find that peace too. She didn't have an easy life, but she left two remarkable little girls behind, and I want them to have that loving childhood their mother craved.

It took a while for me to process everything. I've hardly seen Jack all week. He was away for most of it for hockey, and I skipped his home game last night to finish studying. I didn't spend the night there because I fell asleep at my desk, but we had a quick conversation after his game. It's probably better that we haven't seen much of each other since he opened up to me and Jimmy filled in the missing pieces. I'm excited to see him tonight and shower him in love.

I've been so busy with exams that I haven't had a minute to shop for a gown. I'm meeting my girlfriends to go shopping, and I'm praying we hit the jackpot today. We have limited time to find the perfect dress, but my girls are determined shoppers. I pull my car out of the campus parking lot and make the short trip to the little boutique Ari recommended. I'm there in ten minutes, and my girlfriends are all waiting for me already.

"I can't remember the last time we all got together to go shopping!" I say as I reach my friends and give quick hugs.

Victoria hands me a glass of champagne. This boutique is adorable with a crystal chandelier in the center and purple velvet couches. Clothes and gowns line the walls.

"Oh my gosh, if we can't find something in here, I don't know where else we'd even go."

"It's amazing, right? Caroline, we never see you anymore. Has Jack been tying you up and holding you hostage?" Mel asks, smiling.

"Damn. I wish he'd tie me up and have his wicked way with me."

Victoria chimes in. "Seriously though, babe, you look great! Lots of sex must do something good for your skin."

I can feel myself blushing. Even talking about him makes me feel like a giddy schoolgirl.

"I'm not going to lie. The sex is amazing, he's great, I'm happy, and I am head over heels in love with him."

I'm excited just talking about the guy.

"We're happy for you, Care. You deserve the best! How's Ellie doing?" Ari asks.

"So much better. It was an exhausting few days, but she's back to her adorable sassy self," I say with pride like she's mine. "She told me she loves me, and I literally melted."

"Aww, Caroline, that makes me want to cry. You would be such a good mom to those girls," Sofia replies. "Did their daddy finally tell you he loves you too?"

Ouch. If only they knew how hard this topic is for me right now. I'm going to have to give a little information without divulging too much.

"Not exactly. But he did tell me about Bree, and they were getting a divorce when she died. I was so convinced that he was still in love with her, but then Jimmy and I actually talked, and he gave me some insight on Jack. I think he just needs more time, but I know he loves me."

"Anyone who has spent any time with you two knows how much that man loves you. He'll tell you when he's ready. I mean the guy flew home from a game and went straight to your town house to move Sofia into her new place. Then afterward, he went to your dead mother's birthday dinner and had to deal with Cody's protective ass. A guy who doesn't care isn't going to get that emotionally invested in you," Mel says as she takes another sip of champagne.

"I have to agree, babe," Ari says.

"Plus you've basically moved in. If he's home, you're there, and if he's not home, you still stop by to help his mom or the nanny with his girls. Not to mention you just spent several days taking care of Ellie during her hospitalization," Victoria pipes in.

"And we all saw your pics from the apple orchard. You guys act like an adorable little family. Ellie telling you she loves you comes as no surprise. Those girls adore you, and their daddy looks at you like you walk on water," Sofia says.

"I know you're right. I just want the words. Cody thinks I'm going to get my heart broken. He's not happy with our arrangement and was quite vocal about that when he was here."

My girlfriends know my overprotective big brother extremely well.

"What guy wants to hear his little sister has a fuck buddy? Wait, you didn't tell him that, did you?" Mel asks.

"In different words, yes."

I cringe thinking about it.

"Oh my god. How did that go? I'm sure he wanted to kill Jack!" Victoria exclaims.

"He did. But then they seemed to get along really well at dinner. It was just weird at the end when I left for a minute to use the restroom. I came back and felt like I was interrupting some big private discussion. Cody looked like he wanted to kill Jack, and Jack looked totally distraught. Neither one of them told me what they were talking about, and then Jack got the call about Ellie. We left abruptly after that."

I've talked to my brother a few times since, but every time I bring up Jack, he just keeps reminding me to be careful and won't say anything else.

"I'm sure Cody was just telling him not to hurt you," Ari replies.

"Yeah, it seemed like it was more than that, but I'm probably being crazy."

"Drink up, crazy lady! We haven't had a girls' night in forever," Victoria says.

"Sofia, what's the word on Jimmy? We should all be talking about your sexy hockey player too," Ari says.

"Sofia! What haven't you told me? I love the idea of you and Jimmy together."

I can't believe how out of the loop I feel.

"There's nothing to say. I'm not ready to date, and he keeps asking me out. He wanted me to come as his date to the party with you tomorrow night, but I told him no. The guy literally does not give up."

"Sofia, he's one of the good ones. Trust me, I've gotten to know him, and he's a catch."

I knew he liked her, but I didn't realize that he'd been trying to get her to go out with him.

"They all seem like they're one of the good ones until they aren't. I told you I'm done with men for a while."

Sofia looks defeated. There's so much more she's not saying, but I know this isn't the time to pry. Mel breaks the tension for us.

"Sofia, take all the time you need to yourself. If he's worth it, he'll wait for you to be ready. Caroline, let's get your fine ass a dress. Do you have a color or style in mind?"

We spend the rest of the afternoon drinking way too much champagne. I found the perfect gown almost immediately, and then we spent three hours gossiping and trying on clothes, shoes, and accessories. Everyone is leaving with tons of shopping bags, and we literally never left the boutique. It's one of the best days I've had in a long time, and I'm not going to lie, I'm feeling a little tipsy. We decide to hit up O'Neils for dinner and more drinks.

We're seated toward the back of the sports bar. It's a Friday night, and there's a good-sized crowd gathered. Mel just ordered us a round of tequila shots, and I have a feeling I'm going to have a massive headache tomorrow morning, but I honestly don't care. I'm celebrating the end of my master's program in style. I'm sure we'll end up at a dance club after dinner if we keep up this pace. My phone dings, and I dig it out of my purse.

> Jack: Hey beautiful. Did you find a dress?
>
> Me: Yes. I did, handsome. You're going to love it.
>
> Jack: I'm sure I'll love tearing it off of you even more.
>
> Me: So confident you're going to get some, huh?
>
> Jack: We both know I can't control myself around you. I'll probably be sporting a boner half the night.
>
> Me: Promise?

"Caroline, let me guess. It's Jack?"
Sofia's sitting next to me and glances down at my phone.
"Yeah, sorry. He wanted to know if I found a dress."
I feel rude for looking at my phone during our girls' night. I quickly put it back into my purse.
"Tell him…oh wait. You invited him?" Mel asks.
"No. He doesn't even know we're here."
"Incoming!"
Mel's staring at the front of the restaurant. I turn around. Jack and his crew of guys are standing at the doorway waiting for a table. Our eyes meet. He lights up when he realizes it's me.
"Invite them to join us, Caroline. That man looks like he wants to jump you from the doorway," Ari chimes in.

I wave, and I see Jimmy talking to the hostess pointing toward our table. Leave it to Jimmy. He leads the pack of tall, sexy, muscular men. All eyes are on them, and Jack is still staring at me and smiling, oblivious to the fact that everyone in the building is gawking at him.

It's Jimmy who speaks first.

"Ladies, could we possibly crash your dinner party?"

He's staring straight at Sofia, who is trying to look uninterested.

"The more, the merrier," Sofia replies.

The guys start pulling another table up to ours and moving chairs around. Meanwhile, my sexy man comes over to me and squats down so he's at my eye level.

"You look gorgeous. I've missed you today, but are you sure you're okay with us crashing dinner with your friends?" Jack whispers into my ear.

"I don't think the girls mind, and I'm happy to see you. I've missed you too."

I have butterflies in my stomach. He's wearing a black tight-fitting T-shirt that perfectly outlines his pecs, and the way his jeans hug his ass is absolutely scrumptious.

"I'm so glad we both ended up here. My day just got a whole lot better."

He winks and then leans in to kiss me. It's quick and chaste, but it sends chills down my spine. Seriously, a wink? This guy is too much sometimes.

"All right, you two, why don't you stay and hang out with us for a little bit? Every time we're together as a group, you're fucking in some hidden area," Novotny says, staring right at Jack with a huge grin on his face.

Is this what his friends think of me? I'm just some whore that he's banging? I think back to my only two interactions with Novotny, the nightclub and the impromptu dance party at Jack's house. Yep, both times we snuck away and were totally having sex. My face must be redder than a tomato.

"I'm so embarrassed. I swear I'm not a slut."

I really didn't realize the guys knew what was going on at Jack's that day. I'm mortified.

"You're a screamer, Caroline. We all know, and it's hot as fuck," Jones says as he winks at me.

Another wink like I couldn't have been any more mortified. Jimmy saves the day again.

"Ah, boys, you're just jealous. Why don't we give the lovebirds a break? Plus Hannen's not being a dick to everyone all the time, so it's a win for all of us."

Jimmy laughs as he looks at Jack.

"I'm not a dick all the time. I just don't put up with shit. And speaking of putting up with shit, Jones, maybe you should keep those kinds of comments to yourself. Don't disrespect her again."

Jack's defensive and a little riled up. I put my hand on his thigh and start to gently rub circles with my thumb. He looks at me, and I smile at him.

"Well, babe, they were telling the truth. We do fuck like rabbits," I say.

Mel's mouth drops to the floor.

"Hold up! I know you're a little drunk, but that is not a line our sweet Caroline would ever say! This man has turned you into a nymph!"

Jack looks stunned. He bursts out laughing. I see his shoulders loosening.

"Wow, Jack. She is good for you," Owen Miller chimes in.

I think for the most part, his friends like me. I notice Kelston Green hasn't said much. I'm drunk and feeling feisty, so I go in with guns blazing.

"Hi, Kelston. I haven't seen you in forever! Thank you so much for sending me those dick pics a few months ago. I hadn't seen you since our Michigan days, and I have to tell you, that was totally unexpected."

"Oh shit!" Sofia busts out laughing.

Victoria chimes in. "Wait! You're dick pick guy?" She's smiling ear to ear now. "I have to admit, that was an impressive picture." She turns all her attention to Kelston.

"Wait! Green, you're sending Hannen's girl dick pics? That's fucked up man," Jones pipes in.

"It was months ago! Jack and I hadn't even met yet." I shoot Kelston a glance. "But in the future, Kelston, I wouldn't lead with a dick pic for a woman you haven't seen in years. I also wouldn't tell my teammates that she's a slut who's slept with half of the NFL. Just passing on some helpful advice."

Jack tenses, and I hope I haven't pushed too far. This guy needs to learn some respect, and luckily, I'm feeling loose enough to teach him. Jimmy starts howling. He's laughing so hard.

"Damn, Green. You've pissed off the sweetest woman I've ever met. I didn't even think it was possible for Caroline to get mad."

Jimmy chuckles. Jack pulls me in closer and studies my face.

"The pictures were a joke. I was drunk," Kelston exclaims. "But if any of you pretty things want a ride, you just say the word," he says as he looks straight at Victoria and licks his lips. "And as far as the NFL shit, I was just repeating a rumor I heard. I didn't know if it were true or not."

Jack starts to say something when Victoria jumps in.

"I must say that anaconda really was something. But how do we know it was you and not something you pulled off the internet? Ten-inch cocks aren't the norm."

Novotny loses it right after taking a sip of his beer and starts laughing so hard that he sprays beer all over. He's literally choking, and the rest of the table starts laughing.

"To think, I wasn't going to come tonight. This is turning out to be epic," he says.

Kelston smiles at Victoria.

"There's only one way to find out, baby."

The rest of the night flies by. Our round of tequila shots came shortly after the guys were seated, and while they hardly drank because of hockey, the women have continued to get ridiculously drunk. We eat and laugh a lot. Jack and I can't keep our hands off one another. If my hand isn't on his leg, his is around my shoulder. He's kissed my cheek, my head, and my hand. Any excuse we can find to touch one another, we do. The sexual tension is so thick. I think I'm going to explode. When it's finally time to say our goodbyes, I leap into Jack's SUV, leaving my car to be picked up tomorrow. As soon as we shut his car doors, he's on me. Our lips crash into one another, and his hands are in my hair. I put my arms around his neck and pull him close. He's reaching for the center council, trying to move it out of the way with one hand without breaking our kiss. He finally gets it up and pulls me onto his lap. I'm straddling him, grinding against him, when there's a knock on the window. I break the kiss and look over. Jones is peering into the car.

"I just wanted to let you know I'll get a ride back with Novotny, Jack. Don't worry about me."

Jack puts his head back on the seat and puts the window down.

"Thanks, Jones. I'm so glad you interrupted us to tell me that. No, really, thanks for letting me know. Now can I get back to my girl?"

He's laid the sarcasm on so thick. Both Jones and I start laughing. Jones shakes his head and starts walking away from Jack's car. Jack looks annoyed, and it's adorable. But I also have a second to realize where we are.

"Did you drive him here?" I ask.

"Yeah, but he had a million people who could have driven him home. None of us really drank. It's not like I was deserting him."

"All right, babe. Maybe him ruining the moment was a good thing though. Let's finish this at home."

"You don't want me to fuck you in my car?"

"Two minutes ago, I would have said yes, but I've got my senses back, and it doesn't seem like the best idea."

He chuckles.

"No, it doesn't. But we can still play. Unbutton your jeans. I'm going to have you so wet and ready that when we get home, you'll be begging for it."

I never would have thought that having a man speak so dirty or so blunt would turn me on, but with Jack, it just adds to my desire to have him. I quickly obey, and he reaches his hand down my pants and into my panties. I gasp. He smiles at me as he pulls out of the parking lot. He drives slowly as he caresses my nub. He feels so good. I moan as he slides a finger inside me and find myself rocking my hips even with my seat belt on and his hand down my pants.

"That's right, beautiful. Fuck my hand."

He adds a second finger and increases his rhythm as he continues to drive us home. I'm so close to coming, but every time I think I'm about to explode, he backs off.

"Dammit, Jack."

I'm breathless, and he knows exactly what he's doing to me.

"Almost home, beautiful. How's that feel?"

"I want to come, and you keep stopping."

"I promise I'll get you there, but I want to feel you come around my cock. We're home."

This dominating alpha male thing he's perfected is so hot. He pulls into his driveway, and I see his parents' car is already there. He hits the button for the garage door opener, and I tear my seat belt off and straddle him again.

"I need you to take me right here, right now. You have me all worked up, and I can't wait for your parents to leave."

His smirk says it all as his lips meet mine, and he pulls me further on top of him. I reach down and unbutton his jeans. I can feel his erection already through the denim. He quickly lays me down on the front seat and starts tearing my pants off. I help him pull them down. Once they're off, he throws them on the ground and pushes his own down to just above his knees. He sits back in the driver's seat, and I once again straddle him. He puts his hands on my ass, and I center him over my opening. I'm so wet. I'm dripping. I bring myself down over him, taking him all in one quick move. He hisses and starts bucking his hips up and down using his hands on my ass to help me thrust in and out of him. Our bodies move as one, and although this is fast, furious, and fun, I know it's just the beginning of the night. I can feel myself getting close. I'm on the verge of losing myself to this man in every way imaginable.

"Yes, Jack! Oh my god. You feel so good!"

My orgasm tears through me, and I can feel Jack's eyes on me the entire time. His pace quickens, and in three more deep thrusts, he releases himself high inside of me. We sit there panting, staring at each other, neither one wanting to move.

"I feel like the luckiest man in the world when I'm with you."

He brushes his nose against mine, and I melt.

"But we need to get in before my parents realize we're in here," he whispers, looking up at me with a cocky grin.

I force myself off him. We redress quickly and head inside the house. I immediately worry that they're going to know exactly what we just did in the garage. But if they do know, they don't let on. Kathy and Jack Sr. hug me as soon as I enter with their son.

"Hi, honey. I'm so glad to see you. Did you find a dress?" Kathy asks me, genuinely interested.

In the short time I've been with Jack, his mother has come to mean so much to me. She's warm and welcoming, and she makes me feel loved every time I see her. I think her love is what's molded Jack into the father he's become to Ellie and Rosie.

"I did, and it's gorgeous. I can't wait to show it to you!"

I'm hoping she's okay with my plan.

"I was actually hoping to get ready over here with Rosie and Ellie. My girlfriends are coming over and offered to do our hair and makeup.

"You mean Ellie and Rosie will be getting all done up with you?"

She looks so touched.

"Yes. I bought them a few little goodies like nail polish and some glittery hair clips. The nanny is going to babysit for us to give you and Jack Sr. the night off."

I reach into my purse and hand her an envelope. I've been so excited to give this surprise to her and was hoping I'd see her tonight so I didn't have to give it to her tomorrow morning.

"What's that?" Jack asks as he watches our exchange.

"Your mom will have to open it and find out."

I turn to Kathy. She smiles and opens the envelope. There's an anniversary card I picked out for them with a gift card to Cibo as well as the dinner reservation confirmation. Cibo is the same restaurant Jack, Cody, and I went for my mom's birthday dinner. It's so difficult to get into that Kathy has been waiting for over a year. I pulled some strings with a friend who works in the kitchen to get this reservation for them. Kathy starts crying.

"Sweetheart, I can't believe you did this! It's too much!"

"I wanted you to have a glamourous night out tomorrow too. You've welcomed me into this family with open arms, and I wanted to do something special for you."

Jack Sr. looks at his son and then looks at me. He has tears in his eyes when he gives me a huge hug.

"You are really something special, Caroline. Thank you."

He kisses my cheek.

"It's getting late, Kathy. Let's let these kids get to bed."

He looks at his son, and I don't miss the glance they share.

"You're right. Okay, we'll let you two get some sleep. Caroline, thank you so much. I'm so excited!"

Kathy kisses us both on the cheeks.

"Oh, Kathy, one more thing. We wanted you to get ready with us for your date. Victoria is already planning on doing your hair. If you don't want to, it's totally okay. I just wanted you to know you were invited."

I hope I don't look like I'm begging her to be my surrogate mother. Instead, she starts crying.

"I would absolutely love that. I don't think I've been this excited for something in years."

She hugs me again, and Jack Sr. gently steers her toward the door.

"The girls went to sleep like angels. They shouldn't make a peep for you."

"Thanks, Mom. Thanks, Dad. We'll see you soon," Jack says as they walk out the door.

He turns to me.

"I can't believe you did that for them. My mom may start loving you more than she does her only son."

He pulls me into his arms and kisses my forehead. We stand there holding each other for a minute.

"Let's go to bed, beautiful."

Chapter 28

Jack

I lead Caroline into my bedroom. She never ceases to amaze me. I could have gotten my parents into that restaurant months ago, but the thought never crossed my mind. And of course, my mom would never ask. I had no idea she was even interested in dining there. Not only did Caroline know, but she made it happen. I'm embarrassed to admit that I didn't know it was their wedding anniversary either. They always celebrate together, but that wasn't something my sister or I ever participated in. Leave it to the beautiful, selfless woman holding my hand to once again make me want to be a better man.

I cannot believe the depths of love Caroline has inside of her. When this whole thing comes crashing down around me, it won't just be me and my daughters who are going to lose her. She's become a member of our family. My parents will be devastated. My love for her is like nothing I've ever felt before and continues to grow. If only I could be worthy of her. My father's eyes told me everything I needed to know tonight. He basically told me not to fuck this up with a look. I think he may love Caroline as much as my mom does. I can imagine a life with Caroline by my side, raising Ellie and Rosie. I cannot think of a better role model for them. I can imagine coming home to her every night and waking up to her every morning. I can see her in a wedding gown, declaring our love for one another in front of everyone we hold dear to us, and I can imagine her belly growing with a baby of our own. In a perfect world, that's what I'd get. She'd be mine completely. She interrupts my thoughts.

"I'm going to jump in the shower. I had one hundred different outfits on today, and I still have your come dripping out of me."

That grabs my attention.

"That's hot as fuck, Caroline."

She laughs.

"Yeah, except when your mom was hugging me, it's all I could think about."

I pull her into my arms and kiss her. She silently lifts her arms above her head. I pull her baby-blue, soft cashmere sweater over her head. It only compares to the softness of her skin. She's wearing a strapless, virgin-white bra underneath. I take a deep breath in, and she sees me staring at her chest.

"I wanted something strapless when I was trying on dresses."

She pushes her chest into mine, stands on her toes, and kisses me again. Then she steps away and removes her jeans. She smiles over her shoulder as she walks into the bathroom in nothing but that damn lace white bra and a matching thong. Desire courses through my veins. This woman is going to be the death of me, and in this moment, I don't care.

I tear my clothes off like they're on fire and sneak into the shower. Her back is to me. Her eyes closed. She's facing the water when I come up behind her. I push my chest to her back and wrap my hands around her breasts.

"Hey, you. I was surprised it took you this long to get in here," she says as she rubs her ass against me.

I'm instantly rock-hard. My dick pokes her back, and my hands caress her breasts. I lean in and begin kissing her neck. She leans her head, giving me better access and reaches behind her. She starts stroking my dick, and it feels so fucking good. I flip her around and get down on my knees. I open her stance and tell her to lean against the wall. I lick her slit and realize she's already wet for me. I thrust a finger into her center as I suck on her clit. She moans. I continue fucking her with my tongue, adding a second finger, and stroking her where I know she likes it until her thighs are quivering around me. She cries out.

"Oh my god, Jack."

I slow down my speed and let her come down gently. My dick is throbbing, and I need to get inside of her. I pick her up. She wraps her arms around my neck and her legs around my hips. I push her back into the cold tile and fuck her against the shower wall. She stares at me with every thrust. Our eyes never break contact.

"You feel so good, Care."

Her tits are bouncing with every thrust, and I don't think I've ever wanted anything more than I want her.

"I'm so close again."

I take my one hand from her ass and rub my thumb against her clit. She explodes, clenching my dick like a vise. She's so tight and wet that I follow my own release, spilling into her with such force that my entire body shudders.

"How is it so good every, single time? Jack, you've ruined me for anyone but you."

"It's unbelievable for me too, beautiful. You do something to me."

I lean in and kiss her hard, demanding, unforgiving. My dick starts to twitch inside of her, and she laughs.

"You are insatiable."

"Only for you."

I lift her off me and pull out. I grab the bodywash and begin cleaning her soft skin. We clean each other in silence, rubbing our hands all over one another. It's somehow more intimate than the sex we just shared. We've been having a lot of shower sex lately, and I'm not complaining about it. When we finish, I wrap her in a fluffy towel, and we get ready for bed. I'd prefer to sleep naked, but with two four-year-old girls in the house, I throw on a pair of athletic shorts. Caroline takes one of my T-shirts out of my drawer. It's nearly down to her knees, and she looks so beautiful wearing my things. It warms my nearly cold heart.

*****

I left for practice early this morning but was still running late. I wanted Caroline's sweet pussy for breakfast and got a little carried away before I realized how late it was. She made me a protein shake while I showered and was making pancakes for the girls when I left. We gave the nanny the day off since Caroline is done with school and didn't have any plans for today. The girls were happily sitting at the kitchen island talking to Caroline when I left. I gave them all kisses goodbye and was out the door. It should have been the perfect morning except when I got to the locker room, everyone was already heading on the ice, and I didn't have any of my gear on yet.

"Late night, Jack?" Novotny asks when he sees me rushing in late.

"More like a late morning."

I smile at him and start getting ready as fast as I can.

"Lucky dog. We like her, man. You've got a keeper."

He chuckles.

"Yeah. We'll see."

He shakes his head and heads to the ice. I make it out a few minutes late and don't miss the scowl on Coach's face.

"Hannen! This is the first time you've been late in years. I want to meet this new woman of yours and explain to her that you have to be on the ice on time."

Coach is like a second dad to me. I've been playing for him for the last five years, and he's been there for me through some pretty rough times. I play my ass off for this man, am always early to practice, and am usually the last one off the ice. I think my work ethic is what's allowed me to stay in Chicago all these years.

"You'll love her, Coach. She's sweet as honey."

He chuckles as do a few of my teammates. I don't miss Kelston Green's annoyed look but choose to ignore it. I take off to do my extra laps as punishment for being late and can't help but smile the entire time I think of her. After practice and our team meeting, Coach sends us on our way. Caroline's girlfriends should all be there when I get home helping her and my mom get ready for tonight. My mom texted me again to make sure it was okay that she came over to get ready, and I think she's undeniably excited.

When I get home, I have absolutely no intention of crashing the girls party, but when Ellie calls me over, I decide to sit on the edge of the tub for a few minutes. Caroline's friends are all here.

Raw and Real Love

They've transformed my master bathroom into a salon. Sofia is doing Caroline's hair, Mel is doing her makeup, and Victoria is doing my mom's hair for their anniversary dinner. I haven't seen my mom smile this much in a long time. The women are all talking a mile a minute, and there seem to be fifteen different conversations going on. Ari is curling Rosie's hair, and Ellie is wearing some kind of pink gooey face mask while she waits for her turn to get her hair and makeup done. Apparently, they're getting beautiful to watch Disney movies on my couch tonight. I love that Caroline included all the women in my life. My daughters and my mother adore her. The problem is I do too, and I can't say I've ever adored a woman in my life.

When it comes to Caroline, nothing is simple. I love her. She loves me. It should be a no-brainer. But every time I think about taking that plunge and trying to make something real out of this, I'm hit with a wave of guilt. Bree flashes through my mind. It's always the face that I saw last the night when I kicked her out—tears pouring down from her eyes with her eye makeup running down her face, her hair messy all over, and half-dressed because it's all she had time to put on before I went fucking crazy. I remember the words I said, and then I remember being called to identify her body. I remember the dried blood matting her hair down, her lifeless eyes staring straight ahead, her gray skin, and blue lips. I remember standing there staring at her, feeling like my whole world was falling apart. What had I done? She was miserable for years because of me and then died because of me. And now here I am contemplating starting over when Bree will never get the chance. I don't deserve the opportunity.

"Jack, did you hear me?"

My mom's voice brings me back to reality. She's staring at me, and I have no fucking clue what's going on.

"Sorry, Ma. What?"

"I asked you if you could grab the door. The doorbell just rang, and Mel ordered food for everyone."

"Oh. Yeah. Sorry."

I get up and start walking out when I hear the women start chatting again. I'm stressed the fuck out. I put the food on the kitchen counter and make sure everyone knows it's here. Then I slip into the spare bedroom and bathroom where I moved my stuff so I can get ready. I quickly shower and shave. I take my time putting on my tux. I'm just finishing my bow tie when there's a soft knock on the door. Caroline slowly pushes it open and peeks in. She's gorgeous. She's wearing a long, cherry-red dress with matching nail polish and lipstick. I instantly want to taste those bright-red lips. Without a word, she enters the room, locks the door behind her, and saunters over to me. She grabs the lapels of my coat and pulls me into her. I lean down, and our lips connect. I pull her closer, resting my hands on her ass. The kiss deepens, and I feel my cock stiffening. I push her up against the wall, lifting her ass in the air. She pulls her dress up and wraps her legs around me. My dick is aching against my suddenly too tight pants. I start grinding against her. She nips at my ear.

"Get inside me."

I have no idea what has her so wound up, but I quickly set her down and fall to my knees. I push her dress up over her hips and pull her panties down. I start licking her slit, and I realize she is soaked. I put two fingers inside of her, and she moans.

"We don't have much time, and we need to be quiet."

She gives me a naughty grin, and I start undoing my pants. My cock springs free, and she reaches for it. I push her away, and she lies back on the bed.

"This is going to be fast and rough."

"Good. Now get inside me."

This woman is fucking fantastic. I plunge into her, hard. She groans, and I know I should give her a minute to accommodate to me, but instead, I pull out and push myself as far in as I can go until my balls are slapping against her ass. I'm ruthless, fucking out the frustration that she can't be mine. She never breaks eye contact, and when her thighs start quivering around me and she begins tightening on me like a vise, I cover her mouth with my own to muffle her cries. She whimpers into my mouth. I follow after her, my orgasm exploding through me like a cannon.

"I love you," she says as she stares into my eyes.

I swear she can see my soul. She can see the turmoil raging inside me. I stare back at her. I want to tell her how I feel. But then what? I'll have to tell her that I'm a fucking mess and killed my wife. I pull out and kiss her.

"Let me grab you a towel to clean up, beautiful."

I see the pain in her eyes and the disappointment on her face. I wonder how much longer she's going to subject herself to me and all my fucked-up ways. I grab a towel and run it under warm water. I wring it out and bring it over to her. I gently wipe her. When I look up, she has a single tear falling from her eye. I take my thumb and wipe it away.

"Please don't cry. I'm so sorry."

I feel like the world's biggest asshole. She takes a big breath and then stares me down again.

"No need to apologize, just like I'm not sorry that I broke the rules and fell in love with you, Jack."

She puts her arms around my neck and kisses along my jaw. I'm towering over her on the bed, my arms encasing her underneath me. I'm too numb to move.

"I don't know what to say," I whisper.

I can hardly get the words out. She reaches up and cups my face in her hands. She kisses the tip of my nose. She brushes her hands against my face, and I realize that she's wiping away tears, tears I didn't realize had fallen. We're statues there for quite some time before there's a knock at the door. Ari shouts from outside the door.

"Umm, Jack, your parents are heading out. I'm not sure if Caroline's with you, but I wanted to let you know."

I let out a big sigh and move off the bed. Caroline runs her hands down her dress, straightening it. I pull up my pants, realizing that they're still tucked around my ankles and the rest of my tux never even got removed. Caroline fixes my tie. I don't move. I just stare at her. I'm rooted in place.

"Take a minute, handsome. I'll go say goodbye first."

Chapter 29

Caroline

I think I pushed him too far. He's hardly said a word in the car, but he also hasn't let go of my hand. I can usually read him. However, he almost looks robotic as he drives along. He's regal in his tuxedo, and it's not the first time I've wondered how he can be so gorgeous. I study his freshly shaven face, square jaw, perfect nose, high cheeks, and ice-blue eyes. His eyes look stormy, like the ocean after a hard rain, as he stares ahead at the road. His broad shoulders fill his tuxedo, and it looks like it was made for him. When we arrive at the Ritz, he pulls into the circle drive, past the fountains, and stops in front of a valet. We get out of the car, and he silently places a kiss to my forehead. He still doesn't speak, and at this point, I'm uneasy. I've never seen him like this. He grabs my hand, and we head inside.

The room is breathtaking in its opulence. There's a large crystal chandelier in the center of the room. The tables are covered in crisp white linens with gold chargers and gold silverware. There are red poinsettias everywhere. Each table has an elaborate, tiered arrangement of poinsettias and white candles on gold candlesticks. There is a bar in the front and the rear of the large room. The team has a few days off, and most of the guys are enjoying a drink. I see Jones with a busty brunette who's wearing a dress that's about a size and half too small and four-inch stilettos. I'm still taking the room in as he makes his way over to us.

"Jack! Caroline. Good to see you. This is Mandy. She's a dancer too, Caroline."

The guys do one of those one-armed, half-handshake, half-man hug things that they do. Mandy looks me over like she's sizing up the competition while I smile politely.

"Hi, Mandy. Maybe we'll have to show these guys some dance moves after dinner."

She laughs and gives me a one-word answer.

"Totally."

"Jack, Coach was looking for you a few minutes ago. He's over by the bar," Jones says as he pulls Mandy back into his arms.

"Great. We'll head over there. I could use a drink anyways. See you around, man."

We walk away, and I turn to Jack.

"Mandy seems nice," I say, trying to make conversation.

Jack looks at me with an all-knowing smirk.

"Yeah, Mandy's pretty popular at the Pussy Cat Lounge."

I immediately recognize the name of the gentlemen's club showcasing exotic dancers. Somehow, I'm not surprised at all by this information. I smile up at Jack just as we run into Coach.

"Coach! Nancy! Happy holidays, you two!"

Jack leans down and hugs Coach and his wife.

"Jack, it's always so nice to see you. You look fantastic!" Nancy says, flashing a beautiful white smile.

"Thank you. You look great too. This is my friend, Caroline."

I try not to cringe as he introduces me as his friend, but I guess I don't know what else I expected him to say. Girlfriend? Lover? Fuck buddy? Yeah, maybe just Caroline would have sufficed. I plaster on a smile and shake hands.

"Caroline! Are you the one responsible for making this jackass smile again? He's the happiest I've seen him in years."

Coach slaps Jack on the back. Jack chuckles, but I can see the war he's raging inside. He's off tonight, and I know I'm responsible. I realize I have to answer Coach, so I do so honestly, hoping Jack realizes my reply is directed more toward him than it is Coach.

"Coach, it's so nice to meet you! I've heard so many good things about you. But I don't think you can credit me with Jack's happiness.

I truly believe we're responsible for our own happiness. It's a choice we make."

"Smart and beautiful. You've done well, Jack."

"Thanks, Coach."

That's all he says. He changes the subject off me, and we stand there making small talk for a few minutes before a server comes over and offers me a glass of champagne. I gladly accept the flute and say a little prayer for courage. We all take our seats for dinner shortly after. Luckily, everyone we're sitting with is wonderful. I haven't met as many of the guys' wives as I would have liked to, and they're all so welcoming. I'm almost able to enjoy myself except Jack is virtually ignoring me. He's talked to everyone at the table but me. He's hardly made eye contact with me, and while he usually can't keep his hands off me, he hasn't touched me a single time. After dinner, it's more of the same. I feel like an unwanted shadow and excuse myself to the bathroom. After taking a few long big breaths, fixing my makeup and chatting with a few of the women, I realize I've taken about as much time as I can in the restroom and head back to find Jack. He's standing with a group of his friends with his back to me. I don't mean to eavesdrop, but I walk slowly as I overhear their conversation.

"Jack, I think this is the longest I've seen you with a woman. What happened to hit and quit it?" Jones asks.

"Eh, lay off him. He found the right girl," Novotny says. "Plus let's be real. Any man would want her in his bed."

"Enough you guys. We're just fucking. That's all this is. I told her I didn't want more," Jack says, and the words are like a knife to my chest.

"Yeah, okay, Jack. We're not idiots. It's pretty fucking obvious you developed feelings along the way," Jimmy says as he takes a sip of his drink.

"I'm serious. I know you all think she's an angel, but let's be real. We started fucking in a nightclub, and I've pretty much gotten laid every night since. I'm not offering her a picket white fence, and I'm certainly not looking for a replacement wife and mommy. I just really, really enjoy her pussy."

I cannot even believe he just said that. I'm numb. Fuck him and his self-sabotage. Don't mess with a scorned woman. I take a deep breath. Jimmy sees me first.

"Caroline! He didn't mean it. You know he didn't mean it."

Jimmy actually looks like he's going to be sick.

"Yeah, we were just joking, Caroline."

This comes from Novotny.

Jack's back stiffens, and he slowly turns toward me as all the men stand there with their mouths hanging open. Jack's eyes are full of remorse, but he doesn't dare speak. I push the tears back. I need to be strong, and I need to get the words out without breaking down. I take another deep breath.

"Gentlemen, can you please excuse us for a minute?"

I don't wait for a reply. I take Jack's hand in mine and yank him out the door of the ballroom and into the foyer of the lobby. When we're safely away from anyone who can hear us, I let go of his hand and let him have it.

"How dare you talk about me with such disrespect?"

I'm so mad. I'm trembling.

"I shouldn't have said that."

"Yeah, you think?"

"Look, Caroline. You're the one who broke the rules. I've been real and honest with you from the beginning. I can't do more."

"Oh, you've been honest with me, Jack?"

"Yeah."

"Honest enough to admit you're trying to sabotage us?"

He looks at me quizzically.

"Did you honestly think I'd love you any less if you had told me about Bree's death? Did you honestly think that I'd blame you for her car accident just because you kicked her out after she betrayed you? Did you honestly think I'd have thought less of you because you said some shitty stuff to her before she died? Do you still honestly think you're not worthy of love? Do you honestly think I'm going to stop loving you because of your past? Do you honestly not see what we have?"

I pause, trying to hold the tears back. He looks shocked. He had no idea I knew about the demons in his closet.

"Caroline, please just stop."

His plea is barely a whisper. But I trudge on.

"No! I won't stop. I won't stop loving you because you tried to hurt me just now. I'll continue to love you every single day. I'll love you enough for both of us. I'll love you while you figure out a way to deal with your past. I'll love you while you continue to push me away. I'll never stop loving you. But tonight, you deserve a big fuck you."

"Caroline, please."

His face is pained. His strong shoulders sag, and he drops his head.

"Figure your shit out, Jack. Stop hating yourself and allow yourself some happiness."

I pull my shoulders back and march out the front of the building. I don't look back until I'm out the door. He hasn't moved. We had gotten a hotel room and were planning on staying here tonight. I don't bother using my room key to go back upstairs and grab my bag. Instead, I take my phone out of the pocket of my dress and text Sofia to see if she can come pick me up. Her new place is close, and I know she can be here in under ten minutes. It's freezing outside, and I left my coat at coat check. I don't even care as the snow pelts down on me.

*****

Jack

There's movement around me, but I've turned to stone. I can't move if I want to. I feel hollow. I didn't think I could feel any worse than I've felt these past few years, but I've found a new low. She knows. She knows everything, and she still loves me. How? How the fuck could she have known? I hear my name being called, but I can't seem to answer. I feel a hand on my shoulder.

"Jack, you've been out here forever. Everything okay?" Jimmy asks me.

Rage boils through me. He's the only one who fucking knew besides my parents, and they promised me they'd let me tell her on my own. It had to be him. I push his hand off my shoulder.

"You fucking asshole! You told her!"

I shove him hard. He looks shocked.

"Jack, calm down. What are you talking about?"

"No, fuck you. You're the only one who knew."

I shove him again. He stumbles back. Jimmy's a big fucking guy, and if we go to blows, one of us is going to get seriously hurt. I don't care. I see red. Some of my teammates are starting to gather around.

"Jack, calm down. I don't want to fight you."

"Fuck. You."

I shove him again. He shoves me back this time. I hear someone else tell me to calm down. I lunge at Jimmy. Suddenly, I feel arms grab me from behind. I try to break free, but there are too many people holding me back.

"What right did you have to fucking tell her?" I shout.

I see realization flicker over his face as a few of our teammates hold him back. He knows what I'm talking about.

"She was a mess, Jack. She loves you so fucking much, and you couldn't be real with her. You can't be real with anyone. She was blaming herself. So yeah, I told her. I'd do it again too."

"Fuck you! You don't have a clue what I've been through."

"Actually, I've stood by your side through it all. I was there when your wife cheated on you. I was there when she died. I was there when you couldn't get out of bed. I was there to get you back on the ice. I was there when you woke up in the morning feeling like an asshole because you didn't know the name of the chick you fucked the night before. I was there when you thought you were going to have another kid, and you didn't even remember the fucking pregnant woman calling you her baby's daddy. So yeah, I know what you've been through, you asshole."

"It's not your life. You don't know shit."

"I know that you finally found someone who accepted you with all your flaws, and you pushed her away because you're a fucking coward. Fuck you, Hannen."

He's right. I drop my fist and stop trying to break free. I feel the arms on me loosen.

"Let me go."

They do. I turn around and walk out the door.

*****

Caroline

I wait until I get into Sofia's car, and the Ritz is out of view, before I let the tears fall. I'm crying so hard that I can barely breathe. I gave him all of me, I gave him my whole heart, and I'm left not knowing if he's ever going to be able to give himself to me. I don't even know if he wants to. Will I ever be enough for the man I love? Will he ever love me enough to be faithful to me? Brandon didn't. This pain is so much worse than discovering Brandon's infidelity. Jack didn't love me enough to let his guard down and open up to me. He refused to let me know the real him. I fell in love with the version of him that I knew. Maybe I'll never know the real Jack. But I refuse to believe it was just sex for him. I see how he looks at me. I know how good he treats me and how attentive he is to me. He treats me like I'm his queen, and I don't believe he can fake the bond that we formed.

Maybe I went about this all wrong. I did everything out of character with Jack. Having sex with a man I barely knew in a nightclub and then agreeing to be friends with benefits? What was I thinking? I can't believe he told his friends "he just really likes my pussy." Oh my god! They all must think I'm such a slut. The thing is even from the beginning, Jack wasn't just some random guy. To me, he was a man whose aunt had become a dear friend of mine over the past year. He was a man who lost his wife too soon and showed his loss in his sad eyes. He was a man who loved his two little girls to the moon and back. He was a man who had followed his dreams and was passionate about his career. He was a man who dedicated his time to charity work. He was a man who came from a loving family, one who welcomed me with open arms.

His father changed my flat tire in the parking lot, and his mother brought baked goods to every single dance lesson for me. His parents became my friends while he was on the road, and I fell in love with them. I can't even think about Ellie and Rosie. His daughters have become a huge part of my world. I can't imagine not seeing them every day. My tears start falling harder, and I think I'm going to be sick. I start to heave, and Sofia pulls over to the side of the road. I open the car door and throw up everything I had for dinner, all the champagne and maybe everything I've eaten over the last week. I puke until there's nothing left, and then I start throwing up bile. Sofia has her hand on my back. She's holding my hair back and hands me a tissue to wipe my mouth. This may be the first time I even registered that she's been here watching me, comforting me, and probably wondering what the hell happened to me.

"Thanks."

Those are the only words I can say.

"Babe, you don't need to tell me what happened. You're safe with me. I'm taking you back to my place. I don't want you alone tonight."

"Okay."

The tears slow, and I try to even my breathing. Sofia pulls back onto the road and begins driving. I feel empty.

*****

I woke up on Sofia's couch this morning with a headache and a broken heart. She had called over the rest of the girls, and we talked for hours. I told them everything, and when I was done talking, I cried some more. My friends are legitimately pissed at Jack. As mad as I want to be at him, I'm too hurt to be mad. I know I need to give him space to figure things out. If he realizes that I'm not the woman he wants in his life, I need to accept that. I've never loved anyone the way I love that man, but I just want him to find happiness. I want him to find peace. Maybe there's something wrong with me because as much as his words hurt, I still love him. I'm worried about him. I know he must be struggling too. I didn't know I could feel this kind of pain, and I just want it to stop. I wish I could just talk to him. I do the next best thing. I pick up my phone and text Jimmy.

> Me: Hi Jimmy. Please take care of him for me, ok?
>
> Jimmy: I'm trying but he's too pissed at the world.
>
> Me: Is he ok?
>
> Jimmy: No, but I hope he will be.
>
> Me: I miss him
>
> Jimmy: He's lucky to have you, Caroline. He'll figure it out. Are you ok?
>
> Me: No
>
> Jimmy: Can I do anything to help?
>
> Me: Just take care of him for me, and the girls.
>
> Jimmy: You have my word.

I drop my phone on the floor and close my eyes. Sofia comes out of her bedroom. She's all dressed and ready for the day.
"Hey, Care. How are you feeling?" she asks, concern written all over her face.
"Empty."
It's the only truth I can speak.
"I'm so sorry, honey. Can I get you anything?"
"No, but thanks for everything, Sofia. I think I'm going to go to the cemetery. I want to talk to my mom."
"Of course, Care Bear."
As soon as she says the words, I start to cry again.
"What did I do?"

"I made up nicknames for Ellie and Rosie. I call Ellie, Jelly Bean, and Rosie is Roly Poly. They call me Care Bear. Not seeing them is going to kill me."

I look down and see my phone is ringing.

"Oh, and look, Kathy's calling me. I have to say goodbye to all of them."

The tears come freer now, spilling from my face at an unprecedented speed. Sofia comes over to me and grabs the phone.

"Do you want me to answer?"

"No. Let it go to voice mail. He can fill her in on the details."

The phone stops ringing, and Sofia sets it on the table. She gives me a hug and then grabs a muffin off the table.

"Try to eat something. I'm sorry to leave you, honey, but I have to get to the studio. Stay as long as you like."

I nod my head and stare at the muffin.

"Thanks, Sofia."

I don't move, but I'm vaguely aware of her leaving the apartment.

CHAPTER 30

Jack

Last night fucking sucked. Caroline walking out nearly killed me. She's everything that's good, right, and just. I wanted to grab her and confess every last feeling I have to her so there's no doubt in her mind that I love her with every bone in my body. I want her to be my forever. I want her to be the mother to my girls. I want the fucking picket white fence and happily ever after with her. I want it all. She knew my darkest secrets, and she chose to love me anyways. She loves me when I can't even love myself. She looked past my dark secrets and accepted me as a man with so many faults. They're deeper than the Mariana Trench of the Pacific. I don't deserve that kind of love. I don't deserve her. How in the actual hell can I try to win her back when I'm so fucked up? She deserves so much better.

I snuck in the house last night long after everyone was asleep and didn't bother coming out this morning. The nanny probably thinks I'm at the hotel with Caroline. She took the girls to the park, and the house is empty. It's almost noon, and I haven't gotten out of bed. My phone keeps ringing, but I'm letting it go to voice mail. There's no one I want to talk to anyways. I hear the front door open, and my mom calls my name. Shit. I get out of bed and walk into the foyer.

"Mom, what's up?"

I try to hide the annoyance from my tone.

"Hey, I'm sorry to come by unannounced. I've been trying to respect your and Caroline's privacy."

Yeah, she actually has been doing a good job at that.

"She's not here."

My mother looks shocked, and it takes a lot to shock her.

"Oh. Okay, I was hoping to thank her for an incredible night last night. I called her, but she didn't answer. I was driving by and wanted to drop this off for her."

"What is it?"

I can't help but be curious.

"I found this little crystal ballerina when I went shopping with Judith this morning, and I wanted to give it to her as a thank-you. I immediately thought of her when I saw it."

"That's nice, Mom."

I don't want to tell her that she'll have to wait until dance class to give it to her.

"Jack, what's wrong?"

I let out a big sigh and run my hands through my hair.

"We broke up, Mom."

I think that's the simplest way to explain it.

"What? Why? What happened?"

She looks like she's going to cry. God, if this is a prelude to telling Rosie and Ellie, I'm fucked.

"I screwed up. Not just a little screw up but a massive screw up. I've got to fix some things before she'll take me back."

"Oh, Jack. Are you going to try and get her back?"

"I don't know if I can, Mom."

My phone starts ringing. I planned to ignore it, but it's Coach.

"It's Coach. I've got to take this."

I answer the phone as my mom stares at me in disbelief.

"Hi, Coach."

I hear the shuffling of papers.

"Hannen, what the hell happened last night?"

He sounds pissed.

"I'm sorry, sir. I lost my temper."

"Get your ass over to my office. We're having this conversation in person."

"I'm on my way."

I hang up the phone and see my mom staring at me with wide eyes.

"Jack, what the hell happened last night that made you break up with Caroline and have Coach make you come in today? And what do you mean you lost your temper?"

Little Miss Detective over here.

"I got in a fight with Jimmy after Caroline walked out. We'll talk later, Mom. I've got to go."

I turn around and head for my bathroom. I'm going to take a two-second shower and get dressed so I don't look like complete garbage when I apologize to Coach for acting like complete garbage.

Fifteen minutes later, I'm walking into the stadium. I make my way to Coach's office. He's sitting behind his desk, and Jimmy is sitting in one of the two chairs in front of it. They're talking about something when they see me in the doorway. They both look up at me, and Jimmy immediately tenses.

"I called you both in here to explain to me why two of my most senior players on the team, *leaders* on my team, are getting in a fist fight at our holiday party. Sit down, Hannen," Coach says sternly.

Jimmy doesn't say a word. He looks at the ground.

"I'm sorry, Coach. I was an idiot. I went after Jimmy. He was being a good friend, and I took my frustration about something else out on him."

Jimmy looks at me in disbelief.

"So we're cool?" he asks me incredulously.

"Yeah, if you can forgive me for being an asshole. I'm sorry, man."

"Don't worry about it. Water under the bridge."

Jimmy's always quick to forgive. To be honest, if we had gotten into it, he probably would have won. He's got an inch on me and almost twenty pounds. We both fight hard, but Jimmy takes it to a whole new level.

"I'm glad you two straightened that out. Now answer this for me, Jack. Why did my wife see Caroline standing alone, outside without a coat on, in freezing temperatures, and waiting for a ride?" Coach asks.

"I messed up there too, Coach."

I don't want to have this conversation a hundred times, but I already know I'm going to have it with several people who are important to both Caroline and me.

"Care to elaborate?"

Coach puts his hands together, interlacing his fingers, and leans toward me.

"She wants a real relationship, and I can't give that to her."

It hurts to even say it.

"Why can't you?"

I guess he's going to make me say it.

"Because of Bree, Coach. I don't want to ruin Caroline's life too. I love her too much. She deserves better."

Jimmy starts shaking his head.

"You're so fucking stupid sometimes, Jack."

Coach looks at Jimmy and then me. He pauses for a minute before he speaks.

"Jack, I screwed up with you. You told me you didn't need to talk to a therapist after Bree's death, and I let you get away with that. Your parents had just moved here, and it seemed like you had a good support system at the time. You were playing well, and although you were much quieter and more reserved, you didn't seem as broken as you do right now. I'm not giving you a choice this time. You're going to talk to a therapist. You should have years ago."

"I'm not going to fight you on it this time, Coach."

Maybe this is what I need to do to see if I can be with Caroline. I'm willing to fight for her. I want to be better for her. I just want her.

"Good. I'll set it up. Plan on going immediately after practice tomorrow."

I nod.

"I'm glad that's established. You two can go home and enjoy your day off. I'll see you early tomorrow morning."

"Thanks, Coach."

We both stand and shake Coach's hand. As we're walking out, Jimmy puts his hand on my shoulder.

"I'm sorry too. I thought I was helping," he says.

"You were right. I was too much of a coward to tell her myself. I'm glad you did. Crazy shit is she didn't even care. She said she loved me more because of it."

"She texted me this morning. She asked me to take care of you and make sure you're okay," he says.

"God, Jimmy. Why can't I just be fucking normal? She's the best thing that's ever happened to me."

"You'll win her back. I have confidence in you."

"I just hope I can get my shit together before some other guy swoops in."

I'm sick to my stomach.

"Nah, she loves you too much. Just make sure she knows you still care."

Chapter 31

Caroline

I'm glad I'm done with school because I wouldn't have made it to class this morning. Graduation is next week. My dad and Cody will be here, which means I'm going to have to figure out what to tell them. Cody's going to immediately know something's up, and he'll know its related to Jack. He still thinks I deserve better than a fuck buddy. I will never tell him the things Jack said that prompted me to end things, but I think enough information will be written all over my face. Right now, I need to focus on one day at a time, and I'll worry about my brother next week.

I'm supposed to teach dance this afternoon. I have jazz and tap this evening. I'm going to have to clear my head before then because I'm a mess right now. I'm curious if Rosie and Ellie will be at class on Tuesday. I'm going to have to figure out what to say to them, and Kathy, if she brings them. Maybe I should text Jack and ask him if he has a preference on what I say to his daughters. I don't want to contradict anything he's told them. No, I know I can't text him. I will not text him. I need to stay strong. This may be the toughest thing I've ever done, but I'm going to do it, and I'm going to come out stronger. We are going to come out stronger. This is not permanent. He's going to apologize and fix this. I have to believe that, or I will collapse in a mound of self-pity.

I finally left Sofia's apartment but not before noon. I stopped at a little street vendor and bought some flowers. I'm heading to the cemetery now. I thought I'd talk to Mom first, but instead, I walk over to Bree's tomb. There's a light snow that's fallen, so I clean it off and pull some of the frozen, overgrown grass and weeds away from the tombstone. Once it's as clean as I can get it, I sit down on the blanket I brought. I bought two flowers for Bree. One is a rose for Rosie, which seemed obvious but also fitting of her personality. The other is a Gerber daisy for Ellie. It's bright pink and a little bit sassy like Ellie. Thinking of them made me smile.

I start to talk to Bree. I tell her how much I love Jack, Ellie, and Rosie. I tell her how beautiful her two little girls are. I tell her about Rosie's love for arts and crafts and books. I tell her about how much she loves cooking with me. I talk to her about Ellie's athleticism and how she loves kicking the soccer ball around the backyard with Jack and spends hours on her bike. I tell her about the girls' ballet class and how it somehow fits both of their personalities. I tell her about Rosie rolling and tumbling all over the place when we do our freestyle dances and how fitting the name Roly Poly is. I talk to her about Jack. I tell her what a wonderful father he is and how he's taking such good care of their girls. I tell her how loving, fun, and sweet he is. I tell her about the voices he makes when he's playing Barbies and how good he's getting at braids.

I ask her to forgive Jack. I tell her about how much grief and guilt he's carried all these years. I tell her that he's having trouble moving on. I tell her how much I love him. I tell her how badly I want to be a permanent part of his life and a permanent part of the girl's lives. I tell her about my mom and how hard it was once I lost her. I promise Bree that if given the opportunity, I'll be the best mother possible to her two little girls. I beg her to let Jack go and let him be free to move forward. After all my begging, I simply sit in silence in front of her grave. Snowflakes start gently falling down from the sky. They're big and fluffy, and it's as if they're being dropped from the heavens. I look up and watch them fall. I know it sounds crazy, but in that moment, I feel Bree's presence. It feels as if she's telling me she hears me and everything is going to be okay. I finally feel ready to leave her grave. I walk to my mom's and put the fresh flowers down on her grave as well. I don't talk to her for as long as I normally would. I think I'm too emotionally drained. But I don't need to. I know, deep down in my core, that Jack is going to come out of this a happier, more fulfilled man. I can't wait to see the real him. I just need to stay strong.

*****

Jack

I'm nervous. I don't remember the last time I've been truly nervous. I get a little anxious before games but not like this. This is a feeling of unease. I've never been great talking about my feelings and shit. Now I've got to tell my life story to a complete stranger. My palms are sweaty. After meeting with Coach yesterday, Jimmy and I went to lunch. I owe that guy everything. He's been a great friend to me, and he hasn't had it easy himself. But he's the guy who's always there when you need him. When I got home, both of my parents were at the house with a million questions. The only thing that seemed to get them off my back was knowing that I agreed to go to counseling. Talking to Rosie and Ellie was the hardest. There were tears and lots of confusion. They begged me to make Caroline their mommy. That part was the absolute worst. I promised them I'd try. I intend to keep that promise, which is why I'm here now.

Coach has me meeting with the doctor in one of our conference rooms. I know a lot of the guys on the team talk with him to deal with anxiety or other shit they're going through. I just never thought I'd have to see a therapist myself. I knock on the door when I get to the room. A guy in his midforties answers. He's got a bit of a beer gut and is balding. He's cleanly shaven with glasses, and he's wearing khakis and a blazer.

"You must be Jack. I'm Dr. Reed. Come on in."

I enter the room. It's got a couch and two lounge chairs on one end, a conference table on another, and a little mini fridge with some snacks and drinks over by the windows.

"Nice to meet you. Thanks for meeting with me."

I gulp. I extend my hand to his. He grabs my hand and gives me a good, firm handshake.

"Great to meet you too, Jack. Have a seat wherever you'd like. You want something to drink?"

I take a seat in one of the leather seats. No way in hell am I going to lie on the couch and start spilling my guts like you see in the movies.

"No, thanks. I'm good."

"I read your bio online. You've been with the Wolves for quite a while now. You've got some incredible stats."

"Thanks."

Am I supposed to start telling him my deepest, darkest secrets now? This is weird.

"Jack, I sense you're a little unsure about being here. We can talk about nothing and anything. It's up to you. We don't need to discuss your entire life in one session."

"Sorry. I've never done this before. Well, I take that back. My wife and I did some couples therapy years ago, but she did almost all the talking, and I did my best to talk as little as possible. I usually just bury my feelings, so talking about them is kind of weird."

"I can see that. A lot of men do that. Don't show emotion. It makes you look weak type of thing, right?"

"Yeah, exactly."

I let out an exhale.

"Do you know why your coach wanted me to meet with you?" he asks.

Is he going to make me start talking now?

"Yeah. Do you?"

"All I know is, and I quote, 'he's got some shit to work through.' That's all he gave me." He chuckles. "Don't we all?"

"I guess we do."

I decide to just go for it. I start talking. I tell my story. He listens, asks insightful questions, and makes me delve into the why I felt the way I did about certain things. I don't have all the answers, and he doesn't give them to me. After an hour, he gives me a homework assignment. It's simple, but it feels hard. He asks me if I'd be comfortable telling Caroline I'm in therapy. I am. I think she should know, and it might make things easier for her while I figure my shit out. So he encouraged me to tell her. I don't think I'm ready to see her. It will hurt too bad. I could call her, but even hearing her voice and the possibility of hearing her cry, knowing that I caused that pain, makes me quickly rule that option out too. I decide for the coward's way out—a simple text.

>Me: Hey
>
>Caroline: Hey you
>
>Me: I just wanted to let you know I'm seeing a therapist. He thought it would be good for me to let you know.
>
>Caroline: That makes me really happy, Jack.
>
>Me: I'm trying, Caroline.
>
>Caroline: I know you are. I can't tell you how much that means to me.
>
>Me: The girls still want to dance tomorrow. Is that ok?
>
>Caroline: Of course. I miss them.
>
>Me: We miss you too.
>
>Caroline: Tomorrow then.
>
>Me: Yeah. Tomorrow. I have a game so Mom is bringing them.
>
>Caroline: Good luck.
>
>Me: Thanks

I set my phone down and stare at the floor. I know I can do this. I want to do this. But damn, facing this shit head-on is going to be the hardest thing I've ever done. A few minutes later, my phone pings with a new text message. I look down.

> Caroline: Would it be ok for me to spend the night at your house tomorrow with the girls? I know you'll be gone for your game, which is why I thought it would be a good time. I've grown really attached and I miss them. I think it would be good for me and them to have some time together. If you think it would be confusing for them, I don't need to come.
>
> Me: I think we would all love that.
>
> Caroline: Thank you

Typical Caroline. Doesn't she realize I should be thanking her? She's the perfect amount of honey, and my world is a much sweeter place with her in it.

*****

Caroline

It's Tuesday. I'm so excited and maybe even a little nervous to see the girls. They come barreling into the studio a little earlier than normal, no doubt to give us a few minutes before class. I've just finished with my previous group when I feel someone hugging my legs. I look down and see Rosie with both her arms and legs completely wrapped around my right leg.

"We miss you."

I can see the tears starting to form in her eyes, and I need to hold my own back. Jack is out of town for the next three days, and I plan to spend them with his girls.

"I miss you too. Would it be okay if I came for a sleepover tonight?" I ask, looking at Kathy.

Kathy nods her head in agreement.

"I think that would be a great idea," Kathy says.

"Daddy said you might spend the night," Ellie says, sounding hopeful.

"Well, I definitely want to. I miss my girls. Plus your daddy said it was okay."

"Really?"

Ellie's excited now.

"Yep. Should we do popcorn and a movie?" I ask, knowing neither one can resist popcorn.

"Yes!" Rosie squeezes my leg tighter. "I'm so happy you're coming over."

"Me too, Roly Poly."

I bend down and give them each a hug. They hand me the artwork they made for me, and I make a big show about how good it is. I give Kathy the biggest, longest hug in the world and am so grateful that she's so supportive throughout all of this. Sofia walks over and gives everyone hugs too. Then she gives me a little squeeze. I think she knows how hard I'm trying to keep it together. Class is about to begin, so I change gears and begin welcoming my other students while everyone gathers in our designated studio. After class, I gather my things, give the girls another hug, and make my way over to Jack's.

*****

Jack

I'm back in town. We played really well as a team, and the positive energy in the locker room has been contagious. It's helping me to stay afloat as I try to navigate these uncharted waters of life without Caroline. I shouldn't say life without her. She's my motivation, but not being able to see or touch her is its own form of torture. I'm figuring my shit out. I just keep telling myself that. She's the lighthouse in the storm, and I just have to find my way back to her. I know she's there waiting for me, and I know she deserves all of me, not bits and pieces.

Caroline has spent the last few nights at home with my girls. I got a glimpse of her when they FaceTimed me, and I think she's even more beautiful now than she was the first time I met her. It sounds pathetic, but I asked her to sleep in my bed while she was at my house. I wanted my sheets to smell like her. I even called the housekeeper to tell her not to change my sheets. If that's not creepy, I don't know what is. But apparently, I'm creepy and pathetic now. I asked Dr. Reed if we could meet again this week now that I'm back.

I'm heading to his office now. Dr. Reed greets me when I walk up to his assigned conference room. I sit in the same chair, but this time, I accept a water. We spend a few minutes talking about this last string of away games. The guy really loves hockey. He asks me if I talked to Caroline about therapy, and I update him. I'm slightly embarrassed, but I even mention the creepy and pathetic bedsheets thing. He nods like he understands. It's a way to feel close to her. We talk about her upcoming graduation. I want to be there to support her, but I question my readiness to be with her. This will be my first time meeting her father, and her brother already thinks I'm an asshole, so I've got some work to do. I plan to attend the ceremony and not go to dinner after, but I'm not sure if she's going to be okay with that. Call me a pussy, but I want to minimize any awkward conversation with her father and brother until Caroline and I are back to where we should be. Dinner would be too much for me.

She loves pearls, and I got her a pair of pearl and diamond earrings. They're stunning, and they instantly made me think of her. They cost a small fortune, but I want her to have them. I've never given her anything before, and I really want to do this for her. Dr. Reed and I talk for the full hour. He actually has to end it so that he isn't late for his next client. He didn't give me a homework assignment because he thinks the graduation is going to be enough for me. I think he's right.

Chapter 32

Jack

Caroline's graduation day has arrived. I haven't spoken with her since she was here with the girls a few days ago. I should probably tell her I'm going. She hasn't texted, asking me, and I haven't let her know in case she doesn't want me there. Honestly, I cannot imagine not being there. I want to be there to support her. I want her to know how much I love her. I want so badly to fix everything I screwed up.

If I thought I was anxious to meet with the therapist, meeting Caroline's father is a whole new level of anxiety. I want to make a good impression, and since I have no intention of going to dinner, I want to get there a little early to try and win Caroline's dad over. Of course, things can't just go as planned. I got into a pretty good fight last night on the ice and had to have a few stitches right above my right eye. I have a fat lip, and I look fucking ridiculous. Then our team meeting ran late, and I didn't bring a suit with me because I thought I had time to go home and change. I really didn't have time to go home, but since I had to, I'm now late. The auditorium is full when I walk in, but I have no problem finding my assigned seat. I shake a few hands of fans on my way down and then take my seat next to Cody.

"Hey, Jack. Cutting it a little close there, huh?"

It must look like I'm late all the time because I was late for the dinner we had a few months ago too. Yet another strike against me.

"Yeah, sorry. It's good to see you, Cody."

I hold out my hand. He looks at me for a minute and then shakes it.

"She didn't know if you'd make it or not. I'm sure she'll be glad you're here."

"I wouldn't miss her special day for anything."

He nods his head and doesn't say anything. Then he turns to the man next to him.

"Dad, this is Caroline's friend, Jack Hannen. Jack, this is my dad, Bruce Britton."

I lean over to shake Bruce's hand.

"It's nice to meet you, sir," I say. "Caroline's told me a lot about you."

"It's nice to meet you too, Jack. I've heard a lot about you, Rosie, and Ellie."

I'm surprised by this. I didn't think Caroline talked to her dad all that much, and I especially didn't expect him to know my daughter's names.

"Caroline has made me believe in love again, sir. She's incredible. My daughters agree."

I hope he knows I'm being sincere and not trying to play him.

"You can quit with the sir stuff. Bruce is fine. Jack, meet Anne."

He puts his arm around the woman sitting next to him, and she looks at him with adoration. She then turns to me.

"Hi, Jack. You're right. Caroline is incredible."

She smiles at me with a knowing look, and I'm confused. I didn't think Caroline's father was in a relationship, let alone with someone who appears to know Caroline so well. Bruce then takes the lead again. It's clear he's a man who is used to having people listen when he speaks.

"I hope I'm not being too forward, but we know you and Caroline are working through some stuff. She didn't give us any specifics, and she didn't even know if you'd come today, but I'm glad you're here. I could tell it was important to her."

Well, shit. Talk about having to dig myself out of a hole.

"I would never miss something important to her, Bruce, and I genuinely mean that."

I should have called her and told her I'd be here. That would have saved me this awkward conversation twice now.

"I wasn't too fond of her dating a hockey player, especially one with your reputation. I'm still not, but I'm hopeful you'll be able to prove me wrong."

This guy is intimidating as fuck. No way am I going to win him over in the few minutes we have to talk before things get started. Just then, the dean of the college takes the podium to announce that the commencement is beginning. I don't get the chance to respond to Bruce, so I give him a nod and turn my attention to the stage. My phone pings, and I silently curse myself for not putting it on vibrate. I quickly check the message.

Caroline: Thanks for coming

I look down at the sea of graduates and see her looking up at me with a small smile on her face. My chest aches, and the longing I feel for her is almost unbearable. I give a little wave, and she waves back at me. It reminds me of that dance recital all those months ago and again the first time I saw her unexpectedly at my game. Suddenly, I don't want to be away from her a minute longer. I will go to dinner tonight, and I'm going to remind her why we're so good together. I'm going to prove to her family that I'm not some dumb jock, and I'm not going anywhere. This might not be the right decision, but I physically can't be apart from her any longer. I continue to stare long after she's turned around to pay attention to the speaker. I don't think I absorbed anything that was said during the entire ceremony. I do remember her gliding across the stage and getting her diploma, with honors I might add, but the rest of it is a complete blur. After the ceremony, we all meet in the foyer of the auditorium. Bruce, Cody, Anne, and I wait for Caroline, and the conversation is again strained. Cody is definitely not trying to make things easy for me. Luckily, we don't have to wait too long before she comes out.

She's glowing. She runs straight for me and wraps her arms around me. She gives me a quick peck on the lips, gives me a wink, and squeezes my arms. She then hugs Cody, her father, and Anne. It was a power play on her end, and I'm so incredibly grateful. She basically told the other men in her life that she's mine and to get used to it. God, I love her. I don't know if she has any idea how much I needed that.

"I'm so excited you're all here! Anne, I haven't seen you in forever! What a pleasant surprise!"

She grabs Anne's hand and gives it a squeeze.

"I'm happy to be here. Congratulations, Caroline."

I'm going to have to ask Caroline about Anne later. We get a few pictures with Caroline in her cap and gown, and then it's time to leave.

"All right, guys, why don't we head to the restaurant where we can all catch up? I'll ride over with Jack, and we can meet you there."

Once again, she makes me her first priority. She's also giving us a chance to talk before dinner. Every little thing she does proves her love for me. I want to be the man she deserves so badly. We head for our cars once Caroline's confirmed everyone has the name and the address of the restaurant. It's only about a fifteen-minute drive, and there's so much we need to say to one another. I grab her hand in mine and lead the way to my car. I wait until we're out of earshot of her family before I start talking.

"Thanks for making me feel so welcome. I wasn't sure you'd want me here," I say it sheepishly like I'm waiting for a lecture.

"Jack, seriously? Of course, I want you here. I would have been really upset if you *weren't* here."

She looks at me like I'm an idiot, but I haven't seen her in person since that night she broke things off, the night I threw it all away.

"I never apologized for the stuff I said at the holiday party."

I swallow.

"No. You didn't."

She looks at me, waiting.

"I am so incredibly sorry for being disrespectful and for hurting you. My behavior was unacceptable. You deserve so much better."

"You're right. I do."

"You mean so much more to me than I let on, and I hope you know how much I care about you."

She's quiet for a minute. She looks at me with questioning eyes.

"Are you working through your shit, Jack?"

"I am. I'm trying really hard."

She lets out a long exhale and squeezes my hand.

"Then you're forgiven. But, Jack, this is the second time you've really hurt me. I'm trying to stay strong for you, and it's hard."

"I'm so sorry, Caroline. You mean everything to me. Please just be patient with me."

We've reached my car. I walk around to her side to open her door. Instead of getting into her seat, she turns toward me, grabs me by my tie, pulls me in, and kisses me. At first, I'm so shocked I don't kiss her back. Then realization strikes. I take my hands off the car door and pull her into my arms. I wrap my hands on the angle of her jaw, enveloping her face in my hands, and I kiss her like it's the last kiss I'll ever get. There's so much passion and love in this kiss that I never want it to end. A car driving by beeps at us, and some guy shouts.

"Get a room!"

Just like that, our trance is broken. We look at each other and start laughing. A huge smile spreads across my face, but after she stops laughing, she looks worried.

"I'm sorry. I shouldn't have kissed you."

"Caroline, I really needed that. Thank you for loving me and believing in me."

She nods. I'm so close to telling her. I just can't yet. I need her to be patient for just a little longer. I'm trying so hard to be the man she needs.

"I have so much I want to say to you, but I just can't yet."

I reach into my coat pocket and pull out the box from the jewelers.

"Congratulations on your graduation, babe."

I hand her the box. She unwraps the silver paper and takes the bow off. She opens the little black velvet box and looks up at me with questioning eyes. When she finally opens the gift, she gasps.

"Oh my god, Jack. These are gorgeous. This is way too much."

"Nothing is too much for you, Caroline. I'd give you the world."

Tears form in her eyes.

"Thank you."

"Beautiful, it's freezing out here. Let's get in the car."

She smiles and scoots into the car. I shut her door and walk around to mine. She's got the vanity mirror down from the overhead visor and is putting the earrings on.

"I can't believe you remembered I love pearls. I think I only mentioned it once months ago," she says as I start the car and blast the heat.

I turn on the seat warmers for us and wait for the windows to clear so I can pull out.

"I store that kind of information away," I say as I tap the side of my head.

She gives me a sad smile and grabs my hand.

"How are you?"

"Miserable. I miss you. This is really fucking hard."

She nods her head slowly.

"Jack, we both know this is for the best."

She leans over and kisses my cheek. The windows are clear enough for me to see out of, and I slowly pull out.

"Caroline, what do your dad and brother know? They both told me you didn't think I was going to show up today. I guess I just want to know what I'm up against."

"I told them I love you with my whole heart, but you're going through some stuff right now, and we needed to take a little break while you figure some things out. Then I told them that you were invited to graduation, but I wasn't sure if you'd be able to make it."

"Okay. What does your dad know about the girls?"

"Just that I love them too, and they've become my world."

I swallow. Not only am I responsible for their mother's death, but I've now sabotaged the relationship they have with Caroline too, a woman who has stepped into the role as their mother without any hesitation.

"Stop blaming yourself, Jack. It's not your fault."

She knew exactly where my mind had gone.

"How long have you known?"

"I ran into Jimmy at the coffee shop right after we talked about Bree. I felt like I was missing some important information and was struggling. I don't know if you realize it, but he and I have talked about you a few times now. He's a big part of the reason I stuck with you in the beginning."

"After you left the holiday party, I figured it was him and lost my shit. I started a fight and was throwing punches when my teammates tore me off him. I was a mess."

"Oh no, Jack, you didn't! He was being a good friend whether you realize it or not."

"I realized that after I cooled off. I apologized. We're good now. I ended up thanking him because I didn't have the courage to tell you myself."

"Nothing you could ever tell me would make me love you less."

"I'm starting to believe that."

I pull into the parking lot.

"Okay. Last question. I thought your dad wasn't in a relationship? Who is Anne, and how do you know her?"

"Anne is my dad's secretary. She's been with him for probably twenty years. She's the sweetest woman in the world. My dad had mentioned that she lost her husband suddenly to a heart attack about a year ago, but he hasn't mentioned her since. She's always been so kind to me and Cody."

I pull up to a valet, and I'm glad that it's available. The parking lot is a slushy mess, and I would have had to carry Caroline so she didn't have to trample through the snow in her heels.

"All right, anything else I need to know before I go inside?"

"I think you got all the major bullet points on the ride over."

I pull her hand up to my lips and give her a kiss.

"Let's do this then."

*****

Caroline

He's here. He made it. He's shown his love for me once again. I know he didn't mean the horrible things he said, and I need to just focus on his actions. The words will come. Trying to balance the myriad of emotions I'm feeling is leaving me utterly exhausted. I know I shouldn't have kissed him, but I couldn't help it. I want to be close to him. I want so badly to just melt into him and tell him all is well. I want to tell him I'll take whatever version of himself he wants to give me even if he can't give me all of himself. But I know I can't. I deserve more than he's giving me, and he deserves more than he's giving himself. I want him to find happiness, and if I don't push him, he's going to continue down this path of self-loathing indefinitely. I'm taking a huge risk of losing him forever here. I just hope my plan ends with us together.

"There they are!" Cody says as Jack and I walk in hand in hand.

Gosh, it's almost adorable how nervous Jack is around my family. I wasn't sure how long everything would take at the graduation, and we are a few minutes early for our reservation.

"Jack, let's go grab a drink at the bar while they get our table ready."

I say a silent prayer that Cody isn't a total asshole to Jack.

"Sure, Cody. Sounds great. Can I get you anything, beautiful?"

"Chardonnay would be great. Thanks, handsome."

He kisses me on the cheek.

"Chardonnay it is. What about you, Anne?"

"I'll have a chardonnay too. Thanks, Jack."

"Two chardonnays. You're making it easy on me. Bruce?"

"I'm all set. Thanks," my dad says as he puts his arm around Anne.

It's interesting. I've never seen them touch each other before.

"All right. We'll be back soon."

Jack turns, puts his hand on Cody's shoulder, and gives a little squeeze. I'm scrutinizing their interaction closely. Otherwise, I don't think I would have heard Jack.

"Before you give me any shit this time, Cody, I love your sister, and I'm not letting her go, okay?"

Cody turns to look at Jack with a huge smile on his face.

"Then I guess I have no reason to be a dick to you."

Wait! Did I just hear that correctly? Did he just tell my brother he loves me? I must have misheard him. Only, my dad is watching them too.

"On second thought, I'm going to get a bourbon."

My dad winks at me and jogs over toward the guys. I'm left standing speechless. Anne nudges me with her hip.

"You hit the jackpot, Caroline. That man is sexy as sin even with the stitches. I may be twice his age, but I'm not blind."

I turn to Anne.

"Did he just say he loves me?"

"That's what I heard. You should have seen him during your graduation ceremony. He watched you like a lovesick puppy the entire time. I don't know how you tamed such a playboy, but it looks like you're the only woman he sees now."

"Anne, he's never told me he loves me."

I'm in a state of shock. I hoped he loved me. I knew he cared about me. Jimmy had told me Jack loved me. My girlfriends all say he does. But that was everyone thinking they knew what he was feeling. It was never from his own mouth. I've been going off his actions. I've been convincing myself that everything he does for me is out of love, and deep down, I believed it to be true. But to hear him say those words to me? I need that. I guess I didn't realize how badly I needed him to tell me until this moment.

"Sweetheart, men are complicated. He'll tell you when he's ready."

I don't know how to respond to her, so I just keep looking at the three most important men in my life. She tries again. This time, the men are too far away for me to hear any of their conversation.

"Your earrings are stunning, Caroline."

"Thank you. Jack just gave them to me."

I smile at her.

"He's got nice taste."

"Yeah, he really does. I love them."

I can't help but reach for them.

"Your dad didn't tell you that he and I are dating, did he?"

That snaps me out of my fog.

"No way! You are?"

She smiles.

"I had hoped he would tell you. Cody seemed surprised to see me too. I really love him, Caroline."

She looks worried, and I don't blame her. I hug her, trying to provide reassurance.

"You're not like the others, Anne. This much, I know."

"Excuse me, ladies? Your table is now ready."

The host interrupts our moment, and we break the hug. I wave the guys over. Jack and my dad are each holding a glass of chardonnay along with their drinks. Once we're seated, my dad lifts his glass.

"I'd like to propose a toast."

Everyone lifts their glass.

"Caroline, I'm so incredibly proud of the woman you've become. I know your heart wasn't in this degree, but as usual, you worked hard and pushed through. Tonight, we celebrate you. We celebrate your success. We celebrate your work ethic, and we celebrate you finding love. We wish you nothing but a life full of happiness. To Caroline!"

Everyone cheers their glasses around, and I feel like this entire evening has been one huge mind fuck. What the hell did Jack say to him? Why would my father be celebrating me finding love if he didn't know Jack loved me? I already told him that I love Jack and his daughters, but I have no idea if Jack's feelings for me even scratch the surface of what I feel for him. I once told Jack my greatest fear was being in a relationship where the depths of my love aren't reciprocated. I just told him I loved him half an hour ago, and once again, he couldn't say it back. I'm trying to hold the tears back, but I'm on the verge of a meltdown. Maybe it would have been better if he weren't here tonight. This is so much harder than I thought it was going to be.

Jack squeezes my hand, and my gaze meets his. I can see the questioning in his eyes, and I want to scream at him. What kind of game is this? Is he trying to break me? My thoughts are interrupted because my dad starts to speak again.

"Cody and Caroline, I've been waiting to tell you this in person. Jack, I'll give you a little history. Anne has been my secretary for twenty-five years. When we started working together, we were both married and very much in love with our spouses. When my wife died, I was a wreck. I had truly lost my better half. Anne was there for me, offering support, inviting me over for meals. Her late husband, Ken, and I golfed together and also became very close. They were my people. Anne encouraged me to start dating again, and I made some foolish decisions. I thought I would marry again for friendship or companionship but had closed my heart off to the idea of love. My last two wives will tell you I was a total asshole, and I'd have to agree. About a year and a half ago, Ken died unexpectedly of a heart attack. It was my turn to be there for Anne. We've always been close, but our losses brought us closer. A few months ago, our friendship blossomed into something more, and I want you kids to know that I've found love again. Anne has opened my eyes that it's never too late to open your heart."

"Good for you, Dad! I was wondering what was going on with you this visit!"

Cody reaches over and hugs them both. Happy tears flow down my face. I get up from my seat and kiss my dad. I pull Anne in for a hug, who's eyes are also glossy. Despite whatever mind games Jack is playing with me, seeing my dad in love and happy is an indescribable feeling. Jack stands, shakes my dad's hand, and also gives Anne a hug. The remainder of the meal is happy and light. Jack is back to his usual self, touching me every chance he gets. His arm is around me. He's playing with my hair. He's rubbing circles on my back.

Our meal ends too soon, and it's time to say goodbye. I don't know where we go from here. Does he think he's coming home with me? I won't invite him. Does he think we're back where we were? Because we most definitely are not there. As we walk toward the door, he answers my questions for me.

"I'm sorry I didn't mention it earlier, but if you all want to come to my game tomorrow night, you're more than welcome. I left tickets under Caroline's name. My parents also said you could sit in their box with them and my daughters, but I wanted to give you options. There's no pressure at all, and I know that you're in town for a short visit, so if you'd rather do something else, that's fine too. I just wanted to extend the offer."

"I'm in!" Cody says. "Does your dad always stock his box with good microbrews, or was that a one-time thing?"

Jack laughs.

"I'll personally see to it that there's a large selection of microbrews for you, Cody."

"Thanks, man. You guys ready to leave?"

"I'm actually going to part ways with you here. Thanks for including me. Caroline, I forgot I have a gift for you from my parents in my car."

Just then, the valet pulls around with our vehicles. My dad drove Cody and Anne, and they head toward his car.

"I'll be right there. I'm just going to grab my gift really quick," I say.

I start to walk toward Jack's car, and he follows after saying his goodbyes. When we get to the car, he pulls me into his arms and kisses my forehead. He looks down at me.

"Your dad's story gives me hope."

That's all he says, nothing more, not *Hey, Caroline, I know I told your dad and brother I love you. Maybe I should tell you too*, or *Hey, babe, it was a great night. I love you.* What? Did he not have hope for us before? I don't know if I'm strong enough to do this. I muster all my courage and say it again.

"I love you, Jack."

He doesn't say it back. He doesn't try to kiss me. He gives me a small smile and then reaches into his car. He hands me a small gift bag.

"When I first saw you in the auditorium today, I thought, God, I want her back. I want her to be mine. I want to remind her of how good we are together. I want her now and forever."

"I am yours," I say it, pleading.

He has to understand how hard this is for me. He leans down and whispers in my ear.

"And I'm yours."

He grabs my hand and walks me over to my dad's rental car. He opens the door for me, and I get in.

"Good night, everyone. Thanks for a fun evening."

With that, he shuts the door and walks back to his own car. I try to hide my emotions. I stare out the car window while the conversation goes on without me. Tears flow silently down my cheeks. Cody puts his arm around me. Does he know? Does he know how fucked up this whole thing is? What is wrong with me? Why can't I find someone who will love me the way I love them?

Chapter 33

Jack

Last night's game was rough. It should have been an easy win, and instead, we got our asses kicked. Caroline and her family started the evening in the seats I got for them but ended with my family in the box. I don't notice these things during the game. I'm focused on what I'm doing on the ice, but my mom always manages to fill me in on the details afterward. She kept going on and on about how much she loves Caroline's family and how happy the girls were to spend the evening with her. I texted Caroline twice today and haven't gotten a response. I know her family is all heading to the airport to head home, so I'm assuming she's just tied up.

I could tell she was confused about her dad's toast. I don't think she knows that I told her dad and Cody exactly how I feel about her, especially when I haven't been able to tell her myself. I don't know how to explain my actions other than to say I wanted the men in her life to know that I'll always love and protect her. I want them to know I'm not a playboy looking for a good time but a man who is dedicated and in love. But once I make that declaration to Caroline personally, it means that I'm able to leave everything with Bree in the past and focus solely on Caroline and our future. I think I'm getting there, but I've been burying this shit for years. Two sessions with a therapist aren't going to undo years of self-hatred.

Listening to Bruce the other night and watching him and Anne did something to me. It made me realize that I *am* allowed a second chance at love. Bruce just needed the right woman to get him there, and I can fully understand that. Caroline is that woman for me. It's time to confront my past before I lose her. I could feel her pulling away the night of her graduation, and it killed me to leave her. I called Dr. Reed and am meeting with him this morning. I want to talk to him about the graduation and everything that happened. That night may have been the final push I needed. When I arrive at our usual meeting spot, Dr. Reed greets me with a handshake. We talk about last night's game. I help myself to a bottle of water, and then I tell him everything that happened the night of the graduation.

Conversation shifts to Bree. We talk about the night of her death. We talk about her funeral and burial. These are things I haven't thought about in years. They're things I've never talked about and I don't want to talk about. But somehow, talking about it and saying this shit out loud is necessary for me to move on. Dr. Reed wants me to go to the cemetery and visit Bree. I haven't been to the cemetery since the day we buried her, and I really don't want to go back. I feel like going there is going to bring me right back to that day, and I've been trying to forget that day for so long. He told me it's not about forgetting. It's about accepting so that I can move forward. That resonated with me, and I agreed to go. Every time I think of Bree, I think about those last heated words I said to her and the names I called her, and I feel sick to my stomach. Since burying the thoughts hasn't worked, maybe facing them head-on is a better approach. I guess I'm about to find out.

I leave our meeting and head straight to the cemetery. I know if I go home first, I'm never going to do this. As I get out of my car, I realize how fucking cold it is out. Christmas is right around the corner, and it's always a hard time of year for me. I feel so much more guilt that the girls don't have their mom at Christmastime. It reminds me that the anniversary of her death is approaching, and this is usually the time I shut down. If I hadn't pushed Caroline away already, I know I would have within these upcoming few weeks. At least now I can admit that.

I was in such a haze the morning of the funeral and burial that I honestly don't remember exactly where her tombstone is located. I walk around for longer than I'd like to admit looking for it. When I get there, I see that someone has brushed the snow off, and there are two flowers resting in front of it. There are footsteps in the snow, and I'm utterly confused. I don't know who would have visited her here. She had no real family. Her mom died of an overdose last year, and I don't think there was anyone else who cared enough about her to visit her grave. That sick realization makes me feel bad for her, and again, I go into my normal mode of wishing I could have given her the life she always wanted.

I stand there staring blankly at the flowers and the tombstone. I want to scream at her for fucking up our family. I want to stop feeling like shit every day of my fucking life. I want to accept that this was all a terrible turn of events and not my fault. I want to accept that this was her fate. I want to be free of this guilt that weighs me down. I want to look in the mirror and not hate the man I see. I want to believe I didn't ruin my daughters' lives by kicking their mother out that night. I want to believe I'm not a monster. I fall to my knees and start sobbing. I don't try to stop. I cry so hard that every muscle in my body shakes. I put my hands on the cold stone and fall on top of it. There's snot, tears, and spit, and my whole fucking face aches. After some time, it stops. I can't find any more tears to let out. I wipe my face with the back of my hand, and I sit up. I drop my ass onto the heels of my shoes, and I sit there, trying to catch my breath. I look up and see a woman in the distance staring at me. She's rooted in place. Even though my vision is still blurred, I know, I just know, it's her. It's my angel, my saving grace, my Caroline.

Once she realizes she's been spotted, she begins walking toward me. She's holding two flowers in her hand, identical to the wilted ones on Bree's tombstone. I don't move. I couldn't if I tried. I sit there and watch the woman I want more than anything in this world walk over to me. I'm suddenly overcome with emotion. The tears start falling down my face again, and I don't try to push them away. This is me. Raw. Real. Fucking broken. This is the man she claims to love. She needs to see me like this. She stops once she's standing directly in front of me, between me and the tombstone, and lets the flowers fall. She drops to her knees and brushes my tears away. She kisses my forehead while she holds my jaw in her hands. I look up into her eyes, and I see so much love. She puts her lips to mine, softly brushing them over the top of mine. She moves over me, straddling me in the cold snow. She puts her arms around my neck and rests her head on my shoulder. I instinctively wrap my arms around her. I let the tears continue to fall. At first, neither one of us speaks. Then I take a breath and begin.

"I've blamed myself for years. I've hated myself for years. I robbed my daughters of a mother. She would have never died if it weren't for me, so I've sabotaged every good thing that came my way. I never thought I deserved it. I couldn't make her happy, so for some fucked-up reason, I don't deserve to be happy."

I pause, but she doesn't move or speak. She gives me the time I need to plunge on.

"And then you came along. You made me feel alive again. You made me feel loved. You made me feel like I might be able to have more. You made me believe that happiness is within my reach. You made me want to be better. You made me want you."

I want to look at her, so I move my hands to her shoulders and push her back. I rest my hands on her shoulders and put my forehead on hers. I stare into her eyes.

"I love you, Caroline, with every fiber in my body. I love you more than I thought was humanly possible. I have loved you for so long, and I have been so afraid to tell you because I was so sure I'd hurt you. Once I claimed you as my own, I'd be sealing your fate, and what if I couldn't bring you the same joy you brought to me? What if I couldn't be the man you needed me to be? What if I wasn't strong enough to fight my demons for you? You deserve everything, my love. You deserve all the happiness this world has to offer. You deserve a man who is always going to put you first. You deserve every single ounce of goodness that comes your way. You are my beacon of light in the dark that's consumed me for so long. I love you with my whole heart. I will never stop loving you. I want you to be my wife. I want you to be a mother to my girls. I want to watch you grow a baby of our own. I want forever with you. I want every single morning and every single night. I want you. I love you."

I brush the tears falling down her face and go on.

"This is me. The real me, full of raw emotion. You've made my walls come crumbling down. You've exposed my every fear, my darkest demons, and all my desires. You saved me from myself. Thank you. Thank you for your patience. Thank you for believing in me. Thank you for seeing the good in me. Thank you for loving me. I am, and always will be, yours."

She pulls her forehead away from mine and cups my jaw in her hands again. We stare at each other with tears covering our faces.

"I have waited for so long to hear you say those words to me."

The tears start coming faster.

"There is no one in this world I love more than you, Jack. There is nothing I wouldn't do for you. But I was so close to giving up. I thought you would never love me the way I love you. You are my everything. This moment, right now, has made all the pain worth it. I love every version of you. The real, raw you. The guy you show to the world and every piece of you in between. I just love you."

It's as if she's answering every prayer I've ever said. I have to tell her again.

"I love you, Caroline Britton. I love you. You are mine. You will always be mine. I will love you until the day I die."

I lean in and kiss her. She tastes like home. She kisses me back, wrapping her arms around me. I hold her tight. I'm never letting her go. I finally know, in this moment, what it feels like to be truly whole.

The end

Epilogue

Caroline

Six months later

Jack Hannen has made all my dreams come true, and next month, not only am I going to marry him in front of all our family and friends in the city we call home, but I'm officially going to become a mother to two amazing five-year-old little girls. My fairy-tale ending is just beginning. I found a man who loves me with his whole heart and soul, and any insecurities I may have had are long gone. It may not have been an easy road to get here, but the reward at the end has been so incredibly worth it. Jack continues to amaze me every single day. He still sees Dr. Reed and is forever trying to be the best version of himself. We officially moved in together almost immediately after he told me he loved me, and I've never been happier. The girls call me mom even though we aren't officially married yet, and I continue to visit Bree from time to time. Life is good.

We decided on a joint-destination bachelor-bachelorette party, and last night, our bridal party and closest friends all landed in St. Lucia. It's the off-season, so the guys have a break from hockey. We are staying at an all-inclusive resort and have no idea what is in store for us. Jimmy has taken his job as best man very seriously, and he and Sofia, my maid of honor, have been planning this trip for months. The two have become really good friends although Jimmy makes it well known on a daily basis that he wants more than friendship. We have strict orders to be in the main dining area for breakfast at nine-thirty so that Jimmy can give us our itinerary. I just woke up and am lying in bed when I feel Jack's hand move up to cup my breast. He nuzzles into my neck.

"Good morning, love."

His morning voice is raspy and perhaps my favorite. He begins teasing my nipple with his thumb and index finger. I instinctively push my ass against his hard erection, and he chuckles. He slides down the bed and settles his face between my legs. He begins by slowly licking up and down my folds, then he focuses in on my clit, and his tongue swivels around it. He sucks it into his mouth and then pushes a finger inside of me. I arch my back and begin fondling my breasts. He pulses his finger in and out of me as he licks, sucks, and nibbles. He adds a second finger and then uses his pinky finger to slowly tease at my back entrance. There's a sensation of such fullness that I lose it. My entire body convulses, and I shudder as I come down from my high. He comes up from between my legs with my juices all over his face. He wipes them off with the back of his hand and lies on his back. He props a few pillows behind his back, and then he pulls me over to him.

"Ride me, beautiful."

I put one hand on each of his shoulders as I straddle him. He leans up and pops my left nipple into his mouth. His tongue swirls around it as he fondles my breast and then does the same to the right. I want him inside of me so badly. I push his shoulders back so that he's lying on the pillows, and I lower myself on top of him. I grind against him tilting my pelvis to get him deep inside of me. I lift myself up on my knees and stare at him as I cup my breasts in my hands. I begin to ride him as he pushes his hips up, matching my thrusts. His hands are on my thighs guiding my movements. We find our rhythm, and I feel myself getting close again. My muscles contract, and the sensation overpowers me. Another orgasm shoots through my core, sending chills down my spine. I fall forward onto his chest, but he isn't done. He pulls out of me and has me lie on my stomach. He pulls my ass into the air and pushes his dick back inside my core, taking me from behind. He thrusts hard and long, and I swear I can't tell where I end and he begins. Another orgasm builds, and I scream out. This time, he comes with me, letting out a long grunt. I can feel him twitching inside of me as he shudders around me. He pulls out and rolls onto his back.

"Fuck!" he pants.

He pulls me into his arms.

"Good morning, handsome."

I smile at him.

"I am seriously the luckiest man on the planet. I love you, beautiful."

"I love you too."

He kisses my cheek and looks at the clock.

"Damn Jimmy and his schedule. We have ten minutes to shower and get to breakfast."

"I'm kind of excited to see what they've planned. Let's share the shower."

He groans and gives me one more kiss before we get out of bed. We shower quickly, throw on our bathing suits, and head downstairs. We're only seven minutes late when I see everyone is already seated at our table.

"Well, how nice of you to join us, Jack and Caroline. You're lucky you're the guests of honor. Please have a seat."

Jimmy is standing at the front of the table and looks absolutely ridiculous. He's wearing some brightly colored blue-and-green Hawaiian print shorts. His shirt has bright yellow, red, and pink birds all over it. He's wearing aviator glasses and an orange ball cap that says "It's five o'clock somewhere." Jack bursts out laughing.

"I'm sorry, but I can't take you seriously in that get up."

Jimmy looks down at himself, shrugs, and grabs his clipboard.

"It's island apparel. Now, Sofia, my gorgeous maid of honor, will you please accompany me up here for announcements?"

Sofia smiles and rolls her eyes, but she gets up from her seat next to Mel and walks over to Jimmy.

"Thank you, sexy."

He winks at her.

"Now, gentlemen, I know we wanted to simply lay out by the pool and drink all day, but my irresistible maid of honor has demanded that we have some planned events because she feels Caroline would enjoy them. So today, we will begin by getting ridiculously drunk at the pool all day. Novotny, I ask that you don't piss in the pool like you did at my house last week."

Novotny shrugs. "Dude, everyone was pissing in your pool. It wasn't just me."

Mel starts laughing.

Sofia takes over. "As my cochair was saying, we will begin with a day at the pool, but tonight, we are going to a pig roast that ends with the locals teaching us a dance native to the island."

"I like this plan," Jack says and puts his arm around me.

He's smiling from ear to ear, and I feel so incredibly lucky.

"Victoria, redheads get sunburnt easily. I'll be responsible for rubbing sunscreen all over that hot body of yours," Jones says, looking over at Victoria, who simply rolls her eyes.

"Tomorrow, the guys have a little fishing trip thingy planned all day. Ladies, we will be enjoying a relaxing spa day and will meet up with the gentlemen in the evening for dinner and drinks," Sofia continues.

"Gorgeous, it's not a little fishing trip thingy. We've chartered a huge vessel to go big game fishing. It's going to be epic."

"If you say so." Sofia shrugs.

Owen Miller raises his hand.

"Yes, Owen," Sofia calls on him like a student in a classroom.

"Sofia, I really think you should try out Jimmy's huge vessel. The guy has been pining over you for months."

Everyone bursts out laughing. Owen is usually quieter and more reserved around us than the other guys, and I can't control my giggles. Jimmy looks at Sofia and puts his arm around her. Sofia just smiles at Owen and then looks Jimmy right in the eye.

"He couldn't handle me." She takes her eyes off him but doesn't leave his embrace. She picks up a mimosa. "Now if you'll all please raise your glasses, let's cheer to Jack and Caroline, who made this trip possible for us and have shown us all that true love can overcome any obstacle!"

As I hold my glass high, surrounded by our friends and the salty ocean air, I look up at my future husband. My heart is full. As individuals, we may not be perfect, but together, we're stronger. Our love is real, raw, and full of promise.

Author's Note

Thank you for reading! I hope you enjoyed *Raw and Real Love*. Stay tuned for book 2 of the *Game of Love Series: Fast and Foolish Love*!

About the Author

Georgia Price is a wife, mother, scientist, and all-around romance novel fanatic. She enjoys novels with complex characters who make her laugh out loud. She particularly enjoys strong female characters with men who have a little bit of an edge. She also loves a good plot twist. She sees reading as an escape from the responsibilities of real life and wants her stories to provide that getaway to readers everywhere. She tries to find imperfect characters who fit perfectly together.

Raw and Real Love is her first novel, and book 1, in the Game of Love series. She initially wrote this book for herself but thought it was such a beautiful story that she wanted to share it with others. She developed a strong connection with the characters and felt that she couldn't just stop after Jack and Caroline's story, which is why she was compelled to turn it into a series. Jack and Caroline's friends deserve a chance at true love too. She truly hopes you enjoy Raw and Real Love.

CPSIA information can be obtained
at www.ICGtesting.com
Printed in the USA
BVHW081220160223
658645BV00001B/114